"Benjamin?" Lynn had no idea what she was asking. The pulse thrumming hard and fast in her throat made her voice breathy. Her fingers moved restlessly on his back, the slippery material of his windbreaker cool and slick. Heat pooled between her legs, and she squirmed to relieve the pressure.

With a groan that was almost a growl, he lowered his head. Her mouth opened in immediate welcome. The kiss started gentle, soft lips and sweeping tongues, but soon the banked embers in her belly roared into open flame. The memories of their incendiary night together, which she'd kept doused under the blanket of motherhood, ignited.

She hooked her calf around his lower leg and rose on tiptoe, trusting in his strength to keep her balanced. Her hands slid up his back and clamped onto his shoulder blades as she fused their mouths, tasting, tempting, teasing. His arms banded around her, one circling her waist, the other under her ass to lift her even closer.

She had no idea how much time passed before he dragged his mouth away and rested his forehead against hers. Their gasping breaths mingled as he eased her down and made sure her feet were planted before loosening his grip. Pressing her palms flat against his chest, she leaned back and stared, dazed, into his heavy-lidded eyes. His heart beat a ragged tattoo under her touch, a drumroll that matched her own.

Passion pressed against the walls of the tiny room like helium in a well-inflated balloon. She had to deflate it before it expanded into more than an impulsive kiss.

She cleared her throat. "Well. That was interesting."

LOVING BETWEEN THE LINES
(Silverberry Seduction Seasoned Romance Series, Book Two)

By Brenda Margriet

LOVING BETWEEN THE LINES
(Silverberry Seduction Seasoned Romance Series, Book Two)

First edition published July 2022
Copyright © 2022 Brenda Margriet Clotildes
Digital ISBN 978-1-7773513-6-6
Print ISBN 978-1-7773513-5-9

Cover Art by K. B. Barrett Designs

Desperate saves, unbelievable goals, bloody determination.
Hockey. It's Canadian, eh?

CHAPTER ONE

Lynn Kolmyn had *not* envisioned this on her first day back after a year of maternity leave.

"I am so sorry." She stood in front of Cynthie Neal's desk, jiggling her wailing son on her hip. Her boss regarded her with raised eyebrows. Panic curdled her belly, and she swallowed. "The daycare had a flood overnight. They've promised me an alternate location will be arranged by tomorrow, but I had nowhere else to bring Oscar today."

Cynthie's matte red lips pressed into a thin line. "As we discussed, I'm not totally adverse to having children at the office for short periods of time, but I don't see how you, or anyone else, will get any work done with this"—she waggled her fingers in Oscar's direction—"going on."

Lynn couldn't blame her. Her son's protests had risen in volume since she'd stepped into the room. The back of her throat burned with frustration.

"Give me one minute." Hurrying to her desk, one of two in the outer office, she scrabbled through the backpack she'd tossed beside it, searching for the baby biscuits she'd shoved in it this morning.

At the other desk, Sarah Little watched, a sympathetic expression on her round, cheerful face. "Need some help?"

Lynn pulled out the foil package and held it up triumphantly. "Got it." She smiled her thanks at Sarah's offer and hustled back to the inner office. Plopping into the visitor's chair, she ripped the package open with her teeth, slid out a cookie, and handed it to Oscar. He grabbed it eagerly and shoved it in his mouth.

Silence fell. The tension banding across her shoulder blades eased a fraction.

She spit the corner of foil into her fist as discreetly as she could. "I feel terrible about this. I thought he'd be happy here for an hour or two. At least long enough for me to get up to speed so I don't waste more time tomorrow. I should have just called." When the daycare had notified her it was closed, delaying her scheduled return to work had seemed unsupportable and bringing Oscar with her the only choice.

Now the squalling had stopped Cynthie's pinched nostrils relaxed. "Yes, you probably should have." Her dry tone held little censure, though, and Lynn saw a gleam of amusement in the other woman's sharp blue eyes.

She slumped back in the seat, relief softening her spine. Thank god Cynthie was a strict but understanding woman. "I promise it won't happen again." It shouldn't have happened once, Lynn berated herself. She *always* had back up plans for her back up plans. But things had changed in the year since Oscar's birth. Some days she was thrilled to make it out of her pajamas, let alone make contingency plans for imaginary scenarios.

"I suggest you head home today and try again tomorrow. But since you're here, there is something I might as well mention." She picked up a pen and slipped it through her fingers, back and forth, back and forth. "The marketing coordinator for the Canyon Cats

8

quit. Peterson Brewster asked if we could help out until a replacement is found. I want you to handle it."

Lynn's main duty as arena event director was to assist the businesses and organizations that rented the facility. Most of the concerts, trade shows, and sports tournaments were single night or once-a-year occurrences. Not so the Prince George Canyon Cats. The junior hockey team played more than thirty games at home from September to March—more if they made the playoffs. Not that they had in recent years, but that was beside the point. What with training camps and practices and other team events, the Canyon Cats were vital to the financial health of the arena—and as such needed to be kept happy.

"What about my regular duties?" The marketing coordinator was a full-time position. How could she add that to her plate and not become an absentee mom? She needed to work to support her son, but this was more than she'd been expecting. Mind you, she loved her job with all its challenges and her brain was already whirling with promotional ideas for the team, even as her stomach roiled at the thought of being away from Oscar longer hours.

Maybe she wouldn't feel so torn about the conundrum if she'd been in her twenties, but becoming a first-time mom at thirty-nine made every moment with him precious and fragile.

"Sarah can finish the projects she started while covering your mat leave and continue to pick up some of the slack. But it will require more time and effort, I know that. I can't see any way around it. We can't say no to Peterson." Cynthie aligned the pen on her desk perfectly with the edge of her blotter. "Hopefully he will hire someone within a month or so."

She nodded with resignation. "I'll make it work." She rubbed her chin on Oscar's head, inhaling his fresh scent. His hair was finally thickening, the reddish-brown showing a tendency to curl. Sticky fingers gripped her bare wrist, and her heart swelled at the innocent touch. How was she going to survive being away from him all day? "Thanks for the heads up. We can talk about it more tomorrow."

"Sounds good." Cynthie rose and Lynn followed suit. Oscar wriggled restlessly and rubbed his eyes. "Looks like someone is ready for a nap."

"Yes." Neither of them had had a good sleep the night before, which might have accounted for his fractiousness this morning. "Again, I'm sorry about today. I promise to make up for it. See you tomorrow, Cynthie."

Benjamin Whitestone stepped into the concourse of the arena, closed the door to the Canyon Cats team offices behind him, and leaned against the red-painted brick wall. Pressing his fingertips into the rough surface, he squeezed his eyes shut and breathed deeply.

When Peterson Brewster had summoned him to his office, he hadn't been able to suppress the guilty feeling he'd done something wrong. He'd only been head coach of the Canyon Cats for two weeks. Logic dictated he had no reason to worry that his performance had been judged subpar already.

Logic hadn't stopped him from worrying before, and it hadn't this morning, either.

Turned out Brewster had just wanted to welcome him formally to the organization. He'd met the very involved owner during the hiring process, but he'd been out of town since Benjamin's return to Prince George. Now the meeting was over, he could concentrate on his next challenge—his first official practice. Training camp had ended, and the roster was set. The hardest work was about to begin.

Taking one last deep breath, he pushed off the wall and strode toward the stairs leading down to ice level. As he reached the door to the arena administration offices, it swung open. He dodged to avoid being struck by the heavy metal panel. A woman with her arms full of child stumbled into him.

"Careful now." He gripped her biceps to steady her. Two black bags draped off her shoulders and the sharp corner of one thudded against his thigh as she spun around. He released her and rubbed his leg.

"Sorry." She shifted the baby to her other hip and gave him a quick, harried glance before focusing once more on the squirming, squawking bundle.

He'd had little exposure to children but given the length of the legs kicking at her thighs and the arms flailing about her head, this was no newborn. Other than that, he had no clue.

"I should have been more careful when I opened the door," the woman continued. "I hope I didn't hit you."

That voice. Husky and low, it evoked a sudden memory of subdued lighting, sultry jazz, and smoky whiskey. "Lynn?" His palms tingled, remembering the smooth curves of the shoulders he'd just been clutching.

Her chin lifted and their eyes met. For a moment, her expression remained blank. Then she blinked.

"Benjamin?" The baby continued to wriggle and wail and she bounced and jiggled in the age-old way of mothers everywhere. "What are you doing here?"

He could only stare. He'd thought of Lynn more often than a one-night stand deserved. Especially a one-night stand that had occurred two years ago. Of course, it had also been the day after his father's funeral. Maybe the pain of that time and the comfort she'd given him was why she'd stuck in his mind more than any woman he'd slept with—before or since.

She asked you a question. Answer, you dummy. "I'm the new head coach. Of the Canyon Cats."

Her eyes widened. "*You're* Benjamin Whitestone?"

In the dim light of the jazz lounge where they'd met—and later, in the hotel room he'd brought her to— he'd been too caught up in first misery and then passion to remember the colour of her irises, but saw now they were a bright pale blue. "Yes?" He couldn't help the upward lilt, though it made him sound like an idiot. Reeling from this unexpected encounter, he wasn't certain of anything, even his own name.

"I read you'd been hired, but I didn't realize *that* Benjamin was, well, *that* Benjamin."

Since they hadn't bothered to exchange last names at their first meeting that made sense. "I've thought of you. Often." The truth blurted out before he could stop it. "How have you been?"

Her eyebrows quirked up and she shifted the now restlessly dozing baby on her hip. "I'm doing well. This is my son Oscar. He's a year old. Just last week, actually."

His head spun, as if a giant defencemen had laid him out flat with a body check and his skull had bounced off the ice. Scrambling to do the math, he stuttered, "A year? And we...is he..."

"No." Her tone was firm and laced with amusement. "Relax. He's not yours."

"Oh." Surely the rush flooding his body was relief. He'd never wanted to have kids. He'd been a disappointment as a son and couldn't imagine what a mess he'd make of being a father. "So, you're married?" Oh, god. Had she been married when they'd had their night together? She'd said she was single—he remembered asking—but had she lied?

"Also no." The amusement was gone, exasperation in its place. "Before you jump to any more conclusions, let me explain. Though I can't see how it's any of your business." The baby—whose name he'd already forgotten—lifted his head from her shoulder and squawked. She cradled his skull in her hand and joggled rapidly. "I'm in a hurry to get home so he can have a proper nap, so you'll have to save any questions for later. I am not and never have been married. I wanted a child, so I did in vitro fertilization, starting the process a month after we...met. Oscar is the result of that process." The baby's squalling took on a frantic tone. "I have to go. Congratulations on the new job. Good luck."

Before Benjamin could say another word—which was probably for the best, given his foot-in-mouth disease—she was gone.

CHAPTER TWO

Benjamin trudged down the wide flight of stairs to ice level, stunned and dazed by the chance meeting. In his office, he retrieved his skates and hockey gloves. The players would be waiting in the dressing room, but he made his way to the home team's bench instead, needing a moment to settle himself.

He gripped the wide wooden edge of the rink boards. The glistening ice, smooth and unmarked by the lethally sharp skates soon to be powering across it, taunted him. Shaking off thoughts of Lynn, he focused on the reason he'd returned to Prince George.

A battle would be fought on this ice, and on ice just like it in arenas across Western Canada. A battle for redemption. A battle he had to win.

His heart beat heavily in his chest, thundering with the anxiety that was a long familiar companion. Others might view him as washed up at thirty-five, but he'd made a vow to stop thinking of himself that way and taking this job had been the first step.

"Ready, Coach?"

He turned to the man who had appeared at his side. Levi Ghostkeeper stared at him with challenge in his jutted chin and narrowed eyes. As assistant coach of the Prince George Canyon Cats for the past five seasons, people in the know—as well as Levi himself—had expected he'd fill the head coach position. Instead, Benjamin had been hired. Levi had made his displeasure clear from the moment of their introduction.

And continued to do so every chance he got.

"Let's do this." His fingers aching with tension, he released the rail and sat on the metal bench. Removing his shoes, he slid his feet into his skates and laced them up, the motions ingrained and automatic.

Levi vanished down the tunnel leading behind the bleachers, his shouts echoing off the concrete walls and floor. A surge of adrenalin made Benjamin's face tingle, and he lifted his chin to scan the empty arena.

Remembering the rush of six thousand fans cheering when he stepped on the ice, the hometown star that was going to set the hockey world on fire.

Remembering the boos and hisses when he'd failed them all.

Like a gathering storm, he sensed the approach of the young men that had been placed under his authority. Casual profanities and shouted insults, the soft thudding of skates on padded flooring and sharp creaking of protective gear, reached him before the first player came into view. Hiding his trembling fingers inside his bulky gloves, he stood between the metal bench and the wooden boards, nodding at those that made eye contact as they passed, making note of the ones that didn't. It was his job to meld them into a unit, from the sixteen-year-old rookies dreaming of national league glory to the twenty-year-old veterans learning to accept unwelcome reality.

And if he did his job right, give them all the chance to celebrate the success he'd denied himself.

The crisp sound of blades cutting ice did little to fill the huge space. Gazing up at the enormous score clock hanging from the rafters like a guillotine, Benjamin took a deep breath, squared his shoulders, and stepped through the gate, his skates as comfortable as slippers, his strokes swift and sure. He glided to a stop on the Canyon Cats logo in the centre of the ice and blew his whistle.

"Bring it in, boys. It's time to get to work."

Lynn didn't let herself be distracted by thoughts of Benjamin Whitestone until she had Oscar safely tucked in his crib at home. *Sorry, officer. I ran that stop sign with my baby in the back seat because I was reliving the hottest one-night stand I ever had.* That it was her only one-night stand was a moot point. The passion of those hours was seared into her very sinews.

What a morning. First the panicky call from her daycare provider about the flood, the impulsive and ultimately insane decision to bring Oscar to work, and the twist-of-fate meeting with a man who'd haunted her dreams for two years.

In the spare room that doubled as her home office, she unpacked her laptop from her messenger bag, determined to review emails while Oscar slept. Cynthie may have been understanding but Lynn held herself to a higher standard. One she'd completely failed to attain that morning.

Before settling to work, she went to the kitchen to refill her water bottle. As she held it under the stream from the tap, her eye caught the infinity symbol tattooed on her wrist. It was so familiar she rarely noticed it, but today it blazed off her skin like a beacon.

The day she'd had it inked had been the day she'd decided to skip the husband stage of her life plan and move onto the baby stage.

The night she'd had it inked was the night she'd slept with Benjamin. Now known as Benjamin *Whitestone.*

Though she'd been on maternity leave throughout the last hockey season, it had only been good business sense to keep up with the happenings of the organization that was her biggest client. She'd read little more than the headlines regarding the hiring of the new head coach, as in the normal course of events she wouldn't have had much interaction with any of the Canyon Cats on-ice staff. Now she was handling the team's marketing duties for at least a few weeks, she wouldn't be able to avoid them completely. And by *them* she meant Benjamin.

Snorting out a chuckle, she recalled the varied expressions that had crossed his face during their short encounter. He really had made an ass of himself, first in revealing his terror he might be a father, and then jumping to the assumption she was married. He'd given her the upper hand the next time they met. Not that she needed the upper hand. They were both professionals. There was no reason this had to be awkward, especially since she'd cleared up all his ridiculous misunderstandings.

It might still be a good idea to learn as much as she could about him. For business purposes, of course. Nothing personal, and certainly nothing to do with the sparks of lust fizzing in her veins as she relived their night together.

Back in her spare room office, she fired up her laptop and made her way to the website for the local television news station. A quick search brought up the story she wanted. It included a video, so she set it to full screen, plugged in her earbuds so as not to disturb Oscar, and hit play.

The sports reporter, a young man with dark hair and a strong nose, sat at the anchor desk, a graphic of the Canyon Cats logo over his shoulder. He announced the hiring, and then the shot was replaced with video of a hockey game as the anchor went on. "This will be Benjamin Whitestone's first head coaching position. It is also his return to his hometown. A star in the Prince George Minor Hockey Association, Whitestone was drafted by the Canyon Cats as a Bantam, playing his entire junior career here."

The video changed again to what appeared to be a

post-game interview with an unbearably young Benjamin. His sweat-dampened dark hair clung to his forehead, where his helmet had pressed a red line into the flesh. The thin whiskers of an infant beard were scattered in patches across his cheeks. Lynn's heart clutched at the sight, not only at Benjamin's vulnerability but the foreshadowing of a teenage Oscar.

The sports reporter continued. "He held several team scoring records and is well-remembered for his blazing speed. But his most notable claim to fame—or maybe infamy—is for a missed penalty shot on home ice in the final game of the National Championships. A missed shot that cost the Canyon Cats the trophy."

He paused to let the highlight run uninterrupted. The footage from fifteen-or-so years ago showed Benjamin racing to a puck placed on the blue line, before slowing to bob and weave in an attempt to throw off the goaltender. His wrist shot, so quick she almost missed it, sent the puck sailing by the net, wide by at least a foot. The boos and jeers of the crowd rang in her earbuds, shocking in their animosity.

What a weight for a teenager to carry on his shoulders. Lynn couldn't help but feel sympathy for the young man Benjamin had been.

The video cut back to the reporter at the desk. "Whitestone's career in the NHL never matched the potential he'd shown as a junior. He played for five teams in six seasons, and then retired after a hit that gave him his third concussion. After playing in Europe for a short time, he returned to North America and became an assistant coach. Given the Canyon Cats' lacklustre results in the past three seasons, he will have to work miracles to get the team to the playoffs this year."

Lynn closed the video, pulled out her earbuds, and sipped her water. She had a vague recollection of the championship the reporter had mentioned. At the time, she'd been concentrating on her university education with little attention to spare on junior hockey. If she had been more of a fan, maybe she would have recognized Benjamin that night at the jazz lounge. More than likely not—it was a decade and a half later, after all.

And now it's two years after that, she reminded herself. So many changes had happened between then and now, the most important of which was sleeping in the room next to her. She was a mother. Any relationship she might cultivate had to be good for Oscar, not just her.

Which meant another one-night stand was out of the question—no matter how much the idea tempted her.

CHAPTER THREE

Benjamin drew in a deep breath before knocking on the red front door of the two-storey house. Inside, barking erupted along with deep shouts and high-pitched squeals. He took a wary step back.

When Peterson Brewster had approached Benjamin about the head coaching position, his initial reaction had been *hell no*, and not just because he didn't believe he was ready for the responsibility. A return to his hometown would necessitate reforging relationships he'd damaged through avoidance and inaction, and he *knew* he wasn't ready for that.

But Brewster had insisted, and Benjamin had let himself be wooed. The owner's flattery had soothed enough of his battered pride to convince him to take the job. So here he was, back in town and unable to avoid the two people he'd hurt the most.

He'd had one stilted and uncomfortable visit with his mother since his return. But she'd left for Vancouver to care for her sister following hip replacement surgery shortly after, so he had a reprieve on that front for a few weeks.

Her absence forced him to focus on the other fissure in his life, however. So here he was.

The door opened with a jerk. Instead of the canine assault for which he'd been bracing, he was greeted by the tall, lanky form of Jujhar Malhotra. Seated at his side was a wriggling medium-sized puppy. On the stairs leading to the second floor, a boy perched, staring wide-eyed at Benjamin.

"Ben." Jujhar fed treats to the dog like a rapid-fire Pez dispenser. "I'd shake your hand but we're training Barney not to jump on visitors. Come on in." He backed away, the dog following, intent on the goodies coming his way.

He couldn't help but wonder if the dog-training was a handy excuse to avoid contact. Jujhar had been polite but distant when Benjamin had called the day before asking if it would be okay to stop by. Not that he deserved anything different, not after the things he'd said over a year ago. Which was why it had taken him three weeks to get up the courage to call his old friend.

And also why Jujhar's dinner invitation had been totally unexpected. Benjamin had been so shocked he hadn't had time to come up with an excuse and had stuttered an awkward acceptance.

"Eli, take Ben's coat, will you? Don't worry about your shoes. We're eating in the back on the deck. Got to take advantage of the good September weather while it lasts. Sit." At his final word, the dog plopped down on its furry butt. "Good boy." Jujhar fed him several more treats. "Okay, go find Ella and Elaine." After one last hopeful pant, the dog vanished down the hall, feathery tail flying.

Eli, Jujhar's middle child and only son, stood and smiled at Benjamin, revealing a gap in his top row of teeth. "Did you really play in the NHL?"

"Yes." He gave the boy his coat, which he hung on a tall rack positioned at the bottom of the stairs without moving from his step.

"Cool." The hint of hero worship in his tone made Benjamin uncomfortable. Playing a few games in the big leagues didn't make him extraordinary, especially since his career had been less than mediocre. "My dad told me about when you played together. But what I really want to know is—"

"Eli, you can quiz Ben later." Jujhar ruffled his son's black hair in a casual gesture that echoed eerily on Benjamin's scalp. His own father had done the same to him, many times. In congratulations, in encouragement, in condolence. Never with condescension or cruelty. He'd been the best of fathers, and Benjamin would never forgive himself for not being the success his father had believed he could be.

For being the cause of his untimely death.

Dragging the Canyon Cats deep into the playoffs wouldn't bring his father back, but maybe it would ease some of his crushing remorse.

First things first. Healing the rift between himself and Jujhar was one of the many goals he'd set on his return. "Can we talk?" Benjamin rolled his neck in an attempt to ease the tightness cinching his shoulder blades together.

Jujhar regarded him with his familiar calm, dark gaze. That hadn't changed since they'd last hit the ice together, though he hadn't had his flourishing beard then. "Sure. Eli, go play with Barney and your sisters."

"But—"

Jujhar cut off his son's whining appeal. "Go." He waited for Eli to plod out of sight, and then crossed his arms and leaned against the newel post. "So, talk."

I guess we're doing this here. "I owe you an apology."

Jujhar nodded. "Yes, you do."

"You were just trying to help. It wasn't your fault I wasn't ready to accept it." His admonitions had been doubly unwelcome as they were the same ones his father had been expressing at the exact moment he died. Correct that—the moment Benjamin had caused his death. Memories of those two fateful encounters often kept him awake at night, easily dominating the echoes of all his other failures.

"All I did was suggest you take a good hard look at yourself. You were floating, man, just going with the tide. I hate to see you waste your talents. You have so much to give."

He wondered if Jujhar used the same speech on his high school science students when they disappointed him. "I know you were only trying to help." At the time, his belief Benjamin could be *more* had gnawed with sharp, bitter teeth, had been yet another burden laid on his shoulders. He knew now his friend had been offering support, not condemnation.

Silence settled between them, and with it a hint of their former ease. Maybe Benjamin hadn't left it too late. Maybe he could still salvage something from this particular disaster.

"You were right." He blurted out the admission. "I've been lost then since I quit playing." And everything had gotten so much worse after his father died.

Jujhar nodded but didn't say anything. He had been an excellent, dependable defenceman on the ice and a solid, responsible friend off. Their hockey careers had overlapped in Prince George for three years and their connection had survived Benjamin being drafted when Jujhar had not. It had even survived Benjamin bouncing from team to team for six seasons in the NHL, another two in Europe, and the last seven in various bench positions around North America. Well, not all of the last seven. Twenty months ago, when Jujhar had suggested he get his head out of his ass and do something with his life, things had fallen apart. His friend had given up on him, and Benjamin hadn't blamed him.

"I mean it. You were right and I was wrong. I was an ass to be angry with you." It had still taken months for the truth of Jujhar's message to truly sink in. And for him to decide to do something about it.

"You always were too hard on yourself." Jujhar straightened and punched Benjamin on the bicep. "It's all good. Come on, let's get you a beer. Sadie will be wondering what's happening, and you don't want to piss off my wife."

It couldn't be that easy. Still, hope bloomed in Benjamin's chest as he followed Jujhar down the hall into a bright kitchen and through sliding glass doors that led to a wooden deck raised a couple feet off the ground. On the lawn, the puppy gamboled with Eli and two girls, the afternoon sun striking copper sparks in their long dark hair. At the patio table, a tall blonde woman placed a stack of dinner plates down and hurried toward him with outstretched arms.

"Benjamin!" Sadie Maholtra wrapped him in a tight embrace and rocked back and forth. "It's so good to see you. I can't believe you didn't call us sooner." She leaned back, tapped his cheek gently in reprimand, and beamed at him. "Jujhar! Why doesn't this man have a beer yet?"

And then again, maybe it could. If only all his troubles could be solved so painlessly.

Oscar's feet kicked Lynn's hips, and he shouted gleefully in her ear. She tightened the straps of the carrier and readjusted his weight on her back. "Hang on, buddy. Almost ready." Across the parking lot, members of the Silverberry Book Club gathered at the entrance to the apple orchard. Lynn's usual if-you're-not-ten-minutes-early-you're-late motto was one of the many things that had changed since Oscar had arrived in the world.

"Need a hand?" Stephanie Collins closed the back of Lynn's SUV and took two quick strides to her side. Despite the fact she was on her way to pick apples, she wore a sleeveless sundress in impressionistic swirls of blue and green, with strappy flat sandals on her long, elegant feet. Her makeup was artful and discreet and her jaw-length bob smooth and shiny.

"I think I've got it." Lynn grunted as she jostled

Oscar into position. Now she was at work again, she was getting back into the habit of wearing eyeshadow and stylish clothing, but for a while there she'd been happy when she'd remembered to comb her hair. On those days she'd begrudged Stephanie's put-together appearance. Thank goodness she'd kept those disgruntled thoughts hidden from her housemate and close friend. It would have been poor repayment for basically co-parenting those first stressful weeks. "I can't wait until he's walking. On the other hand, I don't think I'm quite ready for all the trouble he'll get into then."

Oscar giggled as if he knew exactly what she was saying. Her heart swelled at the sound. He *had* changed her life, and some of the changes had been difficult. Especially at two in the morning when everything was darkest—both literally and figuratively. But on a sunny Sunday afternoon in September, it was all good.

With her son securely on her back, Lynn followed Stephanie across the pavement to where the Silverberries waited. Members had come and gone since she'd joined two years ago, but the core group remained.

"How's my favourite young man today?" Helen Mansfield reached over Lynn's shoulder to brush Oscar's cheek with one finger. She and her new husband Nathan Speith, standing proudly beside her as she cooed at Oscar, were founding members of the club. Helen owned the studio where Lynn had received her first, and so far only, tattoo, and had actually been inking the infinity symbol when she'd invited Lynn to join.

When she had been stretched to breaking dealing with a newborn, the club had banded around her. She didn't know how she would have gotten through Oscar's first year if it hadn't been for the Silverberries.

"I remember when my boys were that age." Penta Potter's voice was wistful. Short and comfortably rounded with two sons and two daughters of her own, she was a lifeline for Lynn, accepting her phone calls at all hours of the day and night. She was also a single mom, although that was a fairly recent development, her divorce having gone through just a few months before. The scars of that vicious battle still shadowed her eyes. "I can't believe they're in high school now."

Terrance Renfrew, another longtime member of the club, waved hello but didn't take a breath in his conversation with Natalie, the newest person to join. A good friend of Helen's daughter, she, too, was recently divorced.

Maybe Lynn had dodged a bullet instead of missed a goal when her fiancé of seven years had dumped her. At least she wasn't dealing with child support and custody arrangements on top of learning how to be a mom. She could make up for Oscar not having a father if she tried hard enough, she was certain.

Helen directed everyone to the orchard entrance, where a teenage girl put down her phone long enough to smile a greeting. "Hello! Welcome to Northern Lights U-Pick."

"Silverberry Book Club, reporting for duty." Helen snapped a playful salute.

The girl blinked. "Book club?"

Helen winked. "Never judge a book by its cover. Or in this case, a club by its name. We do more than read. Where do we start?"

The girl pointed at a stack of heavy canvas sacks and the Silverberries each chose one before following her directions to the area they'd been assigned to pick. Stephanie joined Terrance and Natalie while Nathan paired off with Penta.

Helen fell into step beside Lynn. "So, how was your first week back at work?"

"I think because so much has changed in my life in the last twelve months, I was prepared for lots of changes at work, too. Instead, it's like travelling back in time, as if I never left." Adding the marketing coordinator duties hadn't been quite the disruption she'd feared. Of course, the regular season hadn't started yet. When it did, she'd have to arrange her schedule around home games in order to run the contests and promotions that happened during stoppages in play and intermissions.

"It's been an adventurous two years for you, hasn't it?" Helen's sleek cap of silvery grey hair gleamed in the lowering sun.

"For you, too. Falling in love with an old friend. Getting married again." The ceremony, held three months ago at Nathan's cabin on a nearby lake with only family and intimate friends in attendance, had been sweet and romantic and still made Lynn's heart ache. She was thrilled for Nathan and Helen, but their happiness only underscored the fact she'd never share such a wonderful moment with anyone herself. She'd discarded that part of her life plan in favour of the one currently babbling happily on her back.

Helen laughed. "I guess we're living proof it's never too late. You never know when love will strike."

A vision of Benjamin skated across Lynn's inner eye. They hadn't spoken since that first day, but that didn't mean she hadn't seen him. During practices, the sounds of slapping pucks and piercing whistles and shouted instructions echoed from the ice surface to the concourse level. Merely opening the administration office door let her know exactly where Benjamin was. And if she snuck into the stands during her breaks and watched for a few minutes, that was just a logical way of killing time, wasn't it?

Because it didn't matter what Helen believed. It *was* too late for Lynn, and it was time she accepted that.

CHAPTER FOUR

The deep bass of the local rock band Lynn had hired to play the Canyon Cats Home Opener Tailgate Party thrummed through the exterior concrete wall. They were doing their sound check before the crowd began streaming into the parking lot for the event that would kick off the new hockey season. She was taking a breather in the office before heading back outside to make sure everything was running smoothly.

She scrolled through the checklist on her tablet, colour-coded by importance, subject, and timing. The tailgate party was an annual event she'd spearheaded—other than the last, of course, as Oscar had just been born—after joining the arena staff several years ago. None of the players or coaches were expected to attend, since it was a game day, but fans would be treated to a live band, food vendors, and other activities designed to boost excitement. Given the Canyon Cats dismal record on the ice the last few years, anything off the ice that put butts in the seats was sorely needed.

In the past, Lynn would have headed home once the game started. Today, in her role as acting marketing coordinator, it would be up to her to direct the in-house announcer and arena host through the contests she'd planned, which meant she wouldn't be done until the second intermission was over, and maybe not even then.

She glanced at the clock in the corner of the tablet's

screen. She had reworked her schedule so she could spend the morning with Oscar before dropping him off at daycare. Stephanie should be picking him up about now. She'd be the one giving him his dinner, watching over him as he splashed in the tub, kissing his downy head goodnight as she tucked him into bed.

Lynn's fingers itched to send a quick text but, if Stephanie was driving, the last thing she wanted to do was distract her. She could wait a little longer, give them time to get home and settled before sending a casual, friendly message. It wasn't being overprotective if she just said hi, was it?

She left the office, locking the door behind her, and strode along the wide concourse. Through the glass doors and floor-to-ceiling windows of the main entrance a buzz of activity was visible, with people and vehicles moving busily to and fro. Inside, a hum of anticipation filled the empty space, as if the very walls knew something exciting was about to happen.

Giving in to impulse, she veered off her route and climbed one of the many short flights of stairs leading into the arena proper. Rows and rows of green seats flowed down to ice level and upward into the rafters. The players had had an optional skate earlier in the day, but the Zamboni had erased all the evidence, and the team logo painted in the centre circle of the frozen surface gleamed smooth and unmarked.

Her fingertips tingled, the same sensation she had when the lights went dim in a theatre signalling a play was about to begin. All that potential—for failure or success—just begging to be unleashed.

Sucking in a deep breath laced with the scent of fresh ice, she turned to go and caught sight of Benjamin in the Canyon Cats players' bench. Head bowed, he leaned on the boards, rocking slowly back and forth.

She didn't want to interrupt an important pre-game ritual, but something about his posture drew her toward him, ready to offer comfort. The video chronicling the vicious reaction he'd received as a player in this very arena streamed through her mind. The pressure to do well as the coach must be intense.

Weaving her way through the bleachers, she unfolded one of the plastic seats that overlooked the tunnel leading from the players' bench to the dressing rooms and sat. For several more moments, Benjamin stayed where he was, contemplating the ice. Then he turned, and though she wore soft soled sneakers and had made little noise when she'd approached, he didn't seem surprised to see her.

"Hi." He leaned his hips against the boards, rested his palms on the top rail, and crossed his ankles. The pose looked casual enough but the tension in the tautness of his shoulders, the flexing of his throat, was unmistakable.

"Hi." The few times she'd seen him in the last weeks, whether on or off the ice, he'd been wearing a nylon track suit and a team ball cap. Tonight he'd donned a navy-blue double-breasted suit with a white button-down shirt. The tails of a colourful tie hung from the breast pocket of the jacket, ready to be knotted into place. His dark hair, which had brushed the collar of his windbreaker, was now cropped high on his nape. He looked professional and competent.

And sexy. Mouthwateringly, gut-clenchingly sexy. Just like he had in the jazz lounge the first time they'd met.

Lynn swallowed and searched for something intelligent to say, but he spoke before she could collect her thoughts. "How's your boy?"

Her belly warmed further, touched that he had a thought to spare for her son on such a personally important night. "Oscar's good. With a sitter." *Well, duh.* She was pretty sure Benjamin could have figured that out for himself. She scrambled to camouflage her awkwardness. "So, are you going to turn things around tonight?" His eyelid twitched and Lynn wanted to kick herself. "Sorry, stupid question."

While this was the Canyon Cats home opener, it was already the third game of the season. They'd played their first two on the road and lost both. It couldn't be the start Benjamin had hoped for.

"It's okay." He shifted on his feet then stilled abruptly, as if fearing any movement betrayed his anxiety. "We'll do our best."

"Simpson is playing well." Lynn had been reading the sports news closely in recent days, telling herself her interest had to do with her return to work and not the new coach.

"Yes." Benjamin's expression lightened. "He's a great kid. Skilled, coachable, respected by the other players. He's going to be the nucleus this year, I think."

Lynn's phone signalled a text. Her heart stopped. A quick check of the screen, however, revealed it was Cynthie asking if all was ready, not Stephanie with a message about Oscar. "Sorry. Duty calls."

From his stance in the players' bench, Benjamin watched Lynn as she checked her phone. He hadn't heard her approach, though a subtle change in the air had roused him from his pre-game reverie. He would have been glad of any distraction from the negative thoughts swirling in his head but had been especially pleased when he'd seen her there.

She looked up from the screen and offered a small smile. "That's my boss. The gates are opening. For the party." Her husky voice settled in his belly, and then slipped lower. He lifted one foot to the metal bench in front of him to hide his reaction.

She made no move to leave. Her rich blond hair gleamed under the huge overhead lights, and she looked neat and tidy in a light blue windbreaker embroidered with the arena's logo and slim black trousers. This wasn't the first time he'd seen her since their impromptu meeting a few weeks ago. He'd noticed her in the stands during practices, even though she always chose an unobtrusive seat in the shadows. She never stayed long, but it was a simple connection that he savoured without pausing to examine why.

He stepped out of the players' bench and stopped in the hall below her. His head was about level with her seat, and he tilted his chin to meet her gaze. "I should let you go, then."

She reached down between the rails separating the bleachers from the hall. "Good luck."

"Thanks. You, too." He clasped her hand. An electric thrill raced up his arm and hardened his body further. How was it possible that the attraction that had had them jumping into bed after only a few hours acquaintance was still there, maybe even stronger? He released her and took a quick step back. "Uh, I have to go. See you around."

Escaping to the cool dimness of the hall under the stands, he paused to draw in a couple of cleansing breaths.

Even if he wanted to renew the relationship, he couldn't. For one, he didn't have time. He needed to focus on the team. Two losses didn't sound the death knell, but he had to stop the slide, and soon. For another, Lynn was a mother. Her priority would be her son—*Oscar*, he repeated, to commit the name to memory—and she would have no interest in exploring anything with a struggling junior hockey coach with a checkered past.

There were other, deeper reasons, but he was distracted from those depressing thoughts by the clicking of dress shoes echoing toward him. Peterson Brewster came into view at the far end of the hall.

"Benny! How's it going?" His hearty, hail-fellow-well-met bellow reverberated off the concrete walls.

Benjamin disliked that diminutive of his name intensely, but he gritted his teeth and nodded a greeting. He would put up with a lot worse for the opportunity Brewster had given him. The Canyon Cats' owner had taken a chance hiring a first-time head coach, and Benjamin couldn't forget it. "The players are ready, sir. Everyone showed up for the optional skate this morning. That's a good sign."

"Excellent." Brewster fell into step beside him. He was several inches shorter and filled out his expensive suit with a comfortable paunch. While he'd never spoken to Benjamin with anything less than jovial respect, his eyes held a sharp intelligence that warned he should be treated with caution.

They made their way under the bleachers to Benjamin's tiny, windowless office. "Don't worry about the slow start. I've been an owner long enough to know junior hockey is made of dramatic ups and downs. There's plenty of time to turn it around. And if not"—he shrugged, the shoulders of his suit jacket shifting silkily—"there's always next year."

It was a relief to have a boss that understood the intangibles of sports and the tension in Benjamin's spine should have eased. But the other man was wrong. *Next* year wasn't an option. Not for Benjamin. He needed to prove his worth *this* year.

He hadn't told anyone about his self-imposed deadline. But after living and breathing hockey since before he was old enough to lace up his own skates, he'd decided it was time to make the call. If he couldn't drag the Canyon Cats into a respectable place in the league this season, he would leave the sports world for good.

What he would do if he did, he didn't know. Maybe take up knitting. But one thing was certain—this year would make or break the rest of his life.

Disappointment groaned from three thousand throats as the puck bulleted past the Canyon Cats goalie and into the back of the net.

"Well, that's that." The man a few seats down from Lynn stood up in disgust and squeezed past her knees to get to the stairs. He wasn't the only one leaving. Around the arena, fans filtered out, emptying the barely half-full stands even further.

Lynn hadn't meant to stay this long. After wrapping up the second intermission contests, she had texted Stephanie to confirm Oscar was sleeping peacefully, and then slipped into an almost empty row near the top of the stands. The Canyon Cats had gone into the third period leading by one and she'd wanted to see Benjamin get his first win. Unfortunately, the wheels had come off and the Cats were now behind by three goals with less than five minutes left.

While she didn't want to be seen as one of the rats deserting a sinking ship, Lynn followed the man out. Nothing she could do would change the outcome of the game, and it was well past the time she should have been home. As she passed the interior window that looked onto the concourse from Cynthie's office she was arrested by a rapid knocking. The vertical blinds that provided privacy were pulled aside and Cynthie beckoned at Lynn in an unmistakable gesture.

Delaying her return yet again, Lynn sighed, punched the keypad to enter the outer office and walked to the inner doorway. Cynthie paced back and forth in front of her window, mumbling to herself, which was never a good sign. "What do you need, Cynthie? I was just leaving."

Her boss halted, spun to face Lynn, and planted her hands on her hips. "Peterson Brewster wants to move the Canyon Cats. He's looking to get out of his lease."

Lynn felt her face go blank with shock. "There's still three years left."

"I know. I wasn't supposed to hear this, so if anyone asks, you know nothing." Cynthie threw herself into her chair and swivelled back and forth in jerky, rapid motions. "He was on the phone, so I only heard his side

34

of the conversation, but it was perfectly clear."

"You were eavesdropping?"

"I didn't mean to. If you want to have a private conversation, don't have it in your owner's box with the door wide open. Anyone could be walking by."

"And you were?"

Cynthie shrugged. "The bathrooms are at that end. I was on my way back to the management box. I don't know who he was talking to, but he made it perfectly clear that he wants to move the team."

Lynn dropped into a visitor's chair, the air escaping from her lungs in a whoosh. "Can he do that? Can he break the lease?"

"That's the other bad news. I just reviewed the contract." She lifted a document off her desk and waved it at Lynn before tossing it aside with disgust. "He can sell the team whenever he likes, but if he wants to move it and retain ownership while the lease is active, he has to pay a hefty fine. However, another clause states if attendance falls below the required minimum, he can get out of the contract without penalty."

"Is *that* why the marketing coordinator left?" If so, Lynn could understand the other woman's point. Who would want to be hamstrung by an owner that didn't want you to succeed?

"I doubt it. I can't imagine he's trumpeting his intention to his junior staff. If this news gets out, it will cause an uproar."

Lynn nodded. "And could derail his plans. If fans knew, they might start attending more games, just to keep it here." Hockey fans could be rabidly loyal when threatened with the loss of their team.

"Now we know, we have to do what we can to stop it. It would be a huge blow to the arena's revenue. We'd probably have to lay off staff."

That aspect hadn't occurred to Lynn. She suppressed a shiver of fear. No job would be safe if the Canyon Cats left, not even hers. "What do we do?"

"There's no need to panic. We can take some time to come up with a strategy. But one thing is for sure— we can't let anyone know that we know. Brewster would have no compunction in accusing me of spying, even if it was by accident. We don't want to give him any ammunition."

It was only later that night, as she lay sleepless in bed, her mind racing, that another angle struck Lynn.

If Benjamin brought the Canyon Cats up to a competitive level, the result would more than likely mean higher attendance. That would play against Brewster's plans.

How far would the owner go to break his contract? Wouldn't he prefer another disastrous season, not a successful one?

And if so, what did that mean for Benjamin?

CHAPTER FIVE

If Benjamin didn't know better, he would have thought someone had conspired to sabotage the start of the Canyon Cats season. Travel would always be an issue for the team, as Prince George was situated a six-hour drive from their nearest competitor, but to start with two games away, two games at home, and then a four game, five-day road trip was brutal.

Which was why he was more than pleased that the team currently had a record of four and four. After splitting the home opener doubleheader, they'd won three out of the four away games. It was a phenomenon he was familiar with—without the distraction of school and billets and other team commitments, the road was a great opportunity to build the bonds needed to succeed.

After the final game—one of their three wins—they had boarded the team bus and driven through the night, arriving in the arena parking lot at six on Sunday morning. The players had scattered to their homes, the younger ones chauffeured by their billets, the older ones driving themselves. Benjamin issued an open invitation to an optional skate that afternoon and then dragged himself to his apartment. He'd managed to nap on the bus, as years of travel had given him the ability to sleep whenever and wherever, but the older he got the trickier that became, and he fell onto the mattress in his rented apartment with relief.

He arrived at the rink half an hour before the optional skate after squeezing in a quick trip to the grocery store while a load of laundry cycled through. Entering through the main doors, he caught the faint sound of a furious wail. Unlike the last time a child's cry had echoed through the rink, he had a good idea who was making his ire known.

Deciding to take a circuitous route to his office, he paced the concourse in the direction of the arena administration offices. The wailing grew louder when a door opened. Lynn emerged, pushing a stroller in which a red-faced, tear-stained Oscar squirmed.

"Someone's not happy." Benjamin took in Lynn's harried appearance but refrained from commenting on her pinched nostrils and straggling ponytail. He rescued the end of her scarf from trailing on the ground, looping it over the shoulder of her parka. She didn't seem to notice.

"*Someone* is running a low fever and has the sniffles. I'm worried he won't be able to go to daycare tomorrow." Lynn sounded exhausted, frustrated, and anxious. "I was hoping he'd hold it together while I arranged a few things so I can work from home if necessary, but he's not cooperating."

He crouched down and rubbed Oscar's pudgy leg. "Not feeling well, buddy? That's rough." Fluid smeared the baby's top lip, and he patted his pockets, searching for a nonexistent tissue. Lynn interpreted his motions and handed him a fresh one. "Let me get that for you." It was easier said than done, as Oscar reared away, kicking out his legs and squalling with irritation.

"It's also nap time." She jiggled the stroller, making Oscar's round cheeks wobble. "I'm going to walk him around the arena and hope he falls asleep. Then I'll sneak back in and get what I need."

"I can do that." Benjamin straightened.

"Do what?"

"Push the little guy around while you work. We

don't have a formal practice today, so I have time."

Lynn bit her lip. "Don't be insulted but...I don't really know you."

Her lack of trust stabbed, though he supposed he couldn't blame her. Other than the night they'd had sex they'd only spoken a couple of times. And it wasn't like he had any experience with children. He'd attended the occasional elementary school event during his years as a player, but that didn't count, obviously. Now he thought of it, the dinner he'd had with Jujhar's family was the longest he'd spent with people under the age of ten in years.

"I understand. I'm pretty much a stranger." He shoved his hands in his pockets and nodded. "Well, I should let you go, then. He won't get any happier standing around."

Oscar's cries had softened to sobs while they spoke but ramped up in volume once more. Lynn straightened her shoulders. "You're not a stranger. You're a...colleague, I guess. If you're serious about this..."

Though his offer had been impulsive, he realized now he really did want to help. But only if she was comfortable with it. "I promise I can be trusted. I won't leave the building. How long do you need?"

"About fifteen minutes." Her gaze flickered from the office door to Oscar to Benjamin and around again. "Are you sure?"

"I'll take really good care of him." A familiar but forgotten feeling warmed his chest, one he hadn't felt in a long, long time. Pride. This was a big deal for Lynn, trusting her son to another person. Yet she was putting her confidence in *him*, Benjamin Whitestone.

He nudged her gently out of the way and took the handle of the stroller. "I'll keep my cell phone close the whole time. You'll need my number." He waited for her to get her own phone out and then listed off the digits. "Text me when you're ready and I'll come straight back."

"All right." She bent to give a tearful Oscar a kiss. "Mommy will be as fast as she can." The smile she gave Benjamin was filled with relief. "With any luck he'll be asleep by the end of the corridor. Thank you so much. I won't take long."

She hustled back into the office and Benjamin set off, pushing the stroller at a brisk pace. Despite Lynn's hopes, Oscar was still wailing as they rounded the far end. He didn't want to walk past the office for fear Lynn would hear, so when he reached the elevators leading to the lower level, he rolled the buggy in and headed down.

"Whatcha got there, Coach?" Garrett Simpson, the Cats' young captain and top player, paused as he came out of the dressing room.

"This is Oscar." Benjamin regarded the crying baby with rising fear. There had to be something more than the need for a nap and runny nose to account for such distress.

Simpson crouched down, looking twice his usual size in his hockey gear. He slipped off his glove and wiggled Oscar's foot. "Want to get out of there, bud?"

That was an idea. Benjamin unbuckled the harness—it had more straps than a chest protector for god's sake—and lifted Oscar out. Immediately his sobs lessened. "I'm taking care of him for a few minutes while his mom gets some work done." It felt like forever already, and though Lynn had sounded certain she'd only need fifteen minutes he knew how fast time passed when you were busy.

He discovered he was bouncing and swaying just like Lynn had been the day they'd met in the arena. Though it must be an ingrained instinct, it gave him a sliver of confidence.

"I wasn't much older than him when my dad took me on the ice for the first time." Simpson spoke from the lofty heights of a seventeen-year-old. "Not that I remember, but he says I loved it right from the start."

"Me, too." Playing shinny with his father was one of

the memories not tainted by what had happened later. He looked down at Lynn's son. "What do you say, Oscar? Want to come skating with us?"

Lynn had always been a planner. She made lists and set goals and crossed off tasks. But since becoming a mother, she'd had to learn to listen to her gut. Oscar hadn't come with an instruction manual and understanding how his hungry cry differentiated from his tired cry from his frustrated cry, as well as all the other little cues he gave, had meant going with her instincts.

This afternoon, her instincts had told her she could trust Benjamin to look after her son for a few minutes.

That trust didn't mean she could lollygag around. She gathered what she needed as quickly as possible and then took a few extra moments to bring her laptop and files out to her car so she wouldn't have to juggle them as well as an angry baby. Despite her hurry, it was closer to thirty minutes than fifteen by the time she texted Benjamin. *Ready. At the main entrance.*

On the ice, he texted back. *Can you come here?*

What the hell did he mean by that vaguely terrifying message? She hustled down the stairs that led to ice level, screeching to a halt at the sight of Oscar's empty stroller, abandoned under the bleachers near a gate that led onto the rink.

That couldn't possibly mean what her tumbling thoughts told her it meant. Her knees wobbled and she raced past the stroller to the opening.

Benjamin stood in the middle of the ice, Oscar perched in his arms, surrounded by a whirling hurricane of large men wearing knife-sharp skates, wielding weapon-like sticks, and bulleting hard rubber pucks.

Her mouth opened and closed soundlessly as prickles raced up her neck and cheeks, her heart beating with the force of a thousand drums behind her breastbone. Before she could launch into a full-scale panic attack, Benjamin saw her. He waved, glided through the throng, and came to a brisk stop near the boards, a shower of snow kicking up from his skates. "Look who's here, Oscar. Mommy came to watch you skate."

She could only stare. Oscar's head was encompassed by a blue bike helmet with *City of Prince George* stamped on it. In lieu of a blanket, a man-sized windbreaker with the Canyon Cats logo on the dangling sleeve protected him from the chill emanating off the ice. He gurgled and grinned, clapping his hands together with glee. Fury swamped her relief at seeing him unharmed. "Give him to me. Now."

Benjamin held Oscar out. Her son leaned against his shoulder, apparently unwilling to make the switch, and jealousy rose like bile in Lynn's throat. She dragged him out of Benjamin's arms, her heart rate slowing once she held him on her hip. "What the hell, Benjamin? What were you doing with my son?"

His welcoming smile faded. "He wasn't settling down. I thought he might be soothed by skating."

"During a hockey practice?" Releasing Oscar from the security of the stroller to comfort him was one thing. Taking him out onto slippery, dangerous ice with hulking young men blazing by and firing pucks was something else entirely.

"He was perfectly safe, Lynn. If there's one thing I know how to do, it's skate. I even got him a helmet from the public skating supplies."

"Someone could have run into you and knocked you down. Or hit him with a stick. Or shot a puck at him."

"That wasn't going to happen." Exasperation leaked into Benjamin's even tone. "This wasn't a full-bore practice. No one was shooting pucks—the guys are doing stick-handling drills. No one was being reckless."

Oscar reared back, his borrowed helmet knocking

her on the chin, before leaning forward suddenly with his arms outstretched toward Benjamin. She winced and drew in a long breath through her nose. Surveying the rink through calmer eyes, she realized he was right. Her first impressions of danger had been overblown. The players weren't careening around recklessly but sped with dexterity and skill in tight patterns. Pucks weren't flying through the air, but remained on the ice as they were tapped and touched by highly controlled blades.

She wasn't quite ready to forgive him. "You should have asked me first."

Benjamin nodded, his expression serious. "You're right. I didn't mean to worry you, and I'm sorry. To me, skating is just as familiar and safe as walking."

"Maybe so. Still." She shifted Oscar to her other hip, but he continued to wriggle. His nose was running again and his cheeks rosy, either from fever or the chill of the arena, but his eyes were bright, and he showed no signs of distress. Much the opposite, in fact.

Benjamin tilted his head to one side. "He really enjoyed it. He calmed down right away, even laughed a few times."

She'd had every intention of taking Oscar skating. Someday. She tamped down a return of the jealousy. Benjamin had been trying to help, not steal one of Oscar's firsts.

With a feeling of inevitability, she gripped him under the arms and held him out. "Want to take him around again? I'd like to see."

Only when joy washed over Benjamin's face did she realize how hurt he'd been by her distrust. Now two faces looked back at her with happy expectation. Her heart fluttered in a totally different way than its earlier panic.

"Go on, Oscar." She swallowed to hide her sudden tenderness for the man and boy in front of her. "Show Mommy what you've got."

CHAPTER SIX

Lynn wasn't sure how or why, but when the Canyon Cats were on the road, the arena had a completely different feel. It was as if the team took all the vitality with them, leaving the huge building hollow and lifeless.

During the two-week homestand that had started the Tuesday after Benjamin took Oscar skating, her schedule had been erratic and inconsistent as she'd adjusted her days to accommodate the need to be at the rink during games. Now the team was out of town for a short stint, she should be happy to have a few days of nine to five and the weekend free. Instead, she fidgeted restlessly and found it hard to settle into her usual efficient mode.

It had nothing to do with missing Benjamin. It couldn't. How could you miss someone you only said hi to when you passed in the hall or waved to from the stands while he guided his young players through drills and exercises?

Though it was a little more than that, if she were honest with herself. They never just said hello. Benjamin always asked about Oscar, and she would commiserate or congratulate on the most recent game. And her visits during practices had become less stealthy. Now she took a seat near the glass and while she didn't intentionally interrupt his concentration on the task at hand, Benjamin never failed to acknowledge her presence with a nod or a smile.

She forced her attention back to the online calendar filling her screen. The Canyon Cats might be taking up the majority of her time these days, but she had other clients to deal with. Like the music promoter bringing two concerts to the arena in the next month, and the comic con organizer who had booked the facility for next spring.

As she plotted and planned, part of her brain remained consumed with the Canyon Cats conundrum. It was ridiculous that Brewster hadn't yet found a replacement for the marketing coordinator, and she had to assume it was part of his strategy to get out of his lease. That assumption made her work harder to bring people into the stands. So far, things had been hovering around the breakeven point. She needed to come up with something big to get more momentum going.

"Lynn?" Cynthie called. "Do you have a minute?"

"Be right there." Saving a draft of the email she was writing, she grabbed a spiral notebook and pen and headed to Cynthie's inner office. "What do you need?"

Her boss waved her to a seat. "I wanted to update you on the Canyon Cats marketing coordinator position."

"Funny you should mention it. I was just wondering about that."

"I'm sure you can't wait to pass on those duties and get back to normal."

"I suppose." She took the offered chair, oddly disconcerted by Cynthie's comment. While it would be a relief to have a reprieve from the odd hours and lost weekends working with the Canyon Cats required, she would miss the excitement of game nights. And the excuse to talk with Benjamin. "I'm not sure I want Brewster to have more influence over the marketing than he does now. I suspect he asked us because he thought we'd do a lousy job, if only because we wouldn't have the time." She bit the end of her pen thoughtfully. "Do you think he's stalling in the hopes we'll get irritated enough to revoke our help?"

"I wouldn't put it past him. When I talked with him today, his excuse was they hadn't received any acceptable resumes yet." Her sarcastic tone made it clear what she thought of that excuse.

Lynn snorted in agreement. "The last person was fresh out of college and had no experience at all. What is he waiting for?"

Cynthie smiled with tight lips. "Personally, I think you're right on the mark, and he's hoping we drop the ball or give up entirely. I know these additional duties are complicating your life, but I'm glad you agree we shouldn't be in a hurry to return them to someone on Brewster's team. Since you don't work for him, he can't exactly badger you into weaker promotions or cutting back on fan contests. Anyone he hires will be limited by what he allows them to do."

"He's not making things easy." She frowned, recalling the roadblocks he'd placed in her path. "I've been trying to arrange community appearances for the players and coaches, and he's put his foot down on most of them, saying it would be disruptive to the team."

"A team needs to be connected to the community and its fanbase. What have you pitched him?"

"I wanted to duplicate a few things from last year, like a celebrity chili cook off and a charity dunk tank."

"What we need are events that would make the team look bad if they didn't attend. Hospital visits to sick kids, appearances at long-term care homes, that sort of thing."

Lynn nodded. "I like it. When I present to him, I can hint at the negative publicity should he reject the ideas. He may not want too many people in the stands, but he certainly doesn't want a grassroots revolt that would make the team unwelcome in another city."

"Exactly." Cynthie rubbed her palms together as if readying for battle. "Let's get Sarah in here and see what else we can come up with. Brewster won't know what hit him."

It wasn't uncommon for an owner to attend his team's away games. After all, most of them were well-heeled and had the money necessary to travel when and where they wanted. But Benjamin was still surprised to see Peterson Brewster striding down the hotel hallway just as the team was boarding the bus on their way to their opponent's arena for the last game of the road trip.

Brewster didn't have to clear his schedule with Benjamin, of course, and the owner's presence wouldn't influence his actions or decisions in any way. But a little warning would have been nice.

"Benny, I'm glad I caught you." Brewster slapped him on the shoulder in his usual bluff and hearty manner. "Where's Simpson?"

"In his seat." It was one of the reasons Benjamin liked the young man. He was usually the first on the bus and the last off the ice, and his work ethic and leadership made him valuable for more than his goal-scoring ability. He and Benjamin had developed a strong connection that was going to be the bedrock of the team's success.

"I need to talk with him. Go get him, will you?"

A stone formed in Benjamin's gut. "Why?" The single word echoed eerily in his head.

Brewster's jovial expression hardened, and the wily businessman masked behind the good old boy stared out. "Just get him."

Heart thumping, stomach roiling, Benjamin followed Levi Ghostkeeper up the stairs of the rumbling motorcoach. Young men in suits and ties filled the rows. Simpson sat in his usual place, about midway down the bus. "Garret? Can I see you for a minute?"

"Sure, Coach." The lanky youth strode down the narrow aisle. His draft year was coming up and, barring disasters, it was expected he'd go fairly high. Maybe not first round, but second was a definite possibility. That would make him the highest drafted Canyon Cat in several years.

"What do you need him for?" Levi moved into his seat to allow Simpson by. His tone skirted the edge of disrespect, as it usually did. Despite—or maybe because of—the fact the team had bettered their record from this time last year, he still hadn't warmed up to Benjamin.

Hoping against hope he was reading Brewster's request wrong, Benjamin shrugged a wordless response and led Simpson to where the owner waited. Dread dogged his heels at every step.

Brewster wasted no time. "Simpson, I have good news. You've been traded to the Red Devils."

The cloud of apprehension hovering above Benjamin's head thundered down. The worst of his suspicions had been confirmed.

"What?" The teenager looked as stunned as Benjamin felt.

"Pack your bags. You're now a member of the number one team in the league. Congratulations." Brewster beamed, apparently oblivious to the devastation he was wreaking.

Benjamin couldn't believe he was losing his best player. Couldn't believe an owner would make a decision so disastrous to his own team. Couldn't believe he, as head coach, hadn't been given any warning.

Couldn't say a word, as he watched Brewster guide Simpson away, while the future he'd been sweating over crashed down around him.

Lynn tapped her way to the radio app on her phone and placed it on the low coffee table in front of her. Few regular season junior hockey games were broadcast on television, but every team had arrangements with local radio stations, and she'd fallen into the habit of listening to the Canyon Cats, especially when they were out of town. Oscar had been fussy tonight, taking longer to get to sleep than usual, so she was tuning in several minutes past the start of the game.

Stephanie came into the living room, a glass of wine in each hand. Even in the security and comfort of their shared house, Lynn rarely saw her with an unmade face or messy hair or in grubby clothing. Her concession to an in-home Friday evening was to wear silky suit-style pajamas, clear lip gloss and only a single swipe of mascara.

"How are they doing?" She handed Lynn a glass, sat in the plushly upholstered chair set at angles to the couch, and picked up the magazine she'd been reading.

"Down two goals already, with more than half the first period to go." Lynn sipped her drink and frowned. "The announcer mentioned something unexpected happened before the game started, but I don't know what he was talking about." She put down her glass and picked up her crochet project. She'd recently started doing needlework, as it gave her something to do as she listened.

The period wound down and nothing more was said about the pre-game incident, but she realized she hadn't heard Garrett Simpson's name in the play-by-play. "I think something happened to their top player. I hope he didn't get injured." She looped the yarn over the hook and stabbed it into the stitches with nervous fingers, anxious for Benjamin's sake.

The buzzer sounded and the announcer did his recap. "At the end of the first frame, it's the Rapids three, the Canyon Cats zero. Obviously learning that Garrett Simpson had been traded just hours before the game has caused some chaos in the Cats' lineup. We'll take a closer look at the situation during the intermission. Stick around."

Her jaw dropped. "They traded Simpson? Why on earth—" Her teeth clacked together as understanding flooded through her. "That son of a bitch."

Stephanie's neatly plucked eyebrows rose, and she waggled her wineglass in a questioning gesture. "Who's a son of a bitch?"

"Peterson Brewster." Lynn tossed her work to the side, sprang to her feet, and prowled the room, too agitated to concentrate.

"Why? Isn't he allowed to make trades?"

"It's usually up to the general manager, but Brewster's a hands-on owner. His GM does what he's told without question." She couldn't imagine what Benjamin was feeling right now. He'd pinned his hopes on Simpson, built plays around him, worked one on one with him. All that effort, wasted.

All because Brewster was willing to sabotage his own team in order to get out of his contract.

"Doesn't this sort of thing happen all the time?" Stephanie flipped a page of her magazine, unperturbed. Lynn wished she could view the situation with the same equanimity.

"Not like this it doesn't." She was *this close* to blurting out what Brewster was really up to and ground her teeth together to keep the words bottled up inside. Not that she didn't trust Stephanie—Lynn knew she had kept more difficult secrets. But if she was going to break her promise to Cynthie it was going to be to the person most affected, no one else.

Benjamin.

CHAPTER SEVEN

At the team's first practice after the Simpson trade and the seven-nothing shellacking that had followed, Benjamin did his best to cajole his players back into a cohesive unit. There was nothing anyone could do about losing their captain, and they had to find a way to move forward.

Most of the coaching and training staff had been philosophical about the trade. Levi, however, blamed Benjamin. Despite his frequent protestations that he had also been blindsided by Brewster's news, nothing he said assuaged the assistant coach. He remained disgruntled and obstructive. Unwilling to confront him and cause more drama, Benjamin simply set his assignments and then left Levi to his own devices, hoping things would smooth out without a face-to-face duel.

Too bad a similar policy of avoidance wouldn't be possible with the player that had replaced Simpson. From his position at centre ice, Benjamin watched the newest member of the Canyon Cats glide lackadaisically through the puck-handling drills Levi was running.

Valeri Nechayev's reputation as a headcase was one of the league's worst kept secrets. While no one could deny his skill and talent, he was arrogant and intimidating in the dressing room and took stupid, impulsive penalties on the ice. He'd been drafted two years ago but hadn't managed to crack his NHL team's roster. The result was a huge chip on his shoulder and a sense of entitlement that was evident from the moment Benjamin met him.

Left unchecked, Valeri's attitude would poison the team and destroy any progress he had already made. The time to set boundaries was now.

Swallowing down his queasiness at the upcoming skirmish, he blew his whistle. "Water break, guys. We'll work on specialty teams next. Valeri?" The Russian-born player turned to Benjamin, bored dismissal etched on his face. "Bring your bottle over here. I want to talk about where you'll fit in."

With no pretense of enthusiasm, Valeri joined Benjamin on the side of the rink opposite the players' benches, where the rest of the team and staff were gathered. Levi stared across the ice, squinting with suspicion, but Benjamin ignored him. He had bigger problems at the moment.

"Look," he said to Valeri in a conciliatory tone, "I know you're not happy about the trade. It's disappointing to leave a contender for a team struggling to make the playoffs."

"You think?" The young man refused to meet Benjamin's gaze and stared into the empty seats. Behind the clear visor attached to his helmet, his face was set in sullen lines.

"You need to learn to deal with things like this. It won't be the last time your career takes an unexpected turn." Especially if his attitude didn't improve. Being a shit-disturber to throw off the opposition was one thing—being one in the dressing room was frowned upon at all levels.

"Why should I listen to you?" Valeri straightened from his hipshot stance and pinned Benjamin with an icy-blue glare. "It's not like you figured out how to deal. I looked you up. You were a hot shot kid in this tiny little town, but you blew your chance. I'm not going to be like you. I'm going to make it." The guttural traces of his native Russian only highlighted his dismissive tone.

Okay, enough with the sympathy. "You'll listen to me because I am your coach, and if you want to play you'll do what I say, when I say it."

Valeri's eyes widened a fraction though his expression remained belligerent. "I'm the best player on the team. You need me."

Benjamin shook his head. "You forget, no one expects this team to do anything but lose." No one but Benjamin, that was. "If you play and we lose, no one will be surprised. If I bench you and we lose, same deal." He knew he'd have to make good on his threat if Valeri didn't come to the table, and no matter how disruptive he might be, he was still the Canyon Cats' best chance to get into the win column. But Benjamin was responsible for the whole team, not just one player, and if he had to list Valeri as a healthy scratch, he would.

Even if that jeopardized his own goal of reaching the playoffs. He pinched his nose with two fingers to fight off the faint sense of panic that thought sparked.

Valeri studied him. "You're bluffing."

His stomach clenched but he kept his voice firm. "Try me."

The Russian hesitated then gave a brusque nod.

It wasn't much of a concession, but Benjamin would take it. "Okay. Now tell me what you know about our power play unit."

Lynn paced back and forth under the bleachers, invisible to anyone on the ice but close enough to hear the action. The practice was coming to an end, and she was lying in wait to snag Benjamin for a private conversation.

She'd been awake much of the night debating whether to tell him about Peterson Brewster's hidden agenda. If Cynthie found out, she'd be furious. But she'd seen the devotion and drive Benjamin brought to the team. Didn't he deserve to know how the cards were stacked? It wasn't fair for him to be labouring so hard and not know his owner was working against him.

Or was it better he *didn't* know so he could keep his focus where it belonged—on the team, not on the boardroom drama?

She'd teeter-tottered back and forth all night long. Even now she wasn't one hundred percent sure telling him was the right thing, but she'd committed to that decision and was sticking to it. If their roles were reversed, she knew she would want to know.

The players streamed off the ice and down the hall leading away from her, heading to their locker room. The four years between sixteen and twenty and the youths' random growth patterns were evident in their varied heights and bulk. Some seemed tall enough to touch the rafters, others only coming to their teammates' shoulders. The training and coaching staff followed, with Benjamin the last to appear.

She stepped out of the shadows. "Hey."

Lifting his attention from the tablet he carried, he smiled. "Hey, yourself. I didn't see you in the stands today."

Knowing he'd looked for her warmed a hidden part of her heart but did nothing to allay the butterflies dancing in her belly. "Can we talk?"

His attention sharpened. "Of course. Is everything okay with Oscar?"

The ember glowed brighter. "Yes, he's great." She led Benjamin to a room under the stairs that climbed to the main concourse level. It was a catchall location for broken chairs and old posters and various other discarded bits and pieces. She shut the door behind them, barricading them into the claustrophobic space.

"I have an office, you know." Confused amusement lit his dark eyes.

"We can't talk about this anywhere someone might hear."

His alarm returned. "What's going on?"

"You can't tell anyone else what I'm about to tell you." She twisted her hands together.

"You're freaking me out, Lynn." The lines at the side of his mouth deepened.

"It's just..." She took a deep breath. "I'm not supposed to know this. If you let on that *you* know, I could get into big trouble."

He took a small step forward, dipping his chin to make direct eye contact. "I promise I won't tell anyone. And I promise to help with whatever it is."

His solemn oath solidified her wavering intention. "Peterson Brewster wants to move the team."

He was still for a moment, and then his shoulders slumped. It seemed an admission of defeat and it made her realize there might be layers to this news she hadn't considered. It was too late to back down now.

"That's his prerogative." Even his tone was resigned. "Why all the secrecy?"

Lynn explained how Cynthie had learned of the plan. "The thing is, Brewster still has three years left on the contract with the arena. The only way he can move the team before it expires is if the city fails to honour any commitment in the agreement. One of those commitments is fan attendance. If it falls below a certain level over the course of a given season, the contract can be ended without penalty."

It took him barely the blink of an eye to reach the same conclusion she had. "He traded Simpson to hamstring any progress I've made so far." He raked a hand through his hair and a tousled curl fell onto his forehead. "And brought in Nechayev to be a distraction at best, a liability at worst."

Benjamin wondered if his own expression was as miserable as Lynn's. She stared with wide, worried eyes, her fingers snaking together in a Gordian knot.

"I don't know for sure why he traded Simpson. But it seems rather suspicious." She gnawed her upper lip with her lower teeth. "I hope I did right, telling you. Maybe you would have rather not known."

"No, it's better this way. I think." His mind raced. There were so many angles and aspects to this news he needed more time to process it.

"You understand why you can't let on that you know."

He dragged his thoughts away from all the ways Brewster could screw up the team and Benjamin's own plans to concentrate on Lynn. "Other than the fact your boss found out by eavesdropping, which I can see would be regarded as unprofessional? Am I missing something else?"

"If Brewster knows we know, he has nothing to lose by being even more obstructive than he is now. At the moment, the only leverage I have is that hc has to act, at least some of the time, as if he's here for the long haul."

"He's being obstructive?" His teeth clenched at the thought of Brewster making Lynn's life difficult, his protective instinct kicking in.

"Nothing I can't handle." She rolled her shoulders. Her light cardigan was unbuttoned to expose a silky V-necked blouse. The blue material, shiny in the harsh overhead fluorescents, shifted over her full breasts.

Benjamin quickly returned his gaze to her face. "Let me know if there's anything I can do to help."

Her smile flashed, there and gone like sun rays dancing across water. "You worry about what happens on the ice, I'll handle off."

"Community activities aren't only good for the community, you know." Her light floral perfume overlaid the scent of concrete and disinfectant permeating the small room and he resisted the urge to lean in and sniff her neck. "Team appearances build camaraderie and connection among the players.

Nechayev might need some...encouragement...fitting in. It would be good for him to get out with his teammates."

She tilted her head. "Are you saying you'd put your support behind such an event and do your best to prevent Brewster from kiboshing it?"

"We both have stakes in this game." Lynn needed to keep people in the seats, and he needed to build a winning team. Neither would happen if Brewster's scheming went unchallenged. "I don't see a downside to working together."

"Awesome. Thank you." Smiling widely, she stepped forward and hugged him.

His arms encircled her waist, and he rested his chin on the crown of her head as if he'd done it a thousand times before. Though their night together had been more than two years ago, his body remembered the feel of her lushness pressed against him, the texture of her hair against his throat, and instantly reacted.

She had to have felt the swelling of his cock. He immediately loosened his hold so she could escape his embarrassing response. Instead of retreating as he expected, she lifted her chin and stared up at him.

CHAPTER EIGHT

Lynn couldn't help it. She pressed her hips against Benjamin's erection, bulging beneath the thin nylon of his athletic pants. His dark eyes, framed by stubby ebony lashes, widened.

"Benjamin?" She had no idea what she was asking. The pulse thrumming hard and fast in her throat made her voice breathy. Her fingers moved restlessly on his back, the slippery material of his windbreaker cool and slick. Heat pooled between her legs, and she squirmed to relieve the pressure.

With a groan that was almost a growl, he lowered his head. Her mouth opened in immediate welcome. The kiss started gentle, soft lips and sweeping tongues, but soon the banked embers in her belly roared into open flame. The memories of their incendiary night together, which she'd kept doused under the blanket of motherhood, ignited.

She hooked her calf around his lower leg and rose on tiptoe, trusting in his strength to keep her balanced. Her hands slid up his back and clamped onto his shoulder blades as she fused their mouths, tasting, tempting, teasing. His arms banded around her, one circling her waist, the other under her ass to lift her even closer.

She had no idea how much time passed before he dragged his mouth away and rested his forehead against hers. Their gasping breaths mingled as he eased her down and made sure her feet were planted before loosening his grip. Pressing her palms flat against his chest, she leaned back and stared, dazed, into his heavy-lidded eyes. His heart beat a ragged tattoo under her touch, a drumroll that matched her own.

Passion pressed against the walls of the tiny room like helium in a well-inflated balloon. She had to deflate it before it expanded into more than an impulsive kiss.

She cleared her throat. "Well. That was interesting." Her fingers still trembled with the aftershocks of desire, and she masked it by smoothing the slick material of his jacket.

His eyes narrowed. "Interesting? Is that what you'd call it?"

"Would unexpected be a better word?" She couldn't let him believe her lusty response was a sign they should resume where they'd left off two years ago. "Apparently, we are still attracted to one another, but we aren't the same people we were that night. I'm a mom. You're building a new career. Neither of us has time for a relationship. This was just a relapse. Something we needed to get out of our system. Right?"

"Right." He released her, stepping out of arm's reach, and she resisted the urge to lean in as if he was magnetized. "So, what are we going to do about Brewster?"

She blinked and struggled to remember what he was talking about. That fiery kiss had burned away her short-term memory. Hiding her wobbling knees by resting against the tall metal shelf at her back, she gripped the wire slats and did her best to re-wrap her cloak of professionalism. "I don't know yet. I'll come up with something he can't refuse, and we'll go from there."

He nodded. "Okay then." His hand drifted up, his fingers extended as if he was going to trace them along her jaw, but dropped to his side before he touched her. "Let me know when you do. See you around."

He opened the door and disappeared, leaving it ajar. Lynn's breath whooshed out as if he'd taken all the oxygen with him. She sank into a chair boasting two missing casters and balanced gingerly on the seat.

His rapid departure left her dizzy and disoriented. One second, she'd been enfolded in his arms, her mouth locked to his. The next, he was gone.

Something important had just happened, but she didn't know what. Figuring it out would have to wait. Sarah and Cynthie might be wondering where she was.

But first she needed a minute to recover her equilibrium.

Maybe two.

I'm a mom. *You're building a new career.*

Lynn's words reverberated in Benjamin's bones during the next few days.

What had he been thinking, giving into the impulse to kiss her? Yes, his body had reacted to her embrace, but that didn't mean his mind shut off.

Except he'd been unable to resist the taste of her, the lush globes of her ass, the soft warmth of her pressed against his hardness. Sensations he relived with his hand around his cock late at night.

She was one hundred percent right. Neither of them had time for a relationship. Especially now he knew about Brewster's machinations. His redemption would be even harder to achieve with an owner actively working against him. He couldn't allow himself to be distracted from his goal.

To say nothing of her reminder that she was a parent. That had been better than a bucket of cold water. A relationship with Lynn meant a relationship with her son. And as cute as the kid was, he deserved a better father figure than Benjamin.

By the weekend, she had yet to approach him with any ideas on circumventing Brewster's plans. He didn't know whether to be relieved their next encounter was delayed or concerned she hadn't come up with any solutions yet. The two absolutely lousy games the Canyon Cats played Friday and Saturday did nothing to unravel his tangled thoughts. He wanted to lay most of the blame on the disrupting influence of Valeri Nechayev, but worried his preoccupation with Lynn may have caused him to lose focus. He couldn't let thoughts of what the skin behind her knees might feel like detour him off his route to the playoffs.

Sunday was Halloween, and Sadie had coerced Benjamin into assisting Jujhar in handing out goodies while she took their children trick-or-treating. "I can't trust him to hear the door," she had said, "not while the hockey game is on." Jujhar's two favourite teams were playing each other. "Maybe between the two of you at least some kids will get their candy."

After that first, less awkward than he'd thought it would be dinner, he and Jujhar had kept in touch. Despite Sadie's warm but mostly wordless encouragement, they had yet to slip completely back into their old friendship. He was determined to do nothing that would jeopardize their reconciliation, which meant that, though he wasn't feeling the least bit festive after the week he'd had, he couldn't renege on his promise to Sadie.

He dragged himself off the couch in his barren apartment at the appointed time, and a few minutes later pulled to the curb outside the Malhotra home, parking behind a newer model bright yellow Volkswagen Bug—an ironically cheerful reminder of the other reason he was leery about this evening.

His mother had been invited, too. As she was to all Malhotra family events.

Jujhar had been billeted with Thea and Ron Whitestone for his last year with the Canyon Cats and the three had grown close. While Benjamin had been doing his best to crack the NHL—and failing—Jujhar had taken advantage of the junior league's excellent educational incentives and gone to the local university. There he had met Sadie, and instead of returning to Surrey where he'd grown up, they'd married and built a life in Prince George, with Thea and Ron as surrogate grandparents to their children.

He was a much better son than Benjamin.

Swallowing down his jealousy, he clasped the bag containing the full-sized chocolate bars he'd brought for the kids and headed up the path to the front porch. Three jack-o-lanterns with misshapen eyes and square teeth rested on the stoop, candles flickering inside their hollowed-out skulls. He drew a deep breath, rolled his shoulders, and let himself in.

Toeing off his shoes, he draped his coat over the newel post and followed the sounds of playful growls, whining protests, and raised voices down the hall.

No one noticed him, not even Barney, who had a swatch of black and teal material clenched in his jaws and was in a tug of war with Eli. *Some watchdog you are.* He stood in the entry leading to the open plan kitchen and family room and surveyed the chaos.

Chaos might be too harsh a word. The confusion wasn't much worse than the locker room after a practice. But compared to the stillness and silence of his own single bedroom apartment, it was overwhelming.

Jujhar stepped in to end the battle between Eli and Barney, freeing what turned out to be a hockey jersey from the puppy's maw and helping his son don it over the shoulder pads he already wore. Sadie soothed Ella, tearful for an unknown-to-Benjamin reason, as she set a princess tiara on the little girl's head. Elaine stood next to them, proclaiming they would miss all the good treats if they didn't go soon, wearing a one-piece navy-blue snowsuit with round circles and stars sewn on it and holding a snowmobile helmet under her arm. An astronaut, he presumed. In the corner of the sofa, watching it all with a tender, amused expression, was his mother.

Despite the tears and insanity, it was a welcome, homey scene. And it made Benjamin's chest ache so hard he had to rub his fist on his breastbone to catch his breath.

Thea saw him before the others. "Benjamin!" She sprang from the couch and hurried forward. "It's so good to see you." Her quick hug left him wishing for the courage to gather her in for another squeeze, but he let her go.

"You, too, Mom." His Auntie Janet had suffered complications after her hip surgery and his mother's planned two-week stay had extended to almost two months. She'd only arrived home Friday and he'd used the Canyon Cats games as an excuse to avoid her a little longer. She'd said she'd understood in her calm practical voice, which had, perversely, irritated him. She should have berated him for not making time to see her. He deserved her condemnation, not her tolerance.

For so many reasons.

He intended to change that. He was making his peace with Jujhar, now he had to heal his bond with his mother. He'd spent far too many years away, and while his career might send him across the continent again someday, he wouldn't waste this opportunity to at least try and be the son she deserved. To make up for cutting short her time with her husband.

"Okay, picture time!" Sadie's shout interrupted him before he could add to his pathetic greeting. Thea smiled and turned away and frustration gnawed at him. Maybe now wasn't the best night to make amends, but he should have managed *something*.

The children bunched by the back door and Sadie snapped photos for posterity, despite Elaine's scowl and Ella's red-rimmed eyes. Eli was wearing a jersey from one of the many teams Benjamin had played for, one so big it reached his knees. It was only when the boy turned to follow his sisters out the door that he saw *Whitestone* stretched from shoulder to shoulder.

He strode forward and stopped him with a gentle hand. "Where did you get the jersey, Eli?"

He looked up with his gap-toothed grin. "I have one from each of your teams. Dad got them for me." Before he could get over the shock of that, Sadie and Thea ushered the children out the door and it shut with a solid click.

"Thank god. Finally, some peace and quiet." Jujhar dropped into the squashy sofa and lifted the remote to unmute the television, already tuned to the sports channel. The doorbell rang and he groaned.

"I'll get it." Benjamin hurried down the hall and opened the door to a motley group of children chanting the age-old refrain. He tossed candy from the bowl waiting on the lowest tread of the stairs into their pillowcases, shut the door, and hurried back to the family room. "How did you get my jerseys?"

"Hmmm?" Jujhar remained focused on the screen.

"How did you get my jerseys?" Only top names like Crosby and McDavid and Petterson had memorabilia widely available.

"Ordered them online from the team stores." Jujhar didn't take his attention from the play. When the doorbell rang again and he didn't move, Benjamin realized Sadie hadn't been exaggerating. He went to answer it and was kept at the entrance through several groups of children.

His thoughts whirled. Jujhar had gone to significant trouble to attain his jerseys. It was a show of support he hadn't expected. And the fact that Eli wanted to go *as Benjamin* for Halloween was even more touching. Or dismaying. He wasn't sure which.

The horn for the first period sounded and Jujhar followed its echo down the hall to join Benjamin at the front door. The parade of kids had been so steady he hadn't bothered to go back to the family room, instead taking up residence on the stairs leading to the second floor.

"Hey, man. I'm supposed to be doing this." He nudged Benjamin over and took a seat on the tread next to him. "Don't tell Sadie."

"I think she knows." Jujhar grinned at his dry tone. "It's okay. I'm kind of enjoying it." That wasn't a lie. Seeing the kids, especially the tiny ones, in costume warmed a long-ignored corner of his heart.

Jujhar answered the next knock. After distributing the candy, he closed the door on the bitter October night and Benjamin asked something that had been niggling at him for a while. "Did you ever imagine a life like this when we were playing hockey together? A wife, kids, in-laws?"

Jujhar laughed. "Of course not. Then I grew up. Don't get me wrong—there are days I want to escape to the mountains and never come back. But they are far outnumbered by the days I can't believe how lucky I am."

Women had come and gone in Benjamin's life. Once or twice, he'd thought he might be in love, but the moment the subject of children came up he'd run the other way. His dad had been an amazing father, and he knew he'd never be able to live up to that example. Especially since he hadn't managed to be a half-decent son, even before that last, devastating phone call.

But not wanting kids didn't mean he wanted to spend his life alone, and the older he got the stronger his urge to find someone to share his life with. Someone who shared his intention never to have children.

How ironic he was now obsessing over a woman who was already a mother.

Lynn had felt exactly right in his arms. And not just that—he'd found something in her embrace, something he thought he'd lost long ago. Not that he could put a label on it. But *something* had felt different.

Then she'd reminded him he'd been kissing *a mother*, and his heart had almost stopped. He'd fled as soon as he could. Which was probably why she hadn't spoken with him since. She'd seen his panic and didn't want him anywhere near her son.

As he and Jujhar took turns answering the door for the rest of the evening, he reflected on the brief time he'd been responsible for Oscar a few weeks ago. Lynn's frantic reaction dimmed the memory slightly but wasn't enough to cancel out his joy at introducing the baby to skating. Simpson and the rest of the players had laughed and joked with the boy and been extra careful around him. He wondered if they had all been remembering similar times of camaraderie and fellowship with their fathers, like he had.

One thing was certain. If he wanted to explore his attraction to Lynn, he had to be absolutely sure he was ready to welcome Oscar into his life, too. There wasn't one without the other.

CHAPTER NINE

Technology was a wonderful thing when it worked. Ever since Oscar's birth, it had worked to keep Lynn's parents connected with their third grandchild.

Tonight, she and her son were seated on the couch in front of the television with all the wires and doodads hooked up so Oscar could see Rupert and Minerva larger-than-life on the screen. A true child of the 2020s, he reacted to their presence as if they were in the same room, clapping and smiling and babbling.

"He's getting so big." Minerva's smile was wistful. "I can't wait to snuggle him again."

"Christmas isn't that far away. I missed seeing you last year. Maybe you could come then?" Lynn asked the question for form's sake. She knew her parents—and especially her father—too well to expect a firm answer. Even family holidays didn't stand in the way of her father's goals.

Rupert didn't disappoint. "We'll have to check the schedule and get back to you. You know this is a busy time of year."

It was always a busy time of year in the cruise ship entertainment business. The ships never stopped sailing, just the routes changed. Which was why Oscar had only met his grandparents in person during one fleeting visit several months ago.

"Where are you now?" She'd given up keeping track.

"Cozumel. Five-night route through the Caribbean out of Tampa Bay. Good crowd. We're really building our fanbase."

Her seventy-two-year-old father's dreams of catapulting to music stardom hadn't yet been dimmed, despite the fact he was now singing covers on cruise ships. Lynn wished she could respect his endless optimism, but it just made her tired.

"Shall I read to you, Oscar?" Minerva held up *Goodnight, Moon* and Oscar squirmed and crowed on Lynn's lap.

As Rupert's backup singer and tambourine player, her mother was the sole remaining member of the band he'd formed in the late sixties. Lynn was certain she was only doing the circuit because Rupert refused to quit, not from any personal commitment. Five years ago, she'd put her foot down, though, and the cruise ship gig was a compromise—they kept performing, but at least they had a home base. Of sorts.

Which was more than Lynn and her twin sister Henna had had growing up. The family had travelled from town to town in a decrepit old van, crisscrossing Canada and the United States, rarely staying anywhere longer than a few months. They'd been home-schooled by Minerva, a necessity considering their peripatetic lifestyle, and when neither had shown any musical talent—much to Rupert's chagrin—had filled in as roadies and ticket-takers and other odd jobs once they were old enough.

Minerva finished reading the picture book to Oscar. Rupert, restless as always, returned to a familiar complaint.

"So, Crystal-Lynn—ready to toss all that corporate bullshit and come on the road again?" He had never reconciled himself to the fact both his daughters had chosen stability over what he termed *a life of adventure.*

"I don't think so, Rupert." Yet another affectation her counterculture parent had insisted on. She couldn't wait for Oscar to call her Mama. "I'm happy here."

Lynn and Henna had turned eighteen while their parents were performing at a music festival in Prince George. Sticking to the pact they'd made years before, they found jobs as servers and rented an apartment before breaking the news that they were staying put when the festival ended. Minerva had been resigned—Lynn still wondered if she'd known of her daughters' plans through some sort of parental osmosis—but Rupert had been furious. He'd refused to talk to either of them for months after.

A few years later, Henna had moved to Edmonton. She and her husband had been together for almost two decades and had two teenage children. Lynn—who had dropped the Crystal from her name the day she'd started at the local university—had stayed in Prince George. And despite her plans for a "normal" life taking a couple detours, she truly was content.

Rupert accepted today's rejection with equanimity and for a moment she thought they'd be able to end the conversation on a high note. Until he asked, "Have you spoken with Lance lately?"

The mention of her renegade fiancé no longer hurt as much as it had, but it was never pleasant to be reminded of him. Which her father did on a fairly regular basis. "No, of course not."

He scowled. She wished it was because he was angry at Lance for breaking her heart, but she knew better. It was because her ex was living the life Rupert yearned for. Asking after him was like picking at a hangnail just to make it bleed.

If she'd known her quiet, soft-spoken lover had dreams of being a country music star, she would never have wasted seven years of her life on him. Not that he'd hidden his talent. She'd been drawn to his creative side almost as much as his steady, solid career as an accountant. Which had made his decision to give it all up and chase the music such a shock. Almost as much of a shock as when he had a Top 20 hit a year later.

Knowing her father would soon be ranting about young people having it too easy these days, she offered a distraction. "Did I tell you Oscar went skating a couple weeks ago?"

"You did? Aren't you a big boy." Minerva clapped her hands and Oscar laughed. "Did you take him, Crystal-Lynn? When did you learn to skate?"

"I can hobble around. But it wasn't me. A friend took him."

"Oh?" Minerva's eyebrows arched. At odds to her own unusual lifestyle, her mother held the conventional opinion that a single woman, especially one with a child, was incomplete without a man. "What kind of a friend?"

The kind whose kisses set my soul on fire. No way would she stoke her mother's curiosity with such an admission, however. "The coach of the Canyon Cats. He and I are working together on a couple projects."

It had taken her a week to gather the equanimity to face Benjamin after their encounter in the tiny room under the stairs. He'd been his usual kind, amiable self, though her stomach had twisted and turned the entire time they'd spoken. Her gaze had been constantly drawn to his mouth, remembering the feel of those lips on hers, and she'd had to forcibly remind herself a repeat of the kiss was off the table. Far, far, off. They needed to focus on the professional side of their relationship. Not the personal.

She'd just have to ignore how attractive his person was.

The habits of more than a decade were proving hard to break.

Benjamin knew a better man would have taken Lynn aside and cleared the air in a private conversation. He would have confessed his concerns about Oscar—not about the boy himself, but Benjamin's relationship with him. They would have discussed their attraction rationally and calmly and would have decided either to move forward or remain strictly colleagues.

He hadn't actively avoided Lynn. When she'd requested a meeting to discuss community events designed to defeat Brewster, he'd attended without protest. After all, he'd pledged his help in the campaign. It was immaterial that he had spent much of the conversation distracted by her throaty voice and shining hair, wishing he was brave enough to ask for what he wanted.

Another kiss. And maybe more.

Before encountering Lynn several weeks ago, he'd wondered if the intense memories he had of their night together were a phenomenon of the passage of time. Since their kiss, he realized the months between their meetings had *diminished* his recollection, not exaggerated it.

As he pulled into the arena parking lot on the morning of November 11, he did his best to shove all thoughts of Lynn to the background. The team had lost every game since the Simpson/Nechayev trade, including the last two on the road. They'd fallen below five-hundred and while there were still months to go in the season, Benjamin was already having nightmares of failing. Yet again.

Though it was a weekday, the game was set to start at two o'clock, since all offices and most businesses were closed for Remembrance Day. Pre-game ceremonies would include an honour guard and a salute to veterans and the team would be wearing specially designed camouflage jerseys.

None of which explained the kennels and crates lined up outside one set of rear doors leading onto the arena concourse. He drove past slowly and parked in the spot reserved for the head coach near the staff entrance. Unable to restrain his curiosity, he made his way back along the road.

Several people wearing matching blue jackets moved around the crates. Barks, yowls, and yips echoed between the high wall of the building and the embankment on the opposite side. As he approached, the arena doors opened, revealing Lynn with Oscar on her hip, framed against the dark interior.

Her gaze swept past the river of sound and motion separating them and met his. Her mouth curved in a soft smile and his heart squeezed.

He'd never considered motherhood sexy before. He was considering it now.

She nodded at him but spoke to the round, red-headed woman who seemed to be in charge of the blue jackets. "You can start bringing the crates inside. The area is all marked out in Section N." Once the procession began, she descended the steps and joined him at road level. "Can I interest you in an animal companion? We have dogs, cats, rabbits, and an iguana."

"An iguana?" The light dawned. "Adopt-a-Pet Day?"

"Yes." Oscar wound his chubby fingers into Lynn's ponytail and yanked. She winced and reached back to grip her son's arm. "Ouch. It's gotten a lot of attention from fans, so hopefully it goes well." Another yank, another wince.

"Let me help." Benjamin stepped behind her and set to unfastening Oscar's grip, which the boy thought was a wonderful game. He giggled and kicked and refused to let go. Lynn's hair was silky and cool, and he couldn't help accidentally brushing the nape of her neck with the back of his hands as he worked. "How have you been? Both of you."

"Good. Sorry about the road trip."

It was Benjamin's turn to wince. He didn't want to talk about it. "Yeah." He swept her ponytail to the opposite side, out of Oscar's reach. "There you go."

"Thanks." She turned to face him.

"No problem." The pale November sun highlighted

the tiny creases at the corner of her eyes and mouth. He wondered how old she was. If he had to guess, he'd place her a few years older than him, but birthdays hadn't come up in any conversation yet. Not that knowing the detail would alter the attraction he couldn't suppress.

"Hopefully you can get a win today. I've arranged for Sarah, one of my colleagues, to cover the on-ice activations so I can bring Oscar with me. It'll be his first hockey game."

"I'll see what I can do." He chucked the boy under his chin, making him laugh. He needed to get to his office, start his pre-game duties, but was reluctant to leave. Being with Lynn made him feel grounded and relaxed even as his body hummed with desire. "If you're here for our warmup skate, make sure you bring him near the tunnel so he can see the players go on and off the ice. A couple of the guys have asked about him. They got a kick out of meeting him that day."

"I had to be here to let the SPCA people in and lock up after them, but I'm taking him home for a nap before the game. I'll try and get back in time."

The last crate disappeared inside. The doors were still propped open, and the barking grew faint and distant. "I guess I should let you go then."

"And we should do the same to you." She climbed two steps then paused. Turning back, she laid her hand on his shoulder and leaned down. As she brushed his mouth with her firm cool lips, Oscar patted his cheek with a soft warm hand.

Surrounded by these expressions of affection and acceptance, Benjamin's knees weakened. Lynn raised her head, and he swallowed. The heat in her gaze spoke of more than friendship. Much more.

"Good luck." She rubbed his shoulder. "See you later."

He was still standing, frozen in place, when the doors closed behind her and Oscar.

CHAPTER TEN

Oscar loved the excitement and commotion of the hockey game. Lynn had brought ear protection so the buzzers and whistles and shouts of the crowd wouldn't overwhelm him. She'd chosen seats down by the glass behind the Canyon Cats goal and he stared, wide-eyed and entranced, as the enormous young men crashed and banged right in front of him.

Now the game was over, he was fractious and cranky. She guessed he wouldn't be the only one out of sorts. Benjamin had to be frustrated at yet another loss. She was by no means an expert on hockey, but even she had noticed missed opportunities and lazy mistakes.

The disgruntled fans had melted away and the stands were deserted except for the cleanup crew and a few members of the media up in the press box. Unfortunately, she couldn't take her son home quite yet. The Adopt-a-Pet event had been a great success, but all the animals were returning to the shelter for the night to allow the SPCA time to arrange the adoptions formally over the next few days. She needed to stick around until they were all packed up.

She lugged an increasingly heavy and highly irritated Oscar to the area where the kennels and crates had been set up. He'd started walking a couple weeks ago and though he was still unsteady on his feet could make rapid progress when he wanted. Her choices were letting him risk a fall onto the filthy concourse floor or dropping him as he struggled and squirmed in her arms.

Walking it is. She put him down and he made a beeline for the exterior wall. The window came almost to the floor, and he smashed his hands against the glass, chattering at his reflection.

She kept one eye on her son and the other on the SPCA staff as they hauled crates and kennels outside to waiting vans. The larger dogs were led out on leashes, and one of these, still a puppy by its gangly legs and fish-on-a-line behavior, made a bolt for freedom, yanking out of the attendant's hold. Lynn scooped Oscar up as the puppy raced by.

"Rascal. Come. Come, Rascal." The red-headed leader followed the careening dog. She spoke firmly but calmly and walked slowly. Rascal, true to his name, barked with hysterical glee, his toenails clattering on the polished concrete floor.

If he'd stayed on the concourse, they might have been able to corral him by coming at him from both sides. But he spied the wide stairs leading to ice level and flew down, ears flapping, tail windmilling. Lynn hustled in the wake of the SPCA staff, Oscar in her arms. She sucked in a breath, certain the puppy would lose its footing and take a terrible tumble. That particular disaster was averted, however, and by the time the humans reached the lower level, he was galumphing excitedly down the hall.

Levi Ghostkeeper's accusing stare bore into Benjamin. The coaching staff had gathered in the hallway after the team had disappeared into the locker room.

"This has got to stop." Levi's disgust wasn't a surprise. What concerned him was that the other staff, who had been supportive from the start of the season, couldn't look him in the face. A revolt might be in the works, and if it was, he knew who was fomenting it. "If this doesn't get you fired, I don't know what will."

Lynn had been certain Brewster's plan to break the team's contract was a closely guarded secret, but that hadn't stopped Benjamin from wondering who else might know. Levi's mounting frustration at both the continuing losses and Brewster's refusal to make any coaching changes appeared to confirm he, at least, had no knowledge of the owner's ulterior motive. Benjamin doubted he was that good an actor.

If Lynn hadn't broken her pact with her boss, he would be wondering the same thing as Levi. So, in an odd way he owed Brewster a favour. Knowing he didn't care about the losses—in fact, actively *wanted* them—meant Benjamin only worried about losing his job seventy-five percent of the time, instead of ninety-nine.

It didn't make losing games—especially the way they'd lost today—any easier to take.

As he had no answer for Levi, he ignored him. "I'll handle this. See you all back here tomorrow."

Levi shared a couple more pointed comments but, when he refused to engage, the assistant coach drifted off muttering darkly, followed by the other staff. Benjamin gave himself a couple minutes to gather his thoughts and control his temper before entering the dressing room. What he saw and heard there, however, lit his fuse again.

The players were in various stages of undress, equipment loosened or tossed to the side. Half the team were lazing about in convivial groups while ribald jokes and friendly curses blued the air. The other half were already on their phones checking god knows what. Valeri Nechayev was surrounded by several players, all laughing at something he was displaying on his screen. Not one gave any indication they were upset about the depths of their failure this afternoon.

Benjamin snapped. "Shut the fuck up!"

All talking stopped instantly. Only the tinny music

coming from Nechayev's phone broke the startled silence. Players stared at Benjamin. He had never raised his voice before, used profanity only rarely. That soft-shoe approach was obviously not working.

Nechayev leaned back negligently and crossed his ankle over his knee, skates still on though untied. Since joining the Canyon Cats, his actions on and off the ice had balanced on a knife-edge—not destructive enough to force Benjamin to make good on his threat to bench him, yet not productive enough to bring the team out of its doldrums.

He pointed at the phone. "Turn that off. Now. Or I'll turn it off permanently."

Nechayev hesitated just long enough to show defiance but not quite long enough for Benjamin to snatch the device from his hand and crush it under his heel as he longed to do.

He let his gaze sweep the room, meeting each player's eyes. Many shied away, others held his stare while guilt flitted across their expressions. Only a few showed no emotion.

Intent on keeping the players off balance, he reverted to his usual mild tone, knowing they expected him to yell and shout. "It doesn't surprise me to see how much energy you still have. Not after the little you expended on the ice this afternoon." A couple players shifted restlessly, and he waited for the motion to subside.

"I'm cancelling tomorrow's mandatory practice." That got everyone's attention. Eyebrows raised on almost every face. "Instead, there will be an optional one. At five a.m." He waited through the groans. "I said optional. If you don't want to attend, fine. After all, you seem to think showing up for a game is a choice, so why not a practice, too?"

He spun around and pushed through the dressing room door. The safety hinges prevented him from slamming it shut as he'd like to.

Barking and whistles assaulted his ears. He turned to his left and saw a large, shaggy creature barrelling toward him, several blue-jacketed people in pursuit.

His foul mood left absolutely no room for any more bullshit.

"Sit!" He held up his hand, palm facing the escapee.

Paws scrabbling for purchase, the dog slid to a stop at his feet, planted his butt on the floor, and gazed up with mischievous eyes. Benjamin grabbed his collar.

The SPCA staff, led by a red-headed woman, jogged toward them. "Thanks." She clipped a leash to the puppy's collar. "He was on his second lap."

Lynn and Oscar hovered at the back of the scrum. She spoke over the heads of the crowd. "I think Rascal likes you."

Her wide, amused grin softened his temper. A heavy weight pressed his knee. He looked down as the motley-coloured, long-legged creature slid onto his back, begging for a belly rub. Reluctantly charmed, Benjamin crouched to oblige.

"You wouldn't be interested in adopting him, would you?" the red-headed woman asked. "He's one of the few we didn't match up tonight, and he certainly seems to have connected with you."

Benjamin shook his head. "I'd love to. But I live in an apartment and I'm on the road far too often. It wouldn't be much of a life for the guy." He found the right place and set Rascal's rear leg vibrating.

"That's too bad. All right, Rascal. Time to go home." She tugged and the puppy bounced to his feet.

As the SPCA staff headed back to the stairs, Rascal looked over his shoulder with tragic eyes. Benjamin held firm. Maybe someday he'd have time for a dog. But today was not that day.

"Thanks for the rescue." Lynn stood at his shoulder.

"No problem." Oscar held out his arms and without even thinking about it, Benjamin accepted the invitation, taking the boy from Lynn and settling him on his hip.

"Seems you're the hero for boys and puppies tonight." Her smile held nothing but friendly pleasure. "Sorry about the game."

"I don't want to think about it." He meant it, too. For a few hours he wanted to forget all about unmotivated players and conniving assistant coaches and Machiavellian owners. He heaved a sigh. "Not until tomorrow, anyway."

"Why don't you come for dinner?"

"Tonight?" Her offer sparked a yearning he had trouble swallowing down.

"Not if it's inconvenient for you. But it looks like you could use a break. I have sausage and peppers in the slow cooker. There's plenty."

An evening with Lynn and Oscar or one in solitary splendor in his quiet apartment? It wasn't a contest. "I have a couple things to do here. Can you give me an hour?"

"Of course. I'll text you the address. It's only a few minutes away."

CHAPTER ELEVEN

Lynn unstrapped Oscar from his car seat, shouldered the diaper bag, and raced through the back door into the cramped laundry room that opened onto the kitchen. "Stephanie! Are you here?"

No answer. She didn't really expect one, as she lived in the basement suite. But when she was invited for dinner, as she was tonight, she sometimes came up early.

"We've got to hurry, bud." Discarding the bag on top of the dryer, she sat Oscar on the washer, slid off his boots, unzipped his tiny parka, pulled off his toque, and set him on his feet. By the time she'd divested herself of similar clothing, he had toddled into the living room in search of his toy box. Not bothering to unlock the baby gate at the top of the stairs, she stepped over, hustled down the two short flights, and knocked on Stephanie's door before opening it a few inches.

She called through the crack. "Stephanie! I need help."

The door swung wider, and her housemate came into view. As usual she was dressed with taste and flair, hair and makeup perfect. "What's the panic? Everything okay?"

"Benjamin's coming for dinner." Realizing she was wringing her hands like a Victorian virgin, she took a breath and relaxed her fingers. "My place is a disaster. Can you help me tidy up?"

"Benjamin?" One plucked eyebrow rose. "*That* Benjamin?"

While Lynn hadn't told her about the one-night stand or the kiss, he had come up in conversation occasionally since he'd reappeared in her life. She'd kept it cool, just casual work talk, but Stephanie had obviously caught other vibes. "Yes, *that* Benjamin. There's no time to explain. He'll be here in less than an hour."

"Of course I can help." Stephanie followed her upstairs.

In the kitchen, dirty meal prep dishes and utensils were piled next to the sink and Lynn turned on the hot water. "Will you give the hall bathroom a good wipe and put out fresh towels? And tidy the living room, as much as Oscar will allow you?"

"I'm on it." Stephanie vanished.

Lynn hadn't been out of the arena parking lot before she'd regretted her impulsive invitation. Yet he'd looked so forlorn after what had to be another frustrating loss that her heart had tugged and her mouth had spoken before she'd thought it through. She'd needed to do *something* to take that look off his face. But inviting him for dinner? She scrubbed a dish with unnecessary violence. Bringing him to her home was a level of intimacy she should never have considered, let alone encouraged. At least Stephanie would be around to provide a buffer.

Once she was done the dishes, she laid out the table with placemats and napkins. It looked rather bare and unwelcoming, so she set out a couple of candles as a centrepiece.

And immediately removed them, hiding them in a drawer. She didn't want it to appear even remotely romantic.

Stephanie was distracting Oscar from scattering toys about the now well-ordered living room by reading him a book. Lynn spoke over her shoulder as she headed down the hall. "I'm going to freshen up. I'll be right back."

In her bedroom she tugged off the T-shirt she'd worn to the game and shrugged into a blouse. Tossing the discarded shirt as well as the socks, underwear and other clothing scattered about the room into the hamper in her closet, she tidied the top of her dresser, freezing with her fingers on the lid of her jewellery box.

What the hell was she doing? Benjamin wasn't going to be anywhere near her bedroom. Sinking onto the end of the bed she dropped her head into her hands and groaned. Time to get a grip.

The house she owned and Stephanie shared was in an older neighbourhood with small homes and large yards. She'd bought it shortly after confirming her pregnancy, wanting security for her baby-to-be. It was the second house she'd owned, as she and Lance had bought one together—at Lynn's instigation—after they'd been engaged for a couple of years. But that house had been sold when he'd driven off to find fame and fortune.

Normally she avoided thinking of Lance. Tonight, he was an excellent reminder of why she couldn't wish for anything more than friendship with Benjamin. She'd thought she had a stable, solid future with her accountant ex-fiancé, and look how that had turned out. Coaching junior hockey had to be one of the most *un*stable careers around. She shouldn't even be considering a relationship with someone in that industry.

And yet, here she was, preparing to have a cozy family meal with a man whose kisses tingled all her good parts. Was she really willing to risk heartbreak...again? He wouldn't even commit to a *pet*, for crying out loud. She couldn't expect him to commit to a single mother.

There. That was settled. She stood, smoothed the material of her blouse, and headed back down the hall.

Stephanie looked up from the chair where she and Oscar were cuddled.

"Do you mind keeping an eye on him a little longer? I'm going to make a green salad. It can fill the gaps if necessary." The sausage and peppers she'd prepped that morning bubbled under the slow cooker's glass lid and the savoury scent filled the house. It was more than enough for her and Stephanie—and Oscar now he was eating so much solid food—but she had no idea what Benjamin's appetite was like. She opened the fridge and took out ingredients. "We need a dessert, too. Is there ice cream in the freezer?"

"Take a breath, Lynn." Stephanie's voice carried, disembodied, from the living room. "I haven't seen you this flustered since...well, ever. You really like this guy, don't you?"

Lynn paused in tearing the romaine lettuce into bite-sized pieces. Following Stephanie's advice, she drew in a long, steadying breath through her nose, let it out through her mouth. "I do like him. I just don't know if I should." So much for having made her decision. She was going to give herself motion sickness if she didn't pick a lane.

"What's wrong with him?"

"Nothing. Not in a general sense." She ran the salad spinner under water, whipped the handle, and let it slow naturally as she thought. "He's not a stayer. His entire career he's moved from place to place, and if he wants to make a go of it as a coach that will continue all his life. I grew up that way. I won't subject Oscar to a childhood like that."

As if hearing his name, her son let out a long, irritated squawk. Stephanie carried him into the kitchen. "Is he hungry?"

"Probably. Dinner's going to be a little later than he's used to. We'll have to distract him until Benjamin gets here."

Stephanie stood at her shoulder so Oscar could see

what she was doing. "Is it possible you are using this little man as an excuse? I know dating as a single mom can be tough, but—"

She shot her an ironic glance. "At least he's a valid excuse. What's yours? I don't see you out there in the dating pool either."

Stephanie had been married for several years. During her gender affirmation surgery, her wife had been understanding and supportive even though they'd decided a divorce would be best for both of them. That had all happened well before Lynn had met Stephanie, but she had yet to see her friend go on a date.

"I'm getting there. In fact, I'm having dinner with someone tomorrow night."

Lynn watched in fascination as a blush swept up Stephanie's neck. "Good for you!" She gave her a one-armed hug, holding the knife she'd been chopping tomatoes with far out of Oscar's reach. "I'm so glad."

"Thanks. My point stands. Thinking too far into the future is borrowing trouble. Just take things slow, see what happens. It's not like you're sleeping with the guy."

Lynn's rhythmic motions as she sliced a cucumber stuttered and she hunched her shoulder in a reflexive deflection. Stephanie knew her too well to miss the signs. "You *are* sleeping with him? How did I not know this?"

"I'm not sleeping with him. Now. But I did. Once." Lynn concentrated on dissecting the hapless cucumber. "A couple years ago."

"What?" Stephanie straightened, looming over Lynn, five-eleven in her ballet-slippered feet. "Tell Auntie Stephanie all."

Benjamin checked the house numbers as he drove slowly up the street. Early evening in mid-November meant porch lights were on and curtains closed against the dark. The first snow had fallen a few days ago and still lay in a thin white layer, though warmer temperatures were forecast and there was a good chance it would melt. Winter hadn't quite settled into full-on mode yet.

In an odd touch of serendipity, Lynn's home was only a couple of blocks from the house he'd grown up in and where his mother still lived. He'd passed it on his way, averting his gaze guiltily. He'd only seen her once in the almost two weeks since Halloween, despite his renewed intention to see her often now she'd returned from her sister's. Not that he hadn't tried, but something always seemed to come up to prevent a meeting. He wasn't chalking it up in the loss column yet. He would just have to try harder.

He pulled to the curb in front of Lynn's home and turned off the engine. Solar lights lined the walkway to the front of the house. A wreath made of evergreen boughs and sparkling with shiny red ornaments and white lights hung on the door and a tall rustic wood plank with the word *Welcome* painted on it leaned against the bottle glass side panel. Chinks of light showed through the loosely drawn drapes, winking off and on as if someone was pacing inside.

If he'd had more time, he would have gone home to change out of his game suit. It had taken him longer to wrap things up at the arena than he'd expected, and he hadn't wanted to be late. He'd delayed only long enough to pick up a bottle of wine at the grocery store that was on his direct route.

Gripping the narrow neck, he approached the front door and knocked. It opened almost instantly, revealing Lynn.

"I saw you pull up." She stepped back and gestured him into the foyer. "Come on in."

Short flights of stairs led up and down. A safety gate barricaded the opening on the upper floor. The living room was visible through wooden banisters on the left and a kitchen through an open archway directly ahead.

He stepped to the side to allow Lynn to shut the door and held out the bottle. "I didn't want to come empty handed. I hope you like red."

She took it. "That's great, thanks. You can hang your coat in the closet if you like." Her tone was formal, and he wondered if she was feeling the same awkwardness he was. This was a new stage in their relationship, and he wasn't exactly sure what it meant or where it might lead.

He just knew it was an opportunity he didn't want to screw up. As he'd done with so much in his life.

He shrugged out of his wool overcoat and suit jacket and found an empty hanger. Lynn led him up the stairs and through the baby gate, securing it behind them. "Where's Oscar?" Other than soft acoustic music playing from an unseen speaker, the house was quiet. "Is he in bed?" He'd looked forward to seeing the little guy again and was disappointed he might have missed him.

"Here he is." From a doorway down the hall a tall woman emerged. She wore slim fitted pants and a colourfully patterned blouse and carried a naked but for his diaper Oscar.

"Benjamin, this is Stephanie, my friend and housemate."

"Nice to meet you." Stephanie held out her free hand and shook Benjamin's with a firm grip. "I've heard a lot about you."

"Steph!" Lynn's hissed warning made Benjamin lift an eyebrow.

Amusement gleamed in Stephanie's eyes. "It was all good. Don't worry." Her glance flicked from him to Lynn and back again.

Benjamin wasn't sure what to make of Stephanie's reassurances. What exactly had Lynn said?

"I hope you don't mind if we eat right away." Lynn retrieved the baby from her friend and turned to

Benjamin. "Oscar's hungry and the food is ready."

A faint tinge of red coloured her cheekbones and he wondered again how much she had shared with Stephanie. "Of course not. I'm hungry, too. Lead the way."

CHAPTER TWELVE

Oscar waved delightedly at the bubbles Lynn blew in his direction, chubby bare legs splashing in the shallow water. Through the open bathroom door, she could hear Benjamin and Stephanie's voices but not the words. They were cleaning up the kitchen while she gave Oscar his nightly bath. Letting him feed himself half-naked saved on laundry but required a rigorous wash later.

After Benjamin's initial shyness—one she'd shared—he had fit right into their little family meal. Lynn had broken the ice by recounting his capture of Rascal and the conversation had taken off from there.

Stephanie had quizzed him on all the places he'd lived and when that topic had been exhausted it took a natural turn to Lynn's childhood. He'd been surprised to hear of her unusual upbringing, as most people were, and had noted down the name of her father's band so he could look him up online.

Lifting Oscar from the tub, she wrapped him in a towel and scrubbed him dry. It was his least favourite part of bath time, and he shrieked and fretted, only quieting when she released him. He stumbled across the hall to his bedroom, giggling at his escape, and she followed. Fastening his diaper and wrestling him into his pajamas was the next hurdle, but finally he was ready for bed, sweet and clean.

He tucked his head in the curve of her neck as she

carried him to the kitchen. "Oscar's come to say goodnight."

Stephanie paused in drying the dish she held and kissed his temple. "Night, Oscar."

Benjamin, wiping down the counter, appeared at a loss when she approached him. After a slight hesitation he patted her son on the back with gentle fingers. "Have a good sleep. See you later, little guy."

She laid him in his crib, turned on his music and nightlight, and shut off the overhead light. For a minute or two she stood in the soft dark patting his back, before whispering goodnight and closing the door until only an inch of space remained. By then he was standing again, gripping the rails, but that was all part of the ritual. His wordless complaints followed her down the hall as she rejoined Stephanie and Benjamin.

"Is that it?" Benjamin folded the dishcloth and draped it neatly over the faucet. "He's done for the night?"

"Usually. He'll probably squawk a bit, maybe even cry a little, but generally he goes to bed easily." She lifted the bottle of wine Benjamin had brought, which was still half full. "I wouldn't mind a little more of this. Anyone want to join me?"

"I'm heading home." Stephanie stretched her arms over her head, almost brushing the ceiling. "I'm going to do my yoga, have a shower, and curl up in bed with a good book."

Benjamin's brow furrowed. "I thought this was home."

"I have a suite in the basement, with my own entrance and everything." Stephanie opened the baby gate and stepped through. "It was nice to meet you. I expect I'll see you around." A moment later, the click of the door at the bottom of the lower flight signalled she was gone.

Lynn waggled the bottle at Benjamin. "How about you?"

He didn't answer for a moment, still staring down the stairs as if shocked at Stephanie's rapid departure. Then he blinked and gave Lynn a half-smile. "Not for me, thanks. I have to be at the rink at four-thirty tomorrow morning."

"Four-thirty? What on earth for?" Lynn poured herself a couple swallows and gestured with her glass toward the living room.

Benjamin followed her to the couch and sat next to her. "I may have lost my temper with the team after the game today and scheduled a practice for five."

"That sounds like punishment, all right." She turned on the monitor she kept on the coffee table. Oscar may have been only a few metres away, but it was comforting to be able to see him. He was now sitting down, and even as she watched he flopped onto his side. His sleepy mutters indicated he was well on his way to dreamland.

"It's more of a test." Benjamin slid down on the cushion so he could rest his head against the back, lacing his fingers and resting them on his stomach.

"What do you mean?" She lifted her feet and turned her back against the arm of the sofa. Her toes were millimetres away from Benjamin's thigh and she suppressed the impulse to tuck them under his warmth.

He directed his answer to the ceiling. "I told them it was optional. The players that show up will be demonstrating their commitment to the team. The ones that don't"—he rolled his shoulders in a gesture of resignation—"well, the ones that don't will have to be dealt with. Though what power I have with an owner that is actively *wishing* for our failure is uncertain."

Impulsively, she brushed a strand of hair that had caught at his temple, tucking it back into place. One silvery thread glinted in his short sideburn. He was five years younger than her—a discovery made easy by the internet—but tonight he looked worn and tired and five years older.

He rolled his head toward her and their gazes caught. Her fingers, toying with the silky strands of his hair, were trapped between his cheekbone and the couch and it seemed perfectly natural to let her palm curve against the sweep of his jaw. Her thumb brushed across the bristles forming on his cheek to the corner of his mouth.

His lips opened and the tip of his tongue tickled her thumb.

Lynn's pupils dilated. Benjamin tilted his head a fraction and drew her thumb deeper in his mouth. Her fingers tightened on his skull.

Releasing her with a quiet *pop*, he took the wineglass from her hand and placed it next to the monitor on the table. Oscar lay flat on his back, arms and legs splayed like a starfish, limp in sleep.

He shifted position, his knees pressing into the seat cushion, one elbow on the back of the sofa, the other on the arm behind Lynn. "I have to go soon." He should go *now*. Now, before he did something they'd both regret.

"I know." Her voice was low and throaty.

A rush of desire rippled down his spine. Most of the time he could forget about the night they'd spent together. Most of the time he could suppress those heady, delicious memories.

Not this time.

"I could stay a little longer." He let his eyes drop deliberately to her mouth and then raised them slowly to meet hers again. "If you want."

"I want." Lynn slid her feet past his knees and wrapped her ankles around his calves. Her hands gripped his hips and she gave a tug. "God, do I *want*."

He prayed this wasn't a mistake. When Lynn had recounted tales of her vagabond childhood, it hadn't taken a genius to realize she'd built an adult life that was the complete opposite. She had chosen to grow roots, to settle down, to limit change and upheaval as much as she could. His life, on the other hand, was unpredictable and uncertain, forced to bow to the capricious whims of sport and fate.

He was absolutely the wrong man for her.

He should get up and leave.

He didn't.

Without taking his gaze from hers, he lowered his body, his hips cradled at her core, his elbows supporting most of his weight on the arm of the sofa, his chest ever so lightly brushing her breasts. Her breath grew ragged, puffing against his throat, and she licked her lips.

Then, and only then, did he let his mouth sweep hers.

The heat was instantaneous. It sparked down his nerves, swelled his cock, hammered in his veins. He'd intended to keep the kiss cool, flirty, but that thought melted when she embraced him with arms and legs so tightly, she lifted off the cushions.

Shuffling backward, Lynn clinging to him, their mouths still melded together, he pulled her flat on the wide sofa and stretched out on top. His fingers threaded through her hair and when her tongue touched his they spasmed involuntarily. She gasped.

He dragged his mouth away. "Sorry." He muttered the hoarse apology against her neck.

"No. Do it again." She lifted her chin. "Just like that."

He tugged her hair and she moaned. Her willing surrender surged straight to his hardening cock. Another tug had her rocking her centre against him in short, frantic jerks. He didn't remember turning her on this way two years ago but was more than okay with giving her what she needed now.

Her nipples pebbled, so hard he felt them against his chest through the layers of clothing. Clothing he needed to get rid of. Keeping one hand gripped in her hair and nibbling her neck with tiny bites and teasing kisses, he worked the other hand between their bodies to undo the buttons on her blouse. She gave no objections to his actions, even when he laid her bare.

A lacy bra wrapped her soft, succulent flesh. He trailed kisses from her neck to her collarbone to the upper slope of her breast, and then lapped her nipple, the fabric rough against his tongue. Sliding further down her body, he wound both hands into her hair again and twisted the strands as he engulfed her nipple and gave a strong, sucking pull.

The force of her reaction lifted them both off the couch. She screamed low in her throat, her lips clamped shut, her body wracked with shudders. In awe at her responsiveness, he kept up the pressure until she collapsed, boneless.

"I can't...no more...I need..." Her incoherent panting was an aphrodisiac like no other.

He gave her breast one last, tender kiss and eased his grip on her hair. "Shhhhh. I've got you. Take a minute."

Propping himself up on one elbow, he stared down at her. A red flush heated her chest and neck and she'd thrown one arm over her eyes. The pulse in her throat called for him to kiss it but he resisted.

He hadn't intended things to move so fast. Somewhere at the back of his mind he'd thought they would kiss and cuddle and explore each other slowly. He certainly hadn't anticipated Lynn's sensually violent response.

Now he ached to plunge into her, to take her while she was limp and replete. But they were in a much different place than they had been on their previous night together. Then, they'd been strangers seeking oblivion from the trials of their separate lives. Now, they were friends, with careers that intertwined in multiple ways.

Having sex would more than complicate things. It would create an entanglement no one could unravel.

"Oh. My. God." Her voice was slurred and drunken. "I can't feel my legs."

He kept his voice light, locking away his regretful thoughts. "I assume that's a good thing."

She gave a tiny nod, as if she needed all her energy simply to draw air into her lungs. "I don't think I've ever come that way before."

He rested his hand on her belly and she jerked, but before he could pull away she lowered her arm from her face and trapped his palm against her skin. Her eyes opened, still bleary with satiation. "I need a minute. Then I can take care of you."

"That won't be necessary." His cock jerked in disagreement, but he ignored it. He could still salvage their relationship if he left now. Because as much as he wanted Lynn to be his lover, he *needed* her to be his friend. "I really should be going home. I have to be up in a few hours."

"You could stay."

Her statement ended with an upward lilt that seemed to echo his own reservations. Was she already regretting the last few minutes? "Thanks for the invite. But I don't think so." He shifted to a sitting position, making sure she didn't slide off the cushion and onto the floor as he did so.

She found her balance and perched next to him, hair in a sexy tangle, blouse hanging invitingly open. "Are you sure?" Her eyes dropped to the still noticeable bulge in his pants.

He clung to his decision. "I'm sure." He was also sure of something else.

If his future held more than friendship with Lynn, staying the night would be a mistake. She wasn't ready for that step, and neither was he. It was the wrong thing to do.

And for once in his life, he wanted to do something *right*.

CHAPTER THIRTEEN

Benjamin sat in a shadowy corner in the highest tier of the arena. He'd arranged with staff to have the lights come on at five a.m. precisely, but for now the huge space was shrouded in gloom.

Much like his thoughts.

After Benjamin had challenged the team to the five-a.m. skate, he'd texted his assistant coaches. Not to ask them to attend. In fact, he'd told them to stay away, wanting no witnesses to a potential failure. Instead, he'd told them to prepare for a coaches' meeting at the usual practice time.

So now he waited. Alone. Anxious. Unbearably apprehensive.

His dare to the players could easily backfire. Some players would show up. It was unimaginable that the whole team would stay away. But if Nechayev didn't appear, his dramatic challenge would be a failure no matter who else did.

Since Benjamin had been very clear the practice was optional, he wouldn't be expected to discipline him or any other missing players—a thought that made him guiltily relieved. Sweat sprang on his palms at the thought of benching the star player. Despite his threat, it was an action he really, really, didn't want to take.

This skate would also reveal the level of control Nechayev wielded over his teammates. Despite his bullying and arrogance, he had gathered a cohort of players around him—both those that shared his attitude and those seeking to avoid his negative attention. If that faction followed Nechayev's lead and stayed away, Benjamin would have a true revolt on his hands.

Unable to sleep, he'd pulled into the deserted arena parking lot well before any players might be expected to arrive. He wished he could blame his wakefulness on Lynn. He'd left her home in an uncomfortable state of arousal, one that he'd taken care of in the shower before stretching out on his mattress, and while she hadn't been far from his thoughts through the dark hours, it was the optional skate that continually teased him out of slumber.

His watch ticked over to 4:59. He thought he'd heard muted voices and quiet steps during the forty-five minutes he'd been waiting in his lofty eyrie but couldn't be sure. He held his breath.

A player skated out onto the ice. Dudas, one of the alternate captains, and one of the players Benjamin had been certain would come.

Lights flared, starting at the end of the rink furthest away and sweeping toward him in a wave. A mechanical hum rumbled through the quiet. Dudas sprinted from blue line to blue line, maintained his speed as he swept around the net, and sprinted again.

Another player joined him—Noesen. Then Regula. All three alternates were now on the ice.

Benjamin waited tensely as player after player stepped onto the rink until nineteen of the twenty-two members of the roster were warming up.

No Nechayev. No Chisholm or Piiroinen, his two closest conspirators.

At 5:05, the players gathered in the faceoff circle at centre ice. He caught only random words and phrases, but it was apparent that they believed he'd abandoned them. He wondered if they understood the message he was making with his absence.

You don't show up for me, I don't show up for you.

By 5:10, Dudas, Noesen, and Regula had three drills running. Benjamin couldn't help a stir of pride. *This* is what he was aiming toward—players who were invested in each other, working together not because they'd been told to, but because they *wanted* to.

At 5:15, he gave up waiting for Nechayev and headed to his office for his skates. He'd deal with the defectors later. For now, he had players who wanted a coach.

"I come bearing gifts!" Sarah entered the arena administration office through the door leading from the parking lot, a cardboard tray filled with takeout cups balanced in her grip.

"Caffeine. Thank god." Lynn accepted her large black gratefully. She'd already finished the mug she'd brought from home. Oscar had woken three times during the night, and she'd dragged herself to the office groggy with fatigue.

She cracked open the plastic lid, took a scalding sip, and sighed. It wasn't fair to blame Oscar. Yes, he had gotten her out of bed three times. But she hadn't been sleeping anyway, reliving her too brief encounter with Benjamin.

Sarah distributed the rest of the drinks before taking off her coat and hanging it on the rack next to the exterior door. She dropped into her chair at the desk across from Lynn. "Yesterday went well. You must be thrilled."

For a horrified second, Lynn thought she was talking about the orgasm Benjamin had given her. She took another fortifying sip to cover her reaction. "Yes. The SPCA was really happy. They want to do another before the end of the season."

"It won't be your problem by then. At least it better not be. I can't believe the team hasn't hired a new marketing coordinator yet." Sarah sipped her own coffee and wiggled the computer mouse. "What are they waiting for?"

Lynn made a noncommittal noise. Brewster's plan was still a secret in the arena admin office, and she had full confidence that Benjamin hadn't let it slip to anyone either. "Cynthie heard they are starting to interview next week. They should have someone in place soon."

"I hope so, for your sake. I had fun helping out at one game, but you must be tired of going to all of them." Sarah's phone rang. She answered it and was soon deep in conversation with the organizer of an upcoming Christmas charity event hosted at the arena.

The thing was, Lynn wasn't sure she could stay away from the games, even after she had no official reason to attend. She had become invested in the Canyon Cats. Or more specifically, their coach. She no longer wanted them to succeed simply to thwart Brewster. She wanted them to be living proof of Benjamin's dedication and skill.

She'd been both relieved and disappointed when he'd gently rejected her suggestion he stay the night—and a little guilty, too. It didn't seem fair to let him leave without providing the same shattering experience he'd given her. Her reaction to his touch had surprised and shocked her. It had obviously been far too long since she'd been with a man.

She wondered what he would say if she told him he was responsible for her last human-caused orgasms—orgasms more than twenty-six months apart. The morning after their one-night stand, she'd made an appointment with her doctor to talk about the in vitro process, and she'd been celibate ever since. Sure, she'd had a few dates with her battery-operated boyfriend before Oscar's birth, but since then she hadn't even taken him out of the drawer. She had actually wondered if motherhood had conquered her libido.

Last night proved that wasn't the case, for which she was supremely grateful.

But gratitude wasn't a strong enough reason to have casual sex. That was definitely out of the picture now she had a son to consider. She had angsted enough over having a *friendship* with Benjamin. Moving it to the next level was out of the question.

Wasn't it?

His chosen career was volatile and unstable. Lynn needed a man who could be anchored by her and Oscar, not drag his family from place to place like a ship tossing at sea.

Anchor. What a depressing word. Why had she described herself and her son as a heavy, wearisome weight?

Benjamin, Levi, and the other two assistant coaches were jammed into his dank cave of an office.

Levi had snagged the only visitor's chair by rights of seniority, both in age and in longevity. Ryan Rossi leaned against the wall near the door and Avril Mailloux hitched a hip on a low metal filing cabinet.

"So, how did your little challenge turn out?" Levi's tone was disgruntled. As usual.

Benjamin ignored it. Also as usual. "No Nechayev, Chisholm, or Piiroinen. Everyone else showed."

"I could have told you that yesterday. If you'd asked me." The fact he hadn't obviously rankled.

Out of Levi's sight, Ryan and Avril shared a glance. Benjamin wondered where their support would fall should the conflict between him and Levi escalate. Avril had joined the team the season before Benjamin and Levi treated her with the barest modicum of respect, so might be swayed to his camp. Ryan, however, had worked with Levi for several years and was his go-to guy in most situations. His loyalty would be harder to gain.

He directed his comments to Levi. "It was an excellent practice. One of the best we've had since Simpson was traded. It's plain that Nechayev and his buddies are a disruptive influence. As coaches, we need to devise a plan to get them working on the same page as the other players. Any ideas?"

"You should make him captain." Levi stabbed a finger at Benjamin. "You should have the day he arrived. He's our top player and deserves the recognition."

He had wanted to see how Nechayev fit into the team before giving him that honour and responsibility, which was why he'd named three other players as alternate captains instead. In the last weeks he'd seen no reason to reverse that decision and was certain giving Nechayev the C would cause more problems, not fewer.

Before he could state his opinion, Avril cleared her throat. "I don't agree with that." Her faint French accent hardened the *th*s and lengthened the vowels. She'd been a member of Canada's very successful national women's team for several years, though this was her first coaching job. "He needs to earn captain, and he hasn't done so."

"You could bench him." Ryan had reached the top levels of junior hockey in Ontario but never been drafted. He'd worked his way to the Canyon Cats by coaching various minor teams.

Levi twisted in his chair to stare at him in disbelief. "For Christ's sake. That's ridiculous." He turned back to Benjamin. "Even you couldn't be that stupid."

Ryan flushed and Benjamin held up a placating hand. "I asked for ideas and I want all of them. We're brainstorming here." He took a calming breath. "To be honest, benching him has crossed my mind. I would prefer not to take such a drastic move, but I'm running out of options."

"It's an idiotic idea." Levi's glare challenged Benjamin. "Avril's wrong, too. She doesn't know what she's talking about."

His pulse raced and stomach clenched. Before today

he'd managed to avoid an all-out confrontation with Levi, but if he expected Ryan and Avril to respect him as head coach, he couldn't let those comments slide. He had to take a stand.

"We're all professionals here and bring different perspectives to the job." He kept his voice firm and pressed his palms flat on his desk to hide any hint of nerves. "We're going to have conflicting opinions but denigrating each other won't resolve the issues."

"I don't care how many fancy words you use." Levi flicked a palm dismissively. "I'll say what I need to say how and when I want to say it."

He was forcing Benjamin's hand, and he knew it. Ryan and Avril watched the show play out, faces blank.

Ignoring his roiling gut, he stared at Levi. "If you can't be respectful to your colleagues, I will have to ask you to leave."

"You think you can do this without me?" Levi barked out a laugh. "Who has the most experience here? It's certainly not you." He spit out the last word, his dark, derisive gaze pinning Benjamin as fiercely as a stick speared through his chest.

"Maybe you have more years in, but you're not head coach. I am." He swallowed, a prickling sensation racing up his torso and throat to his cheeks. "Which mean you'll work with me, in a manner I approve of, or not at all."

Levi's chin jerked up. "If you're threatening to fire me, it's a wasted bluff. Only Peterson can do that, and even if you asked he wouldn't. He knows what he owes me."

Any lingering doubts that Levi knew of Brewster's plans evaporated. "I wouldn't count on that." He put every ounce of confidence and determination he could into his tone and expression, wishing he could say more. But he wouldn't put Lynn's job in jeopardy simply for the personal satisfaction of seeing Levi squirm.

Levi stared, his belligerence tempered now by faint caution. Ryan and Avril made no movements, as if afraid to draw attention to themselves. Benjamin waited.

"Fuck you," Levi said, and stormed out of the room.

CHAPTER FOURTEEN

As she crossed tasks off her list that morning, curiosity over how the five-a.m. skate had gone ate at Lynn. She'd peeked at the rink when she'd arrived, but the smooth, unmarked ice told her nothing, since it would have been Zambonied as soon as the practice was over. If it had occurred at all.

Despite her conundrum over the sexual side of their relationship, Benjamin was still her friend. He wouldn't be shocked if she asked him how the morning had gone. Besides, it would be best to get their first meeting after the events of last night over and done with, and inquiring about the practice gave her an excellent excuse. At the start of her lunch break, she wandered down to his office. If he was there, great. If not, no biggie. She'd see him some other time.

She neared the door, her heart tripping in her throat, belying her nonchalant inner monologue. As her hand stretched out for the handle, it swung away. Startled, she shuffled back as a red-faced Levi Ghostkeeper stormed past, the brief glance he shot her fierce and bitter. Eyebrows raised, she peered into the small, square room. Benjamin sat behind his desk, his two other assistant coaches ranged along the wall to her right. All three were frozen in place, staring toward her.

Apparently, now was not a good time. "I'll come back later." She reached for the handle again.

Benjamin blinked. "No. It's okay. Just give me a minute to wrap things up."

"Really, it's not important." She retreated further, pulling the door almost closed.

The assistant coaches shifted out of their statue-like stances, their gazes swinging from Benjamin to Lynn and back again. Lynn had met Ryan Rossi several times over the years he'd worked for the Canyon Cats but had only ever seen Avril Mailloux in passing. She'd been on maternity leave when the other woman was hired and there'd been no reason to seek her out since her return.

"Lynn. Wait. Please."

She hesitated, and then widened the opening. Behind Benjamin's calm expression something fluttered. Something wounded and desperate. She wondered if the assistant coaches saw it, too. "Okay. I'll be right outside."

She shut the door with a quiet click and leaned against the concrete wall. Light from the soaring ceiling of the arena filtered down through the bleachers. As she waited, a figure skating club glided out onto the rink, the voices of athletes and coaches thin and distant, the sound of blades cutting ice crisp and clean.

A couple minutes later, Ryan and Avril exited the office and headed in the same direction Levi had gone. Avril offered a polite smile as she passed, but Ryan didn't give her a glance, his spine stiff and defiant.

Whatever had happened in the coaches' meeting was none of her business. Still, the obvious tension caused her unease. Benjamin had enough on his plate without dissension among his staff, too.

She stepped through the doorway and stood quietly, her hands resting on the back of the visitor's chair. Benjamin's elbows were on his desk and the heels of his hands pressed into his eyes. His chest rose and fell in several deep breaths before he dropped his fists.

His smile was self-deprecating. "It's good to see a friendly face."

She resisted the urge to circle behind and rub his shoulders. "Tough day at the office?"

"Nothing that hasn't been coming for a while now." He leaned his head against the high back of his chair and swivelled back and forth in short jerks. "What can I do for you?"

"I didn't mean to interrupt anything." She dragged her nails over the fabric of the chair in a nervous gesture but stopped when it made a rough tearing sound. "I was just curious as to how this morning's skate went. Maybe you'd rather not discuss it."

"It's not a secret. The players I expected to show, did. The ones I *needed* to show, didn't." He shrugged without lifting his head. "I'll figure it out."

The urge to bring a smile to his face swamped her. She blurted out the first thing that came to mind. "I had a good time last night."

If anything, the frown lines that had creased his forehead since she'd entered deepened. "About that—"

"Don't say it. Don't say you regret it."

His expression darkened further. "I wasn't. I don't. But I do think we need to talk about it."

"I didn't mean to be quite so...over the top. It's just...it's been a while. Since I was with someone." The office was tiny but the space between them yawned wide as a canyon. She had to bridge it. "Since *you*, in fact."

Understanding dawned in his eyes. "Really?"

She tilted her head. "I started investigating the in vitro process the next day and I certainly wasn't going to have casual sex while I was trying to get pregnant."

"Well." Amusement lifted the corners of his mouth and her heart warmed. She'd achieved her goal. "I'm glad to be of service. Both times."

Hmm. She didn't like how that sounded. "I wasn't using you. Our first night was mutually enjoyable, wasn't it? And last night...well, I offered to"—she waved a hand in his direction—"take care of things."

He rose and rounded his desk to stand at her side. "I'm sorry. I was teasing." He tapped his fingertip on her chin. "Yes, our first night was *more* than mutually enjoyable. And I enjoyed myself last night, too. I enjoyed getting to know Oscar better and meeting Stephanie. And I enjoyed how it ended. Giving can be as satisfying as receiving, you know."

Was it her imagination or had the air between them heated, surging with electric pulses?

"Do you ever..." Benjamin paused, started again. "Would you consider having dinner with me? As in a date, and a real one?"

Lynn's palms went damp. So much for her rational decision to avoid anything more deeply personal. She craved more time with him. Even knowing it could end tomorrow, she *craved*. "I would." Her rapid pulse made her slightly dizzy.

"Good. Good."

She waited for him to say more, but he remained silent. Deflated, she turned to go. "All right then. I should get back to work."

Benjamin stopped her with a brush of his fingers on her forearm. "I'm sorry. I'm a little distracted right now. But I will ask you, Lynn. I promise."

"That's okay. We can take things slow. We *should* take things slow." That was the mature, responsible thing to do. She was a mother, after all. She had to be careful who she brought into Oscar's life. He might be too young to remember her relationships now, but that wouldn't always be the case. And as much as she liked Benjamin, she couldn't forget one very important thing.

Someday his career would take him away from Prince George, away from her and Oscar. He didn't fit into the life she'd designed after Lance had left. As fun as it might be to colour outside the lines for a little while, she had to keep that in mind.

Practice had barely started on Monday morning when Brewster appeared in the players' bench. He waved Benjamin over with a curt gesture.

His fingers tightened on his hockey stick as he glided to a stop by the boards. "Good morning, Peterson."

"Benny." Brewster's nod skated on the edge of irritated. "We need to talk. My office in ten." He spun away and strode out of sight.

Benjamin watched him go, his mind shuffling through the reasons Brewster might have for summoning him.

He would have liked to put faith in the owner's hidden agenda. The Canyon Cats' recent run of losses ensured they'd dropped well out of the playoff picture. Only the most loyal fans were attending games and Brewster should have been pleased that there were more empty than full seats, but Benjamin couldn't quite wrap his brain around an owner who *wanted* his team to lose.

Behind him, Levi shouted instructions while the defence ran a drill. The disgruntled assistant coach had made no reference to their altercation a few days ago, but an air of grim satisfaction surrounded him. Given Levi's conviction that Brewster had his back, it was entirely possible he had complained to the owner. Benjamin may have made a grave tactical error deciding not to tell his side of the story first, but he'd thought it would make him appear even more incompetent than he already did.

Then there was Nechayev. Neither he nor his two henchmen had said anything about their absence from the optional practice, but their performances in the defeat the Canyon Cats had suffered through over the weekend spoke volumes about their disdain for Benjamin's leadership. If Brewster had noticed that dynamic, he might want to discuss it. Even if he wanted the team to fail, that didn't mean he wanted to be accused of scuttling a top prospect's career by saddling him with a weak coach.

There was only one conclusion. He was about to be fired. It was the most likely scenario, no matter what he knew of Brewster's schemes.

He drew in several deep breaths before he was steady enough to catch Avril's attention. She skated over and he handed her his tablet. "Brewster needs me. Keep things on track, will you?"

"Of course." Wrinkles formed between her eyebrows and her lips pressed together. "What's it about?"

"I don't know." He'd like to believe her expression indicated concern for him but didn't think he'd done anything to earn such consideration during their short time together. "I'll fill you in later." *If I still have a job* was the unspoken conclusion to that sentence, and Avril knew it, too.

In his office, he unlaced his skates and slid into his street shoes, and then stood in the doorway and scanned the room. Though he'd been using it for several months, he had yet to personalize it, as if his subconscious had known it wasn't worth the effort. His only concession had been a photo of his parents and himself on the day he'd been drafted. It served as both a reminder of what had been and a goad toward what he wanted to achieve.

An objective he would never reach, if this meeting went as he suspected.

Benjamin squared his shoulders, shut the door, and made his way to the Canyon Cats offices. On his way he passed the arena administration. He itched to open the door and seek out Lynn, take comfort in seeing her, speaking with her, but gritted his teeth and passed on by.

He hadn't spoken with her since his lame suggestion they go on a date. He'd had to focus on the team and any fallout from his fight with Levi, not to mention Nechayev's power play. When he'd been at the rink, busy with game day duties, it hadn't been difficult. But between times, during the lonely, quiet hours he'd spent in his bleak apartment, he'd had to sit on his hands to keep from calling her. She deserved better than to be used as a distraction from the mess that was his life. Once he had that sorted out...

Yeah, right.

Inside the team's suite, Brewster's door stood open. Benjamin halted in the opening and tapped on the frame.

The owner looked up from the slim, sleek laptop placed exactly in the centre of his desk. "Take a seat, Benny."

If he was fired, he would insist Brewster call him by his preferred name. He should have said something the first time he had used the distasteful nickname, but he hadn't wanted to make a fuss.

He never wanted to make a fuss. It was exhausting, constantly placating and accommodating everyone, and he was tired of it in more ways than one.

In the armless chair on his side of Brewster's desk, he kept his posture straight and his chin lifted. No need to look as cowed as he felt.

"Levi called me Saturday. Bent my ear for a considerable amount of time." Brewster didn't need a power pose to appear confident. He slouched back in his leather executive's chair and narrowed his gaze. "I understand you threatened to fire him."

"Not in those exact words." Benjamin knew he'd been right to chastise Levi and that gave him enough courage to speak with conviction. "He's disapproved of me since day one, and I can handle that. But the coaching staff has to work together. He needs to be respectful of Avril and Ryan."

"I don't like getting dragged into personnel issues." Brewster scowled. "I expect you to deal with these things without bothering me."

"*I* wasn't the one that bothered you." Benjamin stared, stung at the injustice. "I *was* dealing with it."

"You're *not* dealing with it if a member of your team comes to me with a complaint."

There was enough truth in that to stopper Benjamin's next defensive comment. He swallowed and regrouped. "What would you like me to do?"

"Tell Levi that I have no intention of making any changes to the coaching staff. Tell him you have my full support, and he'll have to figure out a way to work with you. Then leave me out of it. I don't want to hear more about your little tiffs."

He wasn't fired. The office spun dizzily for a moment or two. Even the knowledge Levi would continue to make life difficult—maybe even become more actively combative—couldn't dim his relief.

He still had a chance to make good on his vow. Still had a chance to prove he was a good coach, could get the best out of his players, his staff. Still had a chance to make amends for the failures of the past with glorious success in the future.

Several minutes later he was back on the ice. It was only then that a further revelation hit.

Brewster had confirmed he had no intention of making coaching changes, with the implication that his decision was solid, unchangeable.

Benjamin was safe. He could do his job with no fear of reprisals. If his actions didn't improve the team, that was what Brewster wanted. If the team *did* improve, well—what excuse could Brewster use to fire a winning coach?

He had been given a get-out-of-jail-free card. Now he just had to figure out what to do with it.

CHAPTER FIFTEEN

Benjamin was still searching for solutions ten days later.

Late on Thursday evening, he pulled into the parking lot of a long, low building. He didn't think he'd find any answers here, but it was better than being trapped in his silent, barely furnished apartment.

The Canyon Cats had a lull in their schedule that allowed for a three-day weekend away from the rink. While his instinct was to keep pushing as he searched for the answer that would end their dramatic slump, he reluctantly recognized that time away from the ice might be beneficial for everyone.

He knew he needed it. The tension between himself and Levi and Nechayev made his bones ache as if he had the flu. While he didn't one-hundred percent trust that he wouldn't be fired, Brewster's avowal had given him the courage to try new things. The results weren't yet reflected on the score sheet, though there were signs the team was starting to gel again. It didn't make practices any less fraught, however.

Guilt over Lynn was another weight he carried. He hadn't spoken to her other than brief greetings since she'd come to his office almost two weeks ago. He desperately hoped she understood his recent radio silence was necessary. He *had* to focus all his attention on the team. It was his reason for coming back, after all. Asking her on a date would have to wait.

Popping the trunk, he hefted out his equipment bag. He'd lived in so many places for such short periods of time that he'd stripped his personal possessions to the bare necessities. But he hadn't gotten rid of his hockey gear. It had been an extension of him for too long, even though he hadn't stepped on the ice as a player for years.

That was going to change tonight. He'd finally allowed Jujhar to convince him to drop into one of his recreational league games. His heart beat high in his throat at the thought of playing again.

His bag thudding against his thigh, he climbed the slick metal steps, pushed open the arena door—and stepped into his past. He'd spent many a practice in this building during his years in the Prince George Minor Hockey Association. The arched roof covered a single rink and four meagre dressing rooms. Other than a new paint job and updated posters on the community bulletin board, nothing had changed. The scent of wet rubber mats, freshly cleaned ice, and childish sweat enveloped him. The ghost of his father hovered at his side. He pushed the mirage away, not yet ready to confront it.

Memory propelled him to the second dressing room on the left. The door was propped open, and he paused in the entrance. He'd worried that all the tangled emotions of his checkered hockey career would taint this experience.

Now he wished he'd come weeks before. Despite the fact he'd spent half his life in dressing rooms around the world, this cramped, rough, rather foul-smelling space felt like coming home.

Men sat on the wooden benches lining the walls, gear bags gaping at their feet, equipment scattered around them. They glanced at him but made no comment on his arrival other than a few sharp nods. His spine relaxed further.

"Well, are you going in or not?"

He turned to see Jujhar grinning behind him, teeth gleaming in his luxuriant beard. "Just waiting for you, slack-ass."

They found seats on the far wall and began to dress.

"Glad you finally decided to come." Jujhar pulled a tattered shirt over his bare chest and reached for his shoulder pads.

"Me, too." He didn't realize how much he'd missed this camaraderie. As a coach, he could guide and instruct but he couldn't *do*. That was up to the players. It was a loss of control he still grappled with.

Benjamin dawdled with his skate laces until he and Jujhar were the only ones left in the room. He'd accepted this invitation for more than one reason. Yes, he couldn't wait to get on the ice again. But he needed to say something first.

"I want to thank you."

His words stopped Jujhar on his way to the door. "For what?"

"For welcoming me back. It's more than I deserve." He rose when Jujhar returned and loomed over him.

"Are you still going on about that?" Jujhar frowned. "I thought we'd cleared it all up."

"I accused you of being jealous. Of me, of all people. A has-been NHLer." Benjamin laughed without humour. "You saw I was unhappy and suggested I reevaluate my life, and I lashed out. I should have been grateful you cared." That also held true for his father, who had shared the same message in their last conversation. He couldn't tell that to Jujhar, though, not until he'd confessed to his mother.

Jujhar's eyebrows disappeared into his helmet. "That's bullshit. You don't need to be grateful someone cares about you. You're a good man, Benjamin. You deserve to be liked for *you*, not for what you do between the lines of a hockey rink."

Was that possible? Could he be liked—maybe even loved—even though he'd failed as a player? Was it enough just being himself? He couldn't stop a vision of Lynn from popping into his head. He'd put off apologizing to Jujhar for months for fear of being rejected and look where they were now. He wouldn't make the same mistake with Lynn. He owed her an explanation of his actions over the last several days.

"We good now?" Jujhar tapped his shinpad with his stick. "You worry too much about what other people think. We had an argument. You've apologized. It's done."

"We're good." He cupped his gloved hands on either side of Jujhar's visor and banged their helmeted heads together. "Let's get out there and show these guys who's boss."

Cynthie strode toward Lynn's desk, sliding her arms into her heavy wool coat as she approached. "I just got off the phone with Brewster. I have good news and I have bad news."

Lynn rubbed the back of her neck. The last couple of weeks had been rife with tiny annoyances, both professionally and personally. She was looking forward to a weekend free of obligations or responsibilities and didn't want any more trouble loaded onto her shoulders. "Can it wait until Monday? I was just heading out."

"Me, too. Walk with me. I'll tell you on the way." Cynthie straightened her collar and pulled on thin leather gloves.

She sighed, locked her computer, and took her scarf and hat from a desk drawer. At the exterior door she lifted her coat from the rack and Cynthie waited while she donned her outerwear. Then they headed out in the dark winter afternoon.

"What does Brewster want now?" A bitter wind whirled across the asphalt, snow streaming from the tops of the plow piles like flags. She shivered. All she wanted to do was pick up Oscar from daycare, hole up in her warm, cozy home, and forget about everything else for a while.

"He's hired a new marketing coordinator."

"Finally." That *was* welcome news. Juggling the Canyon Cats schedule and a toddler was wearing her down. And since Benjamin had barely talked to her since the middle of November, it would be a relief to have less opportunities to meet.

She wished for the thousandth time that she knew why he'd backed away so far and so fast. He'd asked if she'd go on a date with him—and then gone into stealth mode. Since then, they'd exchanged only platitudes or silent nods, and when the team had been on a road trip there had been no friendly texts, no casual check-ins.

She'd suggested they go slow. She hadn't meant *this* slow.

If he'd changed his mind, all he had to do was tell her. Her own feelings were mixed and tumbled and she didn't have the energy for the skirmish necessary to sort out their relationship. Having him make the decision for her should have made it easier.

It hadn't. She couldn't stop thinking about him, about *them*.

"That's the good news." Cynthie stopped next to her sedan, its engine already purring. Lynn fished into her purse and found her keys, pressing the buttons to get her own vehicle going. She never remembered to use the remote start. "Here's the bad. The new hire is a university student and won't take on their duties until January."

"For Pete's sake." Lynn huddled in her coat in an attempt to avoid the wind whistling over the sedan's low roof. "Who's training her?"

"It's a him. Given what we know of Brewster's plans, I offered your services, but he refused. Says he'll take care of it."

"Not that it matters." Lynn felt as bitter as the wind

biting at her ears. "We're below the minimum attendance requirement as it is, so whatever I'm doing isn't working. Maybe he'll have better luck, no matter what Brewster wants."

"The team is playing right into his plan, that's for sure. And by playing, I mean losing."

Lynn wanted to defend Benjamin and the Canyon Cats, but Cynthie was right. They were languishing at the bottom of the divisional barrel. And the longer they moldered in the cellar, the fewer fans would show. Who could blame them?

She said her goodbyes and made her way to her own car, parked a few slots down. The interior was fractionally warmer than outside, and she tucked her hands under her armpits, waiting for the heater to take the worst of the chill away.

The arena's staff door slammed shut behind Benjamin and he strode to his car. It was only a few steps away, yet his ears burned with cold by the time he settled in the driver's seat. He blew on his fingers to warm them. One of these days he'd have to remember to wear a hat and gloves. Though he'd grown up in Prince George, it had been a while since he'd endured a true Canadian winter. His previous coaching positions had been in much warmer climates.

There'd been no real need for him to go to the arena that afternoon. But a morning spent examining Jujhar's words from the night before had made him restless and edgy and he'd found himself drawn to the building.

Or rather to Lynn, who was in the building. Now he'd decided to apologize for acting so remote, he wanted to get it done. He managed to stop himself from accosting her at work, locking himself in his own office, but it was about the time she normally left on non-game days, and he planned to catch her as she headed home.

He drove up the road that sloped from the below

ground ice level to the main parking lot. A few vehicles were scattered about, all dusted with the light, dry snow the wind tossed around. With relief he saw Lynn's was still there, but as he watched, she pulled out of her slot and made her way to the main road.

It was his own route out, too, so he followed, trying to decide what his move should be now. She turned left, and so did he. Her brake lights brightened as she pulled to a stop at an intersection and waited for the green. He nosed in behind.

Maybe he should have called her and set up a time to meet. But he'd been too eager to see her to think things through logically, and now he was stuck following her like a spy. Or a stalker.

Could he make things any worse?

The light changed and she rolled forward. Several blocks later she signalled and turned into a church parking lot. Instead of continuing on his solitary way, he turned in with her. He'd come this far. He might as well do what he'd set out to do.

She parked in front of a sign that read "Rainbow Acres Daycare" and the lights on her vehicle went out as he pulled in on the far side. He climbed out of his car to find Lynn staring at him across the roof of her own.

"Why are you following me?" she demanded.

Lynn had noticed Benjamin behind her at the first intersection when she'd stopped for the red light. She'd happened to be checking her rear-view mirror when the beams of a vehicle heading the opposite direction had flashed across his face. She'd only needed that tiny glimpse to recognize him.

She'd had no reason to assume he was deliberately following her—after all, they were travelling on one of the main arteries that ran through the entire city. Until he'd turned into the church parking lot behind her.

His smile was hesitant. "I wanted to talk with you."

She slapped the roof of her car, the report echoing through the empty dark. "After saying nothing more than hello for two weeks?"

"I'm sorry about that." He shut his door, rounded the trunk of her car, and stopped beside her. "That's what I wanted to say. I'm sorry for shutting you out. I was concentrating on the team, but that's no excuse."

"No, it's not. All you had to do was say Lynn, I need to focus on my job. I don't have time for you anymore." She got it. She really did. But she loathed the feeling of coming second to someone's career yet again.

An SUV pulled into the lot, the headlights sweeping across Benjamin like the slash of a knife. "I hate I made you feel that way. That wasn't my intention."

"Well, it's what happened."

The father of one of Oscar's daycare mates stepped out of the SUV. He glanced at them curiously but, at Lynn's nod and smile, continued past with a wave.

Benjamin waited until the door had closed behind him. "Please, Lynn. I promise to never shut you out again. And if there are reasons I can't be there for you, I'll tell you why." He took a short step closer. "I thought about you. A lot."

"You did, did you?" They were only inches apart. The chill of the winter night vanished as if he'd wrapped her in a blanket. She lifted her chin to meet his eyes.

He nodded. "I know I'm not who you're looking for. I have baggage, more than you can guess. I have a career on the edge, one that also takes me out of town for lengthy periods of time on a regular basis."

"I know." He'd said nothing she hadn't told herself before. Her head knew all the reasons why they shouldn't pursue anything further. It was her heart that wouldn't listen to logic.

"I apologize again for not asking sooner. But would you have dinner with me tomorrow night?" His expression in the glow of the church sign was a mixture of hope and hesitancy.

Her pulse pounded in her throat, making it difficult to breathe evenly. She'd had time to think during the echoing silence of the last two weeks, and despite his obviously sincere apology, she couldn't risk being rejected again. Keeping far away from Benjamin was the best thing to do, for herself, for Oscar. For her heart.

She made one last, pathetic attempt to be responsible, to stick with that plan. "You said it yourself. We're not a good match, and I'm not looking for another one-night stand. I'm looking for a father for Oscar, a husband I can rely on."

His shoulders sank. "I understand." He stepped back.

A weight squeezed her chest as the memories of the stark, lonely nights of the last two weeks—and the months before that—pressed down. "But how will I know who that man is without spending time with him?"

He froze.

"Yes, Benjamin, I will have dinner with you tomorrow night."

CHAPTER SIXTEEN

Lynn and Stephanie had joined the Silverberry Book Club about the same time and had hit it off immediately. When Lynn had announced she was pregnant and was buying a house with a full suite to allow for a renter to help with the mortgage, Stephanie immediately asked to be considered. Since their friendship had been new at the time, Lynn had been a little leery about the idea, but had agreed to a three-month trial.

Now, she couldn't imagine any other arrangement. At first, they had pointedly kept to their own spaces, but the line had become blurred after Oscar's birth. Stephanie had stepped in to help during the early days without being asked, and Lynn had been so exhausted and overwhelmed she hadn't had the strength to worry whether it might have negative repercussions.

Luckily, it had only strengthened their bond, though the older Oscar got the more careful she was not to abuse Stephanie's willingness to help. A teenage neighbour took care of him on the rare occasions necessary, but when she hadn't been available for her last-minute date with Benjamin, Lynn had turned to Stephanie.

Now the two of them were in her bedroom trying to decide what she should wear. Oscar was there, too, busily occupied by emptying and refilling her sock drawer.

"You can't go wrong with a little black dress." Stephanie hooked one off the closet rod and held it up for Lynn's inspection.

She shook her head. "Too formal. We're going to a restaurant, not a gala."

Stephanie shrugged and replaced the hanger. "You know me. I'd rather be overdressed than under."

"You always look fabulous." Lynn couldn't help a sly dig. "Peter agrees, given the way his mouth dropped open yesterday when he came to pick you up."

Stephanie continued to flick hangers, but a slight blush reddened her cheeks. "I didn't notice."

"Liar. So, things are going well?" Peter was the date Stephanie had confessed to the night Benjamin had come over for dinner. Lynn had met him twice now and was hopeful he would soon become a regular presence. He appeared sincerely attracted to Stephanie, and though she wasn't one to blab about her feelings, Lynn thought she returned his regard.

"I think so. How about this?" She pulled out a silky red dress with a cowl neck.

Lynn took the hint and dropped the subject. They finally agreed on a long-sleeved, high-necked tunic dress in sapphire blue and black silk leggings in recognition of the below freezing temperatures. A silvery belt sparkled at her waist—a waist that still hadn't quite recovered from pregnancy—and knee-high boots completed the casual but elegant look. Lynn was fastening dangling rhinestone earrings when the doorbell rang.

"I'll get it," Stephanie said, scooping up Oscar. "You can make a grand appearance in a minute."

Her fingers trembled as she secured the earring back. It had been close to ten years since she'd last been on a date. There'd only been a few months between breaking up with Lance and deciding to get pregnant, and she'd been smarting too much to get into the game.

Her night with Benjamin didn't count, of course. A

hookup at a bar wasn't a date.

His voice rumbled down the hall, and while she couldn't understand the words, she could tell from his tone he was talking with Oscar. Not that it was the high and squeaky baby talk most people automatically used. She'd noticed at the dinner he'd shared with them that he spoke to Oscar like an adult, if perhaps slightly slower and clearer. It had struck her as incredibly sweet and was one of the many reasons she'd allowed herself to say yes to tonight.

She examined herself in the mirror one more time, drew in a deep breath, and then went to meet her date.

When Stephanie opened the door, Benjamin's heart tripped, hard. Had Lynn changed her mind?

"Come on in. She's just about ready."

His relief was short lived. She backed away only enough to allow her to close the door behind him. They were much the same height and, when she leaned in, they were nose to nose.

"I like you." She spoke in a whisper, but there was steel in the quiet tone. "So, I'm going to give you some advice. She talks about you, and it sounds like you've been running hot and cold. You need to make a decision and make it tonight." She stepped closer and he fought the impulse to lean away. "If, after this evening, you can't be serious about this relationship, you're going to break it off. Politely, but firmly. She doesn't deserve to be jerked around, and if you're just playing with her...well, don't."

Benjamin met Stephanie's dark gaze square on. The woman's lashes were stubby, lengthened by mascara, and the lids glittered with discreet powder. The makeup did nothing to detract from her fierce protectiveness. "I'm not playing with her. I can't promise forever"— Stephanie twitched, and he braced for a blow that didn't come—"but I can promise to be honest and committed, at least while we see where things go."

The silence between them held for one, two, three beats. Then she nodded and backed off. He pulled in a long breath and followed her up the stairs and through the baby gate. In the living room, Oscar sat surrounded by toys of all kinds.

"Hello, Oscar." He crouched down and picked up one of the blocks scattered in front of the boy. "Can I help you build a tower?"

He chatted with Oscar and ignored Stephanie's looming presence until the sound of a door opening at the end of the hall drew his attention.

His gut curled as Lynn approached. At work she dressed in a casually sophisticated style he suspected took time and effort to put together. Tonight, she glittered and shone. And took his breath away.

He rose to his feet as if drawn by marionette strings. "You look beautiful."

She smiled and, for the first time in the months he'd known her, he noticed a hint of shyness. "Thank you. You look very nice, too."

He'd decided against wearing one of his many suits. Lynn saw him in one every game night, after all. Instead, he'd chosen black slacks and a bright blue shirt with an argyle vest in coordinating colours. "We match."

Her smile brightened. "So we do. Maybe that's a good omen."

A flurry of activity followed, with Lynn kissing Oscar goodnight, Benjamin helping her into her warm wool coat, and Stephanie giving him one last, threatening stare. Then they were out in the chilly winter night, breath steaming as he handed her into his car and joined her inside. It was still warm from his drive over, but he kept the heater on low as they made their way through the streets to downtown.

The restaurant he'd chosen was in a block filled with kitschy, trendy retail shops, all closed at this time on a

Saturday night. Sadie had mentioned it the last time he'd visited, swearing it was one of the most romantic restaurants in town while good-naturedly teasing Jujhar that he never took her anywhere. He had little time to explore the local late-night scene even if he'd wanted to, so it had been the first place to come to mind.

Lynn didn't speak much on the drive down, but her silence was calm and relaxed, so he tried not to worry about it. He found a parking stall and they met on the sidewalk. He wanted to take her hand but wasn't sure how she felt about public displays of affection.

"I've never been here." Lynn paused outside the door, and he reached for the handle. "I've heard good things, though."

"Me, too. A friend of mine recommended it." He ushered her in.

As they waited for the hostess, he gave in and twined his fingers with hers. Her eyes sparked, as bright as the stones dangling from her ears, and for an instant he couldn't breathe, the world around him shrinking to her face, her touch.

Determined not to make a fool of himself by kissing her senseless right there, he sought distraction by scanning the room. Wouldn't it just be his luck if Jujhar and Sadie had decided to come tonight? Romancing Lynn under his friends' eagle eyes would definitely crimp what little style he had.

His gaze skimmed over a couple in the far corner, and then snapped back. Shocked, he could do nothing but stare.

His mother. His mother at an intimate table for two, sitting beside a silver-haired man in a grey suit.

A man he did not recognize.

Lynn had thought Benjamin was going to kiss her. His eyes had darkened almost to black and his Adam's apple had bobbed as he swallowed. When he turned away, she was torn between disappointment and relief.

Moments later, his grip on her hand tightened painfully. She sucked in a breath, but he didn't seem to notice. She followed his wide-eyed gaze to an older couple sitting at a far table. They were doing nothing more dramatic than chatting and laughing and sharing an appetizer. Another glance at Benjamin revealed he had yet to look away.

The hostess bustled up. "Sorry for the wait. Do you have a reservation?"

When Benjamin said nothing, Lynn nudged him. He blinked and eased his hold on her hand. "Oh. Yes. Under Whitestone. Benjamin Whitestone." His tone was flat and uncompromising.

Confused at his sudden change in demeanour, Lynn followed the hostess, Benjamin behind her. He had recovered somewhat by the time they were seated with their menus opened before them, though his eyes kept darting over her shoulder in the direction of the other couple.

She couldn't ignore it any longer. "Do you know them?"

He sighed and quirked up a corner of his mouth. The belt of anxiousness around her heart loosened a notch. "I was hoping you hadn't noticed. Am I behaving that oddly?"

"Who are they?" His gaze dropped and his lips pressed together. She tried not to be hurt by his refusal to answer but his distrust stabbed. "Never mind. I won't pry." She focused on her menu.

"She's my mother."

She flattened the leather folder to her chest so fast a breeze fluttered against her heated cheeks. "Your mother?" Daring a glance over her shoulder she caught a glimpse of dark hair glittering with silver and cut in a shaggy bob. The high, solid chair back hid the rest of her. "Is that your dad with her?"

"No," Benjamin said grimly. "It is not."

CHAPTER SEVENTEEN

It was Lynn's turn to stare, this time at Benjamin. Why did he look so upset?

She suddenly realized how little she knew about his life away from the hockey rink. They'd talked mostly about his career the night he'd come for dinner. Had he avoided mentioning his family on purpose? She assumed his parents were both alive, so did that mean—

Was he implying his mother was having an affair?

"Maybe it's a business dinner?" Even as she suggested it, she knew she was wrong. The scene her fleeting glimpse had revealed was vivid in her mind— the woman feeding the man from her fork, her free hand linked with his on the table, their heads tipped together.

"It's not." Benjamin rubbed a finger up and down the bridge of his nose, pressing so hard his skin went white before the blood rushed back in. "My mother no longer works. And she doesn't volunteer for any organizations, either."

She ignored the urge to turn and get a better look at the couple. "Maybe you should go say hi, then. Find out who he is."

"I suppose." His expression was more than reluctant. His pinched mouth and narrowed eyes implied dread and distaste.

"Do you and your mother"—she searched for a delicate way to put it—"not get along?"

"We don't *not* get along." As she untangled that, he focused on her fully for the first time since they'd sat down. "When you and I met at the bar, we didn't talk much. About personal stuff."

It wouldn't help matters to point out they still didn't. "No. Things moved pretty fast between us." Her emotions that night had centred around resentment toward Lance, irritation she'd wasted so much time on him, and a growing conviction that she was going to take matters regarding becoming a mother into her own hands. "I'd never done that before. Hooked up with a guy for one night."

"I remember you saying so. I even believed you." Amusement lightened the gloom in his face. "I'm afraid I can't say the same. Even for a fourth-line player like me, being part of an NHL team meant women were easy to come by."

"You weren't playing any more by the time we met. Not that I knew about your past, of course. All you said was that you'd been in town for a few days and were leaving in the morning."

"I saw you across the bar and it was like no one else was there. I had to talk to you. I didn't think it would go as far—or as fast—as it did, though."

"Me, neither." The attraction between them had been instantaneous. On Lynn's side, she'd seen a chance to have a final fling before settling into the serious business of getting pregnant. She hadn't considered Benjamin's intentions. Was it possible he'd also had a reason more complicated than explosive sex?

"I was in town because—"

The server appeared, but upon learning they hadn't made any decisions yet, told them to take their time and faded away.

Benjamin drew in a deep breath. He put his menu to one side and gripped his hands together, pressing his forearms into the table. "I was in town for my father's funeral. He died of a heart attack. We'd buried him the day before."

"I'm so sorry." She stretched across and laid her hands on his, feeling the tension in his fists. "I wish I'd known."

"Do you?" His lids flickered. "If you'd known I'd come almost directly from my father's grave to the bar, would you have given me a second look? What kind of son does that?"

"One who is working his way through his grief his own way. One who is seeking comfort in living his life fully."

"You give me too much credit." The bitterness in his tone made her heart ache. "Anyway, that's all a very long explanation for my reaction tonight. My mother is dating again, and she didn't tell me."

"Maybe it's a first date? Maybe she hasn't had a chance to mention it?"

His gaze flicked over her shoulder. "I doubt this is the first time they've met."

His dry tone encouraged her to risk another quick glance.

She shouldn't have worried the couple would notice. They were staring into each other's eyes as if they were alone in the room. Benjamin's mother leaned toward the man and Lynn saw her in profile. She recognized the strong arch of her nose and curve of her jaw. Her almost black hair with its silver streaks was tucked behind her ear and swept in a smooth fall to her shoulder.

She turned back to Benjamin. "Okay, it's a date. But it's been more than two years since your father died."

"It's not that. Not only that, anyway." He shifted in his seat and toyed with his silverware. "One of the reasons I was excited to accept the coaching job here was it would give me a chance to reconnect with my mom. It didn't start out well, because she had to go look after her sister for several weeks shortly after I came back. But once she returned, I thought it would get better. It hasn't. I blamed myself for not trying hard enough, but now I think of it, my mom turned down several chances to get together. Was it because of this guy, whoever he is?"

His voice grew stronger as he worked his way through his thoughts, and anger replaced the dismay in his eyes.

"Settle down, cowboy. Your mother is a grown woman with a life of her own. She doesn't have to get your approval on who she sees."

"Of course not. But she could have been honest with me, instead of hiding him."

For a moment she thought he was going to shove back his chair and confront his parent right then and there. It wasn't her place to intervene, so she held her breath and watched him warily. As quickly as it flared, his temper dampened.

"I'm sorry." His smile was rueful. "I'm sure this isn't what you were expecting tonight."

"Don't worry about it. It's not like you planned to run into your mother."

"No." He closed his eyes, drew in a breath through his nose, and opened his eyes. "There's no way to avoid them. She hasn't seen me yet, but she will sooner or later. It's probably best if I go say hi, civilly and calmly."

"I agree."

He remained rooted in his seat.

Benjamin wondered if he was overreacting to the situation. If he was, he couldn't help it. The sight of his mother in an overtly romantic situation with someone other than his father caused his gut to roil with a bubbling stew of resentment and happiness, sorrow and surprise.

Thank god Lynn seemed to be taking it in stride. Her expression was sincere and sympathetic, and she didn't appear to think he was being a jerk. Though she certainly wasn't letting him feel too sorry for himself.

Right now, she was waiting patiently yet expectantly for him to make a move.

He stood up, his knees watery with nerves. "Will you come with me? I could use the moral support."

"Of course." She pushed back her chair and took his hand. "I've got your back. Let's go."

I've got your back. The simple, casual statement stiffened his resolve and made it so much easier to take the first step. Of course, if she knew the whole story behind his father's heart attack, knew that Benjamin had been the one to precipitate it, she'd think differently.

Which was one reason he would never tell her the truth.

Clutching Lynn's hand, he led her toward his mother.

Her grief at her husband's death had been deep and profound. Benjamin didn't doubt that for an instant.

He was the last person who should be upset she had found love again. After all, she wasn't yet sixty and had decades of life to live. He couldn't expect her to live those years alone.

But he kind of did.

As curious as he was about her companion, he didn't take his eyes off his mother. He drifted to a stop beside the table, Lynn's grip anchoring him as she stood just behind his shoulder.

Finally distracted from her date, his mother looked up with a smile that froze when she realized who was standing at her side. "Benjamin! What are you doing here?"

He bit back a snarky *I could ask the same of you.* "I'm on a date. This is Lynn Kolmyn. Lynn, my mother. Thea Whitestone." He refrained from looking at the man sharing his mother's table.

"Lovely to meet you, Mrs. Whitestone." Lynn shook his mother's hand without releasing her clasp on his.

"And you." Red flags bloomed on her cheeks and her

eyes darted from Lynn to Benjamin to the as-yet-unnamed man and back again. "Kelly, this is my son Benjamin."

Kelly stood up and extended his hand. "Kelly Jarmin. Thea has told me a lot about you."

"Mr. Jarmin." Benjamin squeezed his hand firmly, not in challenge, but in warning. Of what, he wasn't exactly sure. He just knew the other man made his hackles rise.

"Call me Kelly." Jarmin smiled at Lynn and shook her hand as well. He was about Benjamin's height and his thick grey hair swept back from a sharp widow's peak. He didn't even have the grace to be going bald. Neither did he have a paunch or jowls. In fact, he looked disgustingly fit for a man his age.

"Would you care to join us?" He indicated the two empty seats at their table.

"Yes, please do." Thea seemed to have recovered her poise though she was having trouble meeting his eyes.

"No, thank you." Benjamin didn't have to think twice. In fact, he couldn't think of anything more excruciating than making small talk with his mother and this Kelly. Maybe having his toenails pulled out without anesthetic. "We'll leave you two alone. Could I come by tomorrow afternoon, though? I haven't seen much of you lately."

She gave a dignified nod, a flicker of her eyelids revealing she understood what he hadn't said.

"Have a lovely dinner." Lynn stepped back, gently tugging his hand.

"Yes." It was difficult, but he kept his tone agreeable. "Have a lovely dinner. See you tomorrow, Mom."

At their table, the server was hovering. Benjamin quickly scanned the menu, decided he had little appetite, and chose steak and potatoes by reflex. He also ordered a bottle of wine after a brief consultation with Lynn.

"How are you doing?" She rested her elbows on the table, intertwined her fingers, and propped her chin on her hands.

"I'm sorry. Tonight is turning into a disaster." The waiter returned with their wine and nothing more was said until he left.

"I wouldn't say disaster," Lynn said judiciously. "Odd and uncomfortable, perhaps. But you'll talk with your mother tomorrow and get everything straightened out. For now, can we put that aside and start again?"

"I would love to." He didn't deserve her understanding, but he would accept it gratefully. He raised his glass. "To new beginnings."

"New beginnings." The crystal chimed and she sipped. "Did I tell you what Oscar did yesterday?"

CHAPTER EIGHTEEN

Sunday afternoon, Benjamin pulled into the driveway of the home where he'd grown up and turned off the engine. Though December was only a few days away, the lights strung along the eaves and windows were not yet gleaming through the wintery dusk. Tradition held they wouldn't be illuminated until the first of the month.

Despite the fact it was long past the time he and his mother should have had a serious talk, he didn't get out of his car. A few more minutes couldn't make things any worse.

Instead, he contemplated the empty seat next to him. He would *much* rather think about necking with Lynn than have the conversation waiting for him inside.

Their date had, surprisingly, recovered from its rocky start. He'd been able to ignore his mother and Kelly for the most part, and when they left before he and Lynn had finished their entrées, the atmosphere had eased further. By the time they finished coffee and dessert, he was back on an even keel.

He wasn't surprised that she didn't invite him in when he brought her home. He needed to regain her trust, and one date was just the start. Their goodnight kiss began chaste enough but turned fiery in seconds. When she dragged herself away, breathless and tousled with eyes that promised *more* burning through the dark, he clutched the steering wheel to keep from hauling her back into his arms.

"Call me." Her husky voice was deeper than usual and ruffled across his skin like velvet. "Tomorrow."

"I will." He had waited for her to enter her house, and then, for the second time, driven home with an aching erection that needed manual attention.

He hadn't called her yet, but he would. As soon as he'd had it out with his mother.

He climbed out of his car and paced down the side of the house to the back door. Though he hadn't lived there for almost two decades, the habits of his childhood and teen years were deeply ingrained. He turned the knob and stepped inside a small mudroom just off the kitchen.

"Mom?"

"In here."

He toed off his boots and unzipped his parka, hanging it on the back of a dining chair as he followed her voice through the opening that led to the living room. She was sitting in her usual chair, an upholstered rocker placed next to an octagonal table that held a lamp, her reading glasses, and a mug that probably contained tea.

On the other side of the table was his father's empty recliner. Sorrow punched his chest. He wondered if he'd ever get used to the sight.

Thea's lap was covered in fluffy mint-green wool. She was an avid knitter and always had something on the go. When he was a kid, he'd look up from the ice during practices, even games, and see needles flashing from her seat in the stands.

She shifted her feet off the chair's matching ottoman, and he lowered to the squashy surface. He waited as she finished a row, set her work down, threaded her fingers together, and met his gaze squarely. "I should have told you."

He'd half expected her to defend herself, so her blunt admission was welcome. "It would have been a shock, no matter what. But it would have been nice not to discover it in public." He'd had time to think, though, and he'd been able to see her side of things a little more clearly. And realized his peaceful acceptance would be a tiny way of making amends for the tragedy he'd caused. "It's your life, Mom. If he makes you happy, I'm happy for you. Where did you meet?"

Thea's cheeks flushed. "Online."

His eyes widened. "Online? Like, on Tinder?"

"I joined a dating site for people over fifty." Her fingers fidgeted with the blanket on her lap, but she didn't look away. "Kelly contacted me, we messaged for a while, and then we went for coffee. We enjoyed our time together, so we started seeing each other regularly."

"When was this? After you got back from Auntie Janet's?" That would explain why Thea had had little time for him since her return from Vancouver.

"Before that. Before you got your job, actually."

"You've been seeing this guy for *months*?" What other secrets was his mother hiding? Did he want to know?

"I'm sorry. I should have told you. But I didn't think it was worth mentioning unless it grew serious." She picked up the needles, scrunching the loops together as if preparing to start work again, and then dropped it back in her lap.

"And is it?" Had it looked *serious* last night or just flirty?

"It depends how you define serious." He raised an eyebrow, and his mother acknowledged his unspoken reproof with a fleeting smile. "Fine. We're not seeing other people. But we're a long way from moving in together. Does that answer your question?"

The idea that his mother might be having casual sex gave him the shudders. He really, *really* didn't want to hear any further details. "I suppose." He stood, paced to the front window, and stared out at the snow-covered lawn and street. The clouds were heavy and grey, and scattered flakes heralded more was on its way.

"You know I'll never stop loving your father." Thea's voice was quiet and firm. "But he wouldn't want me to sit at home and mourn him forever. We talked about it."

He turned to face her. "You talked about it? Really?"

"Of course we did. I'm sure all married couples do at least once or twice." Her gaze dropped to her knitting, and she smoothed the rows of stitches absently. "Being with someone else doesn't mean I'll ever forget him."

"I would never think that." He took a deep breath, moved away from the window, and with deliberation sat in his father's recliner, perching on the edge. He couldn't put it off any longer. It was his turn to confess. "I would never deny you the right to be happy. Especially since I'm the reason he died."

There. He'd finally said it. The words that ate at his soul, gnawed at his heart.

Thea frowned. "What on earth are you talking about?"

He'd hoped the acknowledgment of his sin would be enough, but she looked honestly confused. She mustn't have heard him. "I'm the reason he died. I caused his heart attack."

He'd never forget the terrible choking that had rattled through his phone speaker, the guttural groan, the heavy thud, the sudden silence. His mother's screams as he'd sat, frozen, impotent, half a continent away.

He'd never forget his father's last, disappointed words. "Maybe hockey isn't the life you should be chasing, son."

It had been the off season, and his father had been trying to convince him to come home instead of hiding in Los Angeles where he had been coaching. What had started as a friendly conversation about family and friends had grown heated when his father had suggested it might be time for Benjamin to look at a new career.

"There are so many other jobs out there. What about teaching? Or sales? I know hockey has been your life for a long time, but if it doesn't make you happy..." He'd trailed off with a sigh.

Though Benjamin had spent the last decade drifting from job to job without purpose or plan, that day he had decided to take a stand. He was accusing his father of giving up on him when the fatal, final noises had interrupted his self-centred diatribe.

"Oh, honey." His mother lifted a trembling hand to her mouth, her eyes glazed. "Do you really believe that?"

"It was me, Mom." His throat was so thick with tears he could barely choke out the words. "I killed him."

"You did no such thing. High blood pressure, too much red meat and not enough exercise killed him."

"I was arguing with him. If I hadn't—"

She rose abruptly, her work tumbling to the floor in a tangled mess. Ignoring it, she planted her hands on his shoulders and gave him a shake. "It had nothing to do with you. *Nothing*. Maybe you had a disagreement, but your father got angrier watching the Canucks play. He wasn't upset, not really. He just wanted you to know it was okay to come home. That you didn't have to keep trying to prove yourself."

A fissure opened in the darkness of his heart and dawn seeped in. "I thought—"

She cut him off again. "If I did anything to make you think I blamed you, I'm sorry. I don't and I never did. And your father would say the same thing if he were here. It was horrible, horrible timing. But that's all your conversation was. A coincidence. Not a cause."

"If I had been a better player, if I had been good enough to make him proud, the conversation never would have happened." It *was* his fault. It had to be. It couldn't just be cruel fate.

Her fingers dug into his shoulders as she forced him to look at her. "He was proud of you, Benjamin. So proud. It had nothing to do with how many pucks you put across the goal line or how fast you could skate from one blue line to the next. You were his son." She said the last word with such fervor she shuddered.

The burden he'd been carrying for more than two years lightened. He blinked back a surge of emotion that made him want to curl into a ball and howl. "Are you sure?"

"I'm sure. You're a good son, Benjamin. I love you. And so did your father."

She was wrong—he wasn't a good son. Not as good as he could be. Maybe that's what made his failure to live up to their expectations so painful. Their quiet faith shouted louder than any words.

For now, he'd take the comfort she offered. He laid his palms over her hands and pressed them. "I love you, too."

She studied his face and, seemingly satisfied with what she saw, patted him once more and returned to her chair. He slid further back in his father's recliner, relaxing into the well-worn seat gingerly but no longer with the sense he didn't belong there.

"Kelly is coming for dinner." She picked up her knitting, untangled it, and set to work. "Would you like to stay?"

Sending Benjamin home on Saturday night had been the right thing to do. Not what Lynn had *wanted* to do, but the right thing.

He'd recovered well, but he'd been overthrown by the discovery his mother was dating. He was hurting and vulnerable and though she believed he would have accepted an invitation to her bed with alacrity, she would have felt as if she was taking advantage of his turmoil.

Sunday was laundry day, and the warm, comforting scents of detergent and dryer sheets filled the house. Between chores and Oscar, she kept busy, though nothing completely prevented her from wondering how it was going with Thea and Benjamin. She kept her phone close, ready for his call—which didn't come until Oscar was in bed.

She was curled on the couch under a soft, fluffy throw with her latest binge-worthy escape streaming on the television. Hitting pause, she swept up her phone and answered.

"Did I catch you at a good time?" Benjamin sounded tired but calm. "I would have called earlier but I ended up having dinner with my mom and Kelly. I didn't get home until Oscar's bedtime so I figured I should wait."

She was struck yet again at his consideration, his total acceptance of Oscar, and had to clear the tenderness from her throat before she could speak. "I appreciate the thought. He's down and out. I have plenty of time to talk now." She plumped a pillow behind her back and slid down the cushions, stretching her legs toward the opposite arm of the sofa. "So, how did it go?"

"Better than I expected. Kelly seems a good guy."

"I'm glad. It must still be hard. Seeing him with your mom." She picked at a loose thread in the blanket and bit back a curse when it unravelled, creating a hole.

"It's weird. He's different than my dad. Loud when he was quiet. Likes to cook when he didn't know how to boil water. I never would have picked him for her."

"As long as he treats her well. That's all that matters, right?"

"Yeah." He sighed, long and slow. "Anyway, enough about my mother. When can I see you again?"

Her pulse kicked up a notch, but she answered in a teasing tone. "Tomorrow at the arena?"

He chuckled. "That's not what I meant. I want to kiss you again. Somewhere more comfortable than the front seat of my car."

Desire glowed low in her belly. "I like the sound of that."

"Friday evening is open." His tone was both hopeful and suggestive.

"Stephanie and I are going to a Christmas party hosted by our book club that night."

"I guess that won't work then." His disappointment rang through the speaker.

"Unless you wanted to come along? To the Christmas party? Don't let the book club part scare you off. I can guarantee it will be not what you expect." She held her breath. It was one thing, going to a restaurant together. It was another entirely to invite him into her life, to meet her friends, her chosen family. Was he ready for that step? Was she? "We wouldn't have to stay late. There'd still be time after to be...alone."

An approving hum rumbled in her ear. "That sounds great."

"Awesome. I'll text you the details." Her fingertips tingled with anticipation.

After a pause, Benjamin said, "I suppose I should let you go."

She snuggled deeper onto the cushions. "Only if you have to. I have nowhere to be." She liked the intimacy of his voice. It made her feel warm and connected.

"Me, neither." Another comfortable pause, and then, "What were you doing when I called?"

She opened her mouth to answer with the boring truth, closed it for a moment, and then started again. "I had just gotten out of the bath."

"Oh?" The fatigue in his tone vanished.

"I'm lying on my bed in nothing but a towel."

"Ohhhh." His response was almost a growl.

Her breasts tingled and she slid one hand under the loose waistband of her pajama pants. She wore no panties, and her centre was warm and wet. Her breath hitched and she moaned. "Should I tell you what I'm doing now?"

"Don't leave anything out."

CHAPTER NINETEEN

Lynn had feared that looking forward to Friday would cause the next few days to drag, but instead they flew by. She was swamped at work and Benjamin had ramped up practices and off-ice training in anticipation of a short road trip the following week. Other than a few quick conversations in the halls of the arena, they had no face-to-face interactions.

The late-night calls had continued, though. And the connection between them had grown deeper as they discussed mundane things like movies and music, favourite colours and food they liked.

Now she paced nervously in front of the living room window as she waited for him to arrive. Not that she was worried about the party. No, she was worried about what would happen after.

Because she'd decided that, if she had anything to do with it, Benjamin would be staying the night. He'd made it clear he wanted time alone with her. She didn't intend to send him home unsatisfied a third time.

The noise of the hot air popper, almost loud enough to drown out her thoughts, cut off suddenly and Oscar's teenage babysitter Makayla came in from the kitchen, carrying a metal bowl heaped with fluffy kernels.

"You look great, Lynn." She plopped onto the sofa and spoke around the mouthful she'd shovelled in. "That dress is awesome."

"Thanks." She smoothed the thin, slinky fabric over

her hips. It was midnight blue shot through with silver threads and the hem just skimmed her knees. The cowl neck drooped low over her breasts, and she'd drawn attention to her cleavage with a chunky silver necklace. Despite the fresh snow and old ice coating the ground outside, she was daring to wear stiletto heels. It would give her an excuse to cling to Benjamin's arm.

Makayla picked up the remote and clicked to Netflix. She'd come over more than an hour ago and taken care of Oscar's bedtime routine so Lynn could get ready without a toddler underfoot. He was now in his crib, though still fussing. Lynn hoped he'd be asleep by the time Benjamin showed up. It made it easier to leave him if he was already out for the night.

She peeked through the curtains—again—and her heart bumped as a car pulled into the driveway, headlights brilliant in the deep dark. Her pulse slowed when Stephanie appeared and lowered herself gracefully through the passenger door. Lynn crossed her fingers, thrilled and nervous in equal parts. Stephanie was bringing Peter as her date—the first time she'd be introducing a friend to the Silverberry Book Club, too.

This evening could be a turning point for both of them.

Five minutes later another set of headlights illuminated the cedar hedge separating Lynn's drive from the one next door. "Benjamin's here." She checked the monitor one more time. "I think Oscar's out now."

Makayla waved a hand. "We'll be fine. Have a good night."

"I'm going to try." She slipped into her three-quarter length white faux fur jacket, picked up the spangled clutch containing her phone and other necessities, and made her way down the stairs as a quiet knock sounded. She opened the door, the bells on the Christmas wreath tinkling.

Framed against the night, Benjamin's shoulders

blended into the blackness. His white button-down glowed like moonlight between the lapels of his open dark wool coat and his short, newly cut hair glinted in the beams falling through the doorway. The faint whiff of a spicy cologne drifted toward her, making her want to lean in and inhale.

"Merry Christmas. Sorry I'm late." He twisted and offered his elbow. "Your sleigh awaits."

She took his arm, tinglingly aware of the lean muscles under the layers of fabric. "Well, thank you, kind sir." She called softly up the stairs. "Phone if you need anything, Makayla."

"I will. Don't worry about a thing." A disembodied hand waved goodbye over the back of the couch.

She shut the door and followed Benjamin to his car. Their breath puffed in white clouds and chill nipped at her bare legs, but once inside she relaxed into the warmth of the heated seat.

He slid under the steering wheel and turned his torso toward her. "You look like a Russian princess in that coat." His appreciative gaze swept over her, warming her from her frigid fingertips to her chilly toes.

"Thank you. I feel like it. It's so soft and luxurious." She combed her fingers through the fur. "Merry Christmas to you, by the way. You're looking very handsome." He was attractive even in his nylon coaching uniform, but she had a feeling that, once she had a good look at him when they reached Helen's, *attractive* might be too weak a word.

She hoped she could wait until after the party was over to jump his bones.

Lynn looked regal and untouchable with her hair piled high like a crown and diamond studs winking in her ears. But her smile was warm and familiar, and Benjamin relaxed. He'd been looking forward to tonight all week.

Looking forward. That did little to describe the anticipation with which he'd prepared for the evening.

She directed him efficiently to a neighbourhood with wide roads that climbed and wound up the side of a hill. "I haven't come this way in years." He turned right, passing large homes, many sporting trendy Christmas decorations that brightened the December dark. "I didn't know any of this existed."

"It's a newer subdivision. Helen and Nathan—the couple hosting the party—bought it after they married this year. They used to be neighbours in a different part of town. That's how they met. But they decided they wanted a place that was theirs, not his or hers."

He glanced over. If he didn't know better, he'd say Lynn was nervous. Was it something to do with Oscar? Or was it him? "Everything all right?"

She bit her lip but didn't answer his question. "It's that one. The house with the tree full of white lights."

He pulled to a stop at the curb and turned off the engine. Her profile was limned by the lights of the house behind her. "I'm sorry if I'm acting weird." She slid him a sideways glance. "I've never brought anyone to this party before. Or to any book club events."

Not Oscar, then. He traced her profile with his gaze. She'd already told him she hadn't dated since their one-night stand, so her confession wasn't a surprise. What was she really trying to say? "Are you worried they won't approve of me?"

She twisted toward him, her eyes widening. "Of course not! I'm worried *you* won't like *them*. These are my closest friends. If you don't..." She trailed off, gnawing her lip again.

It was a novel feeling, being the person with the power to approve, not the one being disapproved of. He tapped the back of her clenched hands with a fingertip. "I'm sure everything will be fine. I promise to be open-minded. I'm not that picky, you know."

"Thanks." Her tone was dry.

He laughed, realizing what he'd implied. "You know what I mean." His heart ballooned, lighter than it had been in a long time. "Stay here." He opened his door and rounded the hood to the passenger side. With a flourish he pulled open Lynn's door, extended his hand, and guided her out. "Can I kiss you? Or would that ruin your make up?"

Her eyes glittered and her mouth curved upward. "Ruin away."

Still, he kept his kiss gentle, his hands on her hips, round and firm under her plush coat. Her lips were cool and slightly sticky from the matte red colour she'd tinted them with. Desire licked flames down his spine to his cock. When her hands clutched his lapels and pulled him closer, he lifted his head. "We should go in."

Her eyelids drifted up, revealing her dazed and dizzy gaze. "I suppose." She blinked and her concentration sharpened. It was fascinating to watch her gather her control around her. "Just one thing."

"What's that?" *Anything*, he thought. *Anything you want.*

"You're coming home with me after the party. And you're staying the night."

His hands clenched her hips. She wriggled closer, brushing her core against him, determination in her expression. Who was he to deny her? Not that he wanted to, of course. "How long do we have to stay?"

This was only the third Silverberry Book Club Christmas Party Lynn had attended. Mind you, it was only the third the club had hosted. The summer Lynn joined, the members had decided to transition from the expected read-a-book, talk-about-a-book club to one that was more active. Sure, once in a while they still read a book they could all agree on, but usually their get-togethers were more along the lines of recent events—the apple-picking excursion in September, the horror movie night in October, and the photography class in November. She'd had to miss the last two because of Canyon Cats games and had been looking forward to seeing everyone at the party.

She stood in the corner of Helen and Nathan's elegant but welcoming living room and sipped the Red Shoe Martini her hostess had shoved into her hand, alone for the first time since she and Benjamin had joined the throng. He was currently chatting with Bennett Ayers, whose husband Terrance Renfrew was a longtime member of the Silverberries. She had no idea what they were talking about, but Benjamin's eyes were bright, and his laughter reached her over the many conversations bubbling around her, as well as the Christmas music playing from hidden speakers.

She clenched her thighs together and drew in a long, slow breath. Only a couple more hours until they could be together. She could control herself that long.

Helen appeared at her side. "I like your young man." She waved her own martini glass in Benjamin's direction. She wore the ugliest of ugly Christmas cardigans over a silver pant suit and a Santa hat was perched on her short grey hair. Lynn often envied her exuberance, wishing she was as comfortable in her own skin as Helen was.

"He's not that young. Only five years younger than me." When she was with Benjamin, she never thought of the age difference, but occasionally it stuck like a burr.

"And more power to you, my dear. No one would blink at that if it were the other way around. So why should it matter?" Helen's smile glittered with challenge and amusement.

Lynn straightened her shoulders. "You're right. It doesn't."

"I also like Peter." Together they turned their heads to regard the couple standing near the artfully decorated Christmas tree. Peter hadn't left Stephanie's side. He was a couple inches shorter than her and his concession to the holiday season was a red and green bow tie. She seemed both flattered and embarrassed by his close attention, a faint flush never quite leaving her cheeks. "Stephanie deserves some romance. She's such a lovely person, if a little shy. Even after knowing her for more than two years I don't feel like she's completely opened up."

Lynn doubted she ever would. Some wounds ran too deep. But she knew for a fact Stephanie felt safe among the Silverberries. "I like him, too. I hope he sticks around."

Helen drained the last of her drink. "It's time for karaoke. Make sure you help yourself to the appies. The bacon-wrapped scallops are to die for." And in her characteristic hurry, she was gone.

A tingle ran over Lynn's skin and her gaze snapped back to Benjamin. He was staring at her with an intensity in his expression that boded well for later tonight. Her mouth dried.

The music cut off, Helen called for attention, and Lynn made a vow.

Five songs. That was it. She and Benjamin would stay for five karaoke songs and then they were out of here.

Enough was enough.

CHAPTER TWENTY

In the end, it was six songs before Lynn could drag Benjamin out of the party, as Helen insisted on a group carol just as she was about to whisper in his ear. But as soon as the tuneless rendition of *Deck the Halls* was completed amid much laughter and teasing, she clasped his bicep and leaned in close.

"I'm ready to get out of here. You?"

The muscles under her hand tensed and he faced her, so close their noses brushed. His dark eyes, framed with short thick lashes, bore into hers with a heat that made her knees weak. "Whenever you want. Whatever you want." The double entendre curled like syrup through her veins.

Lynn shamelessly used Oscar as an excuse when the Silverberries bemoaned her early departure, and in a few short minutes she was seated next to Benjamin as he manoeuvred away from the curb. The console separated them as effectively as the Great Wall and she thanked the lord it would take less than fifteen minutes to get home.

Benjamin seemed to feel a similar compulsion. He accelerated before each green light as if determined not to be stopped, and even snuck through a long amber at one intersection. He pulled into her driveway, and she didn't wait for the engine to die before opening her door and hurrying to the house, Benjamin at her heels.

On the front stoop, she stopped. "I have to send the babysitter home. This will have to hold me." She gripped his skull and drew him toward her. Their mouths met and matched and melded, opening so their tongues could dance. A flush raced over her body. Before she could surrender to the passion and wrap herself around his solid, hard form, she broke away, breath panting. "We have to go in. Makayla would have heard us drive up."

His chest heaved in unison with hers. He sucked in air through his nose and let it out slowly. "Okay."

She turned to unlock the door, almost stumbling through the opening, intensely aware of Benjamin behind her.

"Hey, Lynn." Makayla stood at the top of the short flight of stairs. "You're home early. It's barely eleven."

"Yes." She cleared her throat, ignoring the curiosity in Makayla's tone. "How did it go?"

"Great. Not a peep out of him."

Benjamin helped her off with her coat, his hands lingering on her shoulders an instant longer than necessary. She shivered with anticipation and forced herself to focus on the teenager. "Good. I'll pay you until midnight, like I said. E-transfer as usual?"

"Sweet." Lynn and Benjamin switched places with Makayla. She refrained from making shooing gestures as the girl put on her coat, tugged a toque over her curls, and slid into her fleece-lined boots. "Okay, then. Have a good night." The look she swept from Lynn to Benjamin and back again was far beyond her fifteen years.

"You, too." Lynn waggled her fingers and moved to the front window. Makayla trudged down the drive and she mentally urged her to walk faster. After what felt an age, the girl turned up a walkway three houses down. The door opened and light spilled out, and then shut behind her.

"She's home." She tugged the curtains closed and turned to Benjamin, expectation and trepidation and excitement coiling tightly within her.

Benjamin had heard the expression *the anticipation is killing me* but hadn't fully appreciated it until this evening. He'd been in low-grade torture from the moment Lynn had stated she expected him to stay the night. Through introductions and interesting conversations and impressive and not-so-impressive karaoke performances, he'd been constantly aware of her. Where she was, what she was doing, who she was talking to.

How she tasted.

And now, finally, they were alone. Well, except for Oscar. But if Lynn wasn't worried about having sex with her toddler just down the hall, neither was he.

She took a step toward him at the same time he moved toward her. He'd toed off his shoes when they'd first come in, and though she still wore her heels she was a couple inches shorter than him. It didn't matter. Their mouths lined up perfectly and she fit against his chest like they'd been custom made for each other.

He'd unbuttoned his coat but hadn't removed it and she slid her hands underneath the heavy wool, along his ribs to his spine. Without breaking their connection, he shrugged it off and let it drop carelessly to the floor. She kissed him like she was never coming up for air, making him feel powerful, wanted, invincible.

He scooped her up behind her knees and she gasped against his mouth. "What are you doing?"

"Taking you to bed." He pressed his lips hard on hers and spun toward the darkened hall.

"You'll break your back! Put me down." Despite her demands, she snuggled in closer, biting his neck gently.

He grinned even as a sharp ripple of desire flashed through his veins. "Even that wouldn't stop me from being with you tonight. But don't worry, I work out with the boys most days. You weigh less than I bench press."

The door to Oscar's room was ajar and the soft glow

of a nightlight illuminated the rails of his crib. He paused and listened to the soft, tender sighs of his breathing, and then continued past, his sock feet making no noise on the carpet. At the end of the short hall, he turned left into what was obviously Lynn's room.

It wasn't a large space. The bed with its puffy comforter and piles of pillows took up much of the floor. Unlit candles in various shapes and sizes waited on the dresser and nightstand, and everything was as neat and tidy as a hotel room.

The evidence she'd prepared for his stay caused his already racing heart to kick into a higher gear.

He laid her gently on the mattress, propping her up on the stack of pillows. "Do you have a lighter? Or matches?"

"In here." She rolled over and struggled to open the top drawer of the single nightstand. When he moved to help, she batted his hand away. "No. Don't. I've got it."

Ignoring her, he pulled the drawer wide and saw a barbeque lighter. As well as an open box of condoms and a long, thick, purple vibrator.

She flopped onto her back and draped an arm over her eyes. "I didn't want you to see that."

"The condoms? That's only sensible and I would expect nothing less from you."

"Not that. The other thing."

"The vibrator?" He grinned when she squirmed and pressed her arm tighter over her eyes. "*That* only seems natural for a healthy single woman. Maybe you'll have to play with it while I watch." The idea was intoxicating. He stored that thought for later consideration.

She lifted her arm and peeped out at him. "Really?"

"Really. But not tonight. Tonight, I want you all to myself. Just like the first time." Unlike the first time, though, he intended to immerse himself in her, delight in every sensation. His memories of their one-night stand were confused and frantic, a torrent of lust and heat and sweaty bodies. And while the sex had been fantastic, he wanted something different from her.

He wanted her soul. Even if what they had wasn't for forever, he wanted tonight to *mean* something. To both of them.

He lit the candles one by one until the room flickered with a romantic glow. She watched him, sprawled against the pillows, eyes heavy-lidded, fingers trailing absently up and down her torso, from her belly to her breasts and back again, the shiny fabric of her dress shimmering. When he was done, he stood at the foot of the bed and undid the buttons of his shirt, tugging it out of his pants and slipping it off as he used his toes to pull off his socks. She drew the tip of her tongue along her bottom lip and her gaze dipped to his abs. He wasn't in the prime physical shape he'd been in when he was playing hockey, but he knew he was still in good form. Working out was a great stress reliever, and lord knew he'd had enough stress in his life lately.

Lynn lifted her hips and wriggled her dress out from under her buttocks. Sitting up, she pulled it over her head, disarranging her bun so that it slipped sideways. Tossing the dress aside, she fiddled with her hair, discarding an elastic and several pins on the nightstand. The silky strands fell to her shoulders.

His cock, already hard and ready, hardened further, shifting under his pants. She wore a black lacy bra and matching panties, and still had her high heels strapped on her slender feet.

The silence between them was ripe and full, just like her body. He placed a knee on the mattress, his weight shifting her slightly toward him. Lifting one foot, he worked the tiny buckle on her shoe, slow and deliberate. She moaned low in her throat when he slid it off and kissed the arch, each toe, and then her ankle. Her breath grew ragged as he repeated the procedure on the other foot.

Still wearing his pants, he crawled up the mattress

and stretched out beside her. She rolled to her side so they lay nose to nose, breasts to chest, groin to groin. Her fingers worked his fly, and he felt some relief when the zipper gave way.

Until she took his cock in hand through the silk of his boxers.

His entire body stiffened, heated. She worked him firmly, reading his hissing breath and clutching fingers to give him more of what he liked.

"I should...you..." He couldn't think through the erotic haze.

She read his incoherent utterances correctly. "We'll get to me, don't worry." She slid down until he felt her breath on his thigh. "But you are not going home unsatisfied. Not this time. We'll take care of you first."

She rolled him to his back and worked his pants and boxers off his legs, leaving him naked. Settling herself on her knees between his legs, she bent forward. His hands fluttered on her skull, not directing, not demanding, but he had to touch her somehow, and this was all he could reach.

Warm, wet lips encircled him, and he bucked up. Her approving moan vibrated along his length and up his spine. She took him deeper. Her hands stretched up, scratching lightly on his pecs, teasing his nipples, but he was almost too lost in the sensation building in his cock to notice.

He tasted so good. Musky and spicy, tangy and warm. Lynn savoured his silky strength, going down as far as she could, and then sliding up to tease the tip, making his hips jerk. His hands floated on her skull, and she wanted him to twist his fingers in her hair and tug like he had done before, but this was for him.

She gripped the base of his shaft and cupped his balls. Crouched comfortably between his legs, she felt like she could play with him forever. It didn't take long, however, before she sensed he was close.

He tried once more to take control. "I don't want to finish yet." His voice was hoarse, breathless.

Perfect.

She dragged her teeth lightly over his shaft and let him pop out of her mouth. "We have all night." She swallowed him down, and then repeated the rough caress. "You'll have time to recover. But you deserve this first." She slid her thumb over the head of his cock and stroked.

He arched his head back, the tendons in his neck strong and fierce, the pulse in his throat pounding. His face screwed up in an expression of passion that almost made her come from the sight. With a guttural groan, he gripped the bedsheets, and his release juddered onto his belly and chest.

She softened her touches, feeling the last traces of his orgasm shudder through him as his body relaxed.

"Holy fuck." His tone was reverent.

She curled up at his side, tucked herself under his limp arm, and drew a fingertip through the moisture on his belly. He sucked in a breath through his nose.

"That was..."

It was extremely satisfying he couldn't find the words to describe the experience. "I'm glad."

The hairs on his chest vibrated with the pounding of his heart. He drew in another breath, held it, and then let it ease out slowly. "Let me go clean up. Then it's your turn."

She shook her head, and he kinked his neck so he could make eye contact. "Then it's *our turn*. Don't be long."

CHAPTER TWENTY-ONE

Lynn woke in an instant, reacting to Oscar's cheerfully demanding squawk. It was a familiar early morning refrain.

What definitely *wasn't* familiar was the heavy arm that tightened around her waist, pulling her against a hard chest, and the protesting snort that wuffled into her ear.

"What time is it?" Benjamin muttered.

"Too early." She dragged an arm out of the covers and checked her phone. 5:45. Her son was right on time. "Go back to sleep."

"Okay." His drowsy acceptance made her smile. He snuggled closer, his thighs tucking in behind hers, and a hot, silky length nudged her bare ass.

She pushed down a surge of desire. Oscar wouldn't be patient much longer. By some miracle of fate, he hadn't interrupted them while they'd been...occupied...two more times during the night. But nothing would ruin a morning quickie faster than a toddler screaming for attention.

She wriggled from her right side to her left and came face to face with Benjamin. His hair was deliciously tousled and his eyes slumberous and dark, though they lost some of their sleepiness when his hand slid to her ass. *Maybe if we're really fast...*

A louder shout from across the hall.

"Oscar's getting angry. I have to go," she whispered,

sliding backward off the mattress. His eyes never left hers. She stepped quickly into flannel pants and a worn T-shirt, foregoing underwear for the moment, and gathered her hair into a loose ponytail. A husky groan came from the bed, and she stole a quick look, arms still raised above her head as she secured the elastic.

There was no trace of slumber in his expression now. "You are so sexy."

She laughed. "You can't be serious. I'm a mess."

"But you're *my* mess."

The possessiveness in his tone softened her knees. That was nothing to the dizziness that washed over her when he tossed back the covers and rose to his feet, naked and glorious. She took a deep breath and hurried to the door. "Don't get up. It's far too early. I'm used to it."

"So am I. Too many six a.m. practices when I was a kid." He bent down to snag his pants from the floor and his buttocks flexed.

Lynn fled before she lost all control and tackled him to the ground.

Benjamin grinned as he stepped into his wrinkled trousers. He liked flustering Lynn with unexpected compliments and had strutted his nakedness with the intent of making her eyes glaze over.

Mission accomplished.

She was talking with Oscar in the kitchen. This morning was eons away from the only other morning they'd shared, when they'd both been shy and awkward. Despite the dawn being hours away yet, he felt brighter than he had in a long time. And it wasn't only because his long sexual drought was over.

It was because of the woman who had slaked his thirst. How great would it be to wake up like this every—

He cut off his thoughts. What the hell? This wasn't his life. Couldn't be his life. Lynn was settled, anchored.

She knew what she wanted, and it wouldn't be him. Not a fourth-rate NHLer with a precarious career and a job that took him away from home constantly.

Oscar's giggle floated down the hall and Benjamin's heart clutched. She definitely wouldn't want a man who couldn't meet the fatherhood standards set by his own dad.

Shaking off his unease, he headed for the bathroom. He would have liked a shower—with Lynn, preferably, but that was obviously off the table—but made do with a hot, soapy washcloth. He borrowed her toothpaste and scrubbed his teeth with his finger. By the time he entered the kitchen, the coffee was done and Oscar was ensconced in his highchair doing battle with a bowl of oatmeal.

Lynn greeted him with a steaming mug, her eyes flickering to his chest as he buttoned up his shirt. "I meant it, you know. You really didn't have to get up yet."

He took the coffee. "I know. But now I am, I might as well get going. I have things to do before we leave for the road trip." That wasn't until Monday, but he had to go now. Before the longing to become a permanent fixture in her life grew stronger.

"Of course. I understand." She leaned against the counter and sipped from her own mug, clasping it with both hands, her unfocused gaze now on Oscar, as if she'd sensed Benjamin's withdrawal.

He didn't want her to think he was regretting last night. How could someone regret the best night of his life? "Thank you. Not just for, well, you know, but..." He trailed off, not sure where he was going.

"Right. Thank you, too." The warmth and playfulness they'd shared in the moments before she'd left her bed was gone, dissipated like smoke.

"I'm sorry." For everything. For nothing.

God, he was a mess. He placed his mostly untouched mug on the counter. It was no use prolonging his departure. "Bye, Oscar." The toddler grinned from behind a mask of oatmeal.

Lynn followed him to the front door, fidgeting with the hem of her T-shirt as he shrugged into his coat.

"Have a safe trip." Her tone was cool, dismissive.

Damn it. Maybe they had no future, but he couldn't leave her like this. He cupped her chin in both hands and lifted her face so she couldn't avoid looking at him. "Thank you for inviting me. See you in a week or so." He brushed a gentle kiss on her lips and then stepped away, leaving her warmth. He missed her already, which was ridiculous.

"Wait. That wasn't a proper goodbye." She wrapped her arms around his neck and pressed against him. An echo of his own desperation was apparent in her clutching hands and demanding tongue. She tasted of brown sugar and coffee.

The clatter of a spoon being tossed to the ground and a delighted squeal from Oscar jolted them apart. He pulled away slowly. "I guess that's a sign." He gripped the handle and then paused. "Is it okay if I text you while we're gone?"

Her reply was so swift and sure he couldn't help the surge of relief. "I expect you to. Good luck."

During the days that followed, Lynn had plenty of time to think about what their night together might mean. Her thoughts swayed wildly from *just-another-one-night-stand* to *when-can-we-do-it-again*. The sex had been amazing, but it was the connection and comfort she'd felt the next morning waking up with him beside her that freaked her out a little.

Benjamin's seesaw reaction had mirrored her own uncertainties. While she might have been miffed at him in the moment, she realized later she shouldn't blame him, not when she had her own doubts.

Nothing had changed. Benjamin was still in a volatile job, and she had no intention of ever moving from her comfortable home. She was independent and settled and perfectly capable of caring for Oscar on her own. She didn't *need* Benjamin.

For anything other than sex, that was. Even the power of her vibrator paled in comparison to his touch.

She listened to the games on the radio, pleased when they won a close one, commiserating when they lost the other in an embarrassing drubbing. The team remained inconsistent, but that was often the way of junior hockey. When Benjamin was interviewed, his voice evoked a vision of him in her bed, all seductive eyes and sleep-warmed skin.

He texted her, as he'd promised. Casual, friendly messages about the team or the hotel or asking how Oscar was doing. She always replied, but never initiated a conversation, not wanting to interrupt him at an awkward time. At least, that's what she told herself. It had nothing to do with her uncertainty about their relationship.

Thursday morning, Oscar woke her before her alarm as usual. The team was scheduled to arrive home any minute now after an all-night drive, and her pulse raced at the thought of seeing Benjamin. She fed and changed and prepared Oscar for his stay at the daycare in a glow of anticipation that had nothing to do with her son. Even the blustery wind that scoured the parking lot and encouraged her to hustle from her car to the arena didn't ruin her mood.

In the warmth and quiet of the office, she unwrapped her scarf and draped it over a hook on the coat rack. "Morning, Sarah." She almost carolled the greeting, so buoyant did she feel.

"Morning, Lynn. Did you hear?"

"Hear what?" She unzipped her coat and shrugged it off.

"The Canyon Cats were in an accident last night. The bus went off the road."

CHAPTER TWENTY-TWO

Lynn's coat dropped from her nerveless fingers. "An accident?" she croaked.

Sarah nodded, the gleam of juicy gossip in her eyes. "Just this side of Quesnel. Swerved to miss a deer, hit an icy patch, and ended up in the ditch."

She bent with careful precision to retrieve her coat from the floor, wondering if it was possible for a spine to crack from fright. "Was anyone hurt?" Didn't coaches traditionally sit at the front of the bus? Hadn't she heard that somewhere? If the bus went into the ditch straight on...

"Nope. They spent a few cold hours on the side of the road, though, waiting for another bus. They should be here any minute now."

The tension left her in a dizzying rush. She hung her coat on the rack, gripping the fabric and hanging off it until the world settled. "Oh, thank you, God," she whispered.

"What was that?"

"Nothing." Taking a cleansing breath, she turned and made her way to her desk. "I'm glad no one was hurt."

"Of course." The possibility the accident could have been much worse didn't seem to diminish Sarah's enjoyment in the tale.

Safely in her chair, she wiggled the mouse to wake up her computer in an automatic gesture. Something Sarah had said niggled at her. "They're not back yet?"

"No. The accident happened about five. It took some time to get transportation figured out." A dark bulk glided to a stop outside the wide windows. "And here they are. How's that for timing?"

She remained seated, listening to the growl of the diesel engine, letting relief flood her system. *He's home. He's safe.*

The driver exited the bus and pulled open the doors of the enormous storage recess underneath the seats. Unlike the logoed, semi-luxurious team bus, this one had seen better days, with the evidence of ancient stickers on its side and old-fashioned windows. She didn't care. It had brought Benjamin home in one piece.

As the players trickled off, she gripped her desk and fought the urge to race outside and make sure for herself he was unharmed. Whatever their relationship was, it certainly wasn't at the stage where she was comfortable with such a public display, and she was convinced Benjamin felt the same. Besides, he hadn't texted her after the crash, so wouldn't know she knew. He would have had more important things on his mind.

Levi, Avril, and Ryan followed the players out. Benjamin was the last to stride down the steps, frowning at his phone, a dark satchel slung over his shoulder. Her heart gave an uncomfortable thump at seeing him whole and healthy. He took his overnight bag from the storage compartment, nodded at the crowd still standing near the bus, and headed in the direction of the arena's main doors, just out of her view.

Sarah gave her a surprised look when she jumped to her feet. "Umm, just going to check that set up is on track for the concert tonight. I'll be right back."

Benjamin had been dozing when the bus went off the road. He'd been jerked awake by the sudden swerve, the driver's curses, and his laptop tumbling off the seat.

The motorcoach was a newer model that included

shoulder-strap seat belts, so when it nosed into the ditch and came to a sudden stop everyone was still in place, but he'd done a quick roll call to ensure there were no unexpected injuries. One of the players who had reclined his seat to sleep the trip away hadn't even woken up. Organizing a replacement bus had been more of an annoyance than a worry. He'd been thankful they weren't in one of the many spots along the highway where cell service wasn't available.

As much as he longed for a few hours of sleep stretched out on a comfortable mattress, when the bus pulled up at the arena he headed to his office. The team was scheduled to do dryland training later that day as the ice would already be covered for a concert that night, but he'd pushed it back to allow everyone some personal time. If he got a couple of tasks done now, he could head home for a nap and be rested by then.

Satchel on his shoulder and overnight suitcase bumping behind him, he pushed through the arena doors and headed down the wide stairs that led to the lower level. Rushing footsteps followed him, a woman's heels on concrete, and he turned at the bottom in time to see Lynn swinging around the landing, blonde ponytail flying.

Without a word she barrelled into him, wrapping her arms around his torso, the force of her embrace causing him to take a step back. He released the hold on his suitcase, and it fell over with a clatter.

"Well, hello there." He held her close. Something cold and dark deep in his chest warmed and brightened. It had been forever since he'd had someone greet him after a road trip.

It felt odd and unexpected—and totally awesome.

"I heard about the accident." Her voice was muffled against his coat. "I'm so glad you're okay."

"Is that what this is about? It was nothing, barely a bump." Not that he didn't appreciate her concern. Especially if it meant he could hold her. "Were you worried about me?"

She drew her head back so she could look him in the eye but didn't release her grip on his waist. "Maybe a little." She huffed out a breath. "Okay, more than a little, at least until I heard there were no injuries."

He'd promised never to shut her out, and yet he'd done just that. Guilt flared. "I'm so sorry. I swore I wouldn't keep things from you. I should have texted."

She shook her head. "You had other things to think about. I'm not upset you didn't let me know. Honest." She snuggled back in. "I just needed to see you for myself. I'm good now."

He was having trouble breathing, his chest heavy with an emotion he couldn't define. To be the focus of Lynn's concern was a responsibility and a privilege. He hadn't even thought of her in the chaos of getting things done after the crash, and he regretted the omission fiercely.

"Let me make it up to you." He rested his chin on the crown of her head and peace washed over him. "How about I bring dinner over tonight?"

"You don't have to do that."

A wistful note in her tone gave him the courage to press the issue. "I want to. I want to spend time with you and Oscar. I've missed you. Both of you."

Her hair tugged in his whiskers when she raised her head. "You haven't been home for a week. Wouldn't you rather go to your own place?" Her eyes scrutinized his.

He couldn't tell her that her house felt more like home than his apartment. "It's okay. Pizza sound good?"

"Sounds great."

He leaned toward her, his lips just a breath away from hers, when the tread of heavy steps approached. She stiffened and with reluctance he let her go.

She stepped back, smoothing her blouse. "Tonight, then."

He nodded. "Tonight."

When Benjamin arrived that evening with two large pizzas in hand, Lynn immediately invited Stephanie to join them. It served the dual purpose of fewer leftovers and further delaying the talk that Lynn knew she had to have with him.

During her childhood and teens, it had been the uncertainty that she found most stressful. She had been well into her twenties before she'd come to that realization, not being self-aware enough until then. While her upbringing had been unusual, it wasn't the home-schooling and the travel that had bothered her. It was the sudden changes. One day they'd be settled in a town, the next her father would have a new scheme and away they'd go. If she'd *known* when the changes were happening, she would have dealt with them better, she was sure.

Now she had to remove the uncertainty in her relationship with Benjamin.

Just like the first evening he'd shared a meal with her and Stephanie, Lynn took care of Oscar's bedtime routine while the others cleaned the kitchen. Her heart gladdened at their shared laughter and chatter. It was a little frightening how seamlessly he fit into her life, even with his frequent absences. Stephanie had given her stamp of approval after the Silverberry Christmas party by offering, unsolicited, to look after Oscar anytime Lynn wanted to go out with him.

When she brought Oscar in to say goodnight, her son stretched out his arms to Benjamin, babbling and chortling. After a tiny pause, he took the toddler under his arms and tucked him on his hip. His expression was an interesting mixture of pleasure and trepidation.

Lynn went with her impulse. "Do you want to put him to bed? I think that's what he's asking for."

Benjamin's eyes widened and glanced from her to Oscar and back again. "I suppose I can handle that. What do I do?"

Lynn explained the routine—music, night light, a few minutes of back-patting. He nodded, his lips pressed together in concentration while he swayed from side to side, Oscar clamped securely to his ribs.

She kissed her son's sweet-smelling head. "See you in the morning, honeybun."

Stephanie kissed him, too, and then Benjamin disappeared down the hall with an air of determination. Lynn stared at the empty opening, a hard lump in her throat.

Stephanie nudged her elbow. "I assume it was the night of the Christmas party, since you haven't seen him since then."

She was still caught up in the sight of Oscar in Benjamin's arms. "What are you talking about?"

"When the two of you had sex. For the first time. Again. His car was still in the driveway the next morning."

Her gaze snapped to Stephanie. Her friend's knowing grin made her want to wriggle so she lifted her chin defiantly. "Maybe."

Stephanie's smile widened. "What are you going to do about it?"

"I don't know. It's not only up to me, after all. I'm going to talk with him tonight."

"I'll make myself scarce, then." She headed for the stairs and hesitated, turning back with a serious look. "Just remember. Oscar's taken as much of a shine to him as you have. If Benjamin spends much more time around here..." She trailed off, but Lynn had no trouble filling in the blank.

"I know. Just because he's a baby doesn't mean he won't get attached. But he's so young. He'll never remember Benjamin if it all falls apart."

It was her own heart she was worried about.

CHAPTER TWENTY-THREE

Benjamin followed Lynn's instructions with exactitude. She'd put her trust in him, and he intended to deserve it.

It was possible he was taking the whole routine a little too intensely. If he failed at getting Oscar to sleep, the world wouldn't come to an end. This wasn't a pass/fail test.

It only felt like it.

He counted as he thumped Oscar gently on the back, figuring one-hundred and eighty would be close enough to the required time limit. As she'd warned, the boy stirred when Benjamin stopped patting and stepped cautiously away from the crib, but his lids were heavy and his head dropped back onto the mattress. By the time Benjamin eased the door shut, leaving the requisite two-inch gap, he appeared to be asleep.

Lynn was on the couch in the living room. She had changed out of her jeans and T-shirt, which Oscar had dampened during his bath, and put on a loose dress with short sleeves and a hem that swept to her feet.

She held out her hand, offering the bottle of beer he hadn't finished during dinner. He took it and she lifted her wine glass from the low table in front of her. "Sounds like he's out." She curled up her legs, tucking her feet under the fabric of her dress and shuffling back into the corner of the sofa. He sat half a cushion away. She'd been...not exactly *distant* this evening, but cautious, wary. She hadn't acted like the woman who'd given him such an affectionate welcome home earlier in the day, and he didn't feel he had the right to snuggle up any closer, no matter how much he wanted to.

"I did everything just the way you said." His beer wasn't cold any longer, but he took a sip anyway.

"Yes, well, that's no guarantee. If there's one thing I've learned since becoming a parent, it's that routines don't last. I've learned to be flexible." She quirked a small smile. "And flexibility is *not* one of my talents. I like things neat and orderly and *don't* like surprises and last-minute changes."

I guess we're doing this. A chill trickled down his spine and his gut clenched. The talk he'd been dreading for almost a week was unavoidable now. He wished he knew which way he wanted it to go.

There was nothing to it but to be honest. "Not that I like curve balls, but in sports you learn to go with the flow. Game plans are always changing, adapting. In my personal life, though, I have a bad habit of letting things simply happen, even avoiding issues until I'm forced to do otherwise." Until recently, that was. Taking the job with the Canyon Cats, vowing to get them to the championships, reconciling with his mother and Jujhar—making those decisions had been terrifying. He had been opening himself to failure—again. He sucked in a breath, seeking calm. "I always figured that, if you have no expectations, no goals, you can't be disappointed." Or disappoint the people you love.

"I assume there's a happy medium somewhere." She propped her elbow on the back of the couch and rested her head on her hand. "Here's the thing. I can't toy with Oscar's future. Whatever I do, it has to be good for him."

"I won't argue with that. *Can't* argue with that."

"That being said…" Lynn's gaze flickered past his shoulder, and then focused on him again. The sign of nervousness relieved some of his own growing tension. "He's too young to remember much of anything yet. I comfort myself with that when I screw up, which happens on a daily basis. He's getting used to you, of course, and he likes you, but if you suddenly disappeared I don't think he'd be scarred for life."

He wasn't sure whether she was comforting or cautioning him. What about *her?* Would he be that forgettable to Lynn? "What are you getting at?"

She sipped her wine, and then sipped again. "What I'm trying to say is—I can't use Oscar as an excuse. Not with you. Which means I have to decide what our night together meant for *me.* For us. Was it the start of something—or the end?"

Lynn's chest was tight, her gut watery, an uneasy juxtaposition that made her queasy. She felt vulnerable, exposed, unbalanced. Having a plan didn't guarantee success. Just look at her engagement to Lance. And though she hadn't meant it that way, her question to Benjamin just now had the air of an ultimatum.

His gaze dropped to the bottle in his hand. He picked at the label with a fingernail, shredding the glittery paper.

The longer he remained silent the more fiercely her stomach curdled. She opened her mouth to backtrack, to soften her stance, when he finally spoke.

"What do you want from me?" He slid her a glance from the corner of his eye. "I can promise that you'll be the only one while we're together. I *can't* promise anything more than a day at a time." He didn't have to spell out why. If his career took him to a different city, he wouldn't let their relationship stop him. His chin dipped, further hiding his expression. "I know that's not what you're looking for."

It wasn't, not in the long term. But she'd told the truth when she'd said Oscar had taught her to be flexible. And maybe this was one of those times.

"Here's what I know." She shifted forward and touched his forearm. He looked up from mangling the label and met her gaze. "I like you. You're a good, kind man. You're sexy as hell. You make me feel desirable and beautiful."

"You are. Anyone that doesn't see that is blind."

Her heart swelled. "Be that as it may, all those things put together make me want to take a chance on you. I know everything could change tomorrow." She swallowed down old fears. "For now, day to day is good enough for me."

"I don't know if I deserve that. Deserve you."

She searched his face. His eyes were solemn and sincere and wistful. She slid her fingers up his bicep to his shoulder, to the taut column of his neck—

—and pinched his earlobe.

"Hey!" He flinched away. "What was that for?"

"That's for selling yourself short. You deserve to be happy. I deserve to be happy. Maybe we can't guarantee how long that happiness will last, but coming into any relationship with that outlook will doom it from the start."

He rubbed his earlobe and scowled at her, but he'd lost the rather pathetic look that had irritated her. "You sound like Jujhar."

"Who?"

"A friend. He said much the same thing a little while ago."

"He sounds like a smart guy." She placed her wineglass on the coffee table and knelt on the cushion, bringing herself closer to his heat, his scent. "I'm all for a sensitive man. I like that you're modest and not some arrogant asshole that expects everything to fall into his lap. But I have one son. I'm not looking for another child to coddle. I want a man who is strong and determined and willing to fight for what he wants. Is that the kind of man you are?"

No. I'm not.

Benjamin was thankful his instinctive denial

remained unspoken. It wasn't what Lynn wanted to hear.

It also wasn't the truth. Not completely, anyway.

He'd been strong and determined and willing to fight for his goals once. But the vagaries of sport and life, including mistakes and injuries and plain old bad luck, had battered him, eating away at his confidence so slowly he hadn't even realized it. Not for years. Not when his father had challenged him with love and pride. Not when Jujhar had told him so with blunt affection.

He was working on getting it back. Getting the Canyon Cats to the playoffs would be the first step. Winning the championship would be the next. After that...who knew?

Maybe he had something to learn from Lynn. Something about making goals and being flexible—and taking chances.

She was waiting for his answer. Lines creased her brow, and the fierceness had faded from her eyes.

He wanted to bring it back. Wanted to feed off her passion and vigour and conviction.

"Yes." It didn't come out as firm as he wanted. He cleared his throat. "Yes, I am that kind of man. I think."

She shook her head. "Don't waffle. Don't temporize. If you're in, you're in all the way, for as long as we have. If circumstances change, we'll deal with them then."

"I'm in." He straightened his spine, the bottle gripped in his hand like a torch, like a spear. "You said I was good and kind and sexy. That I make you feel beautiful." She opened her mouth. He held up a palm. She closed it. "I could say the same about you. Maybe not the beautiful part"—a smile tugged the corner of his mouth, and he saw an answering one on her lips—"but the rest for sure."

"Okay then. We're agreed." All of a sudden, his lap was full of warm, soft woman as Lynn straddled him, hiking her skirt up so he caught a flash of bare thigh. "We're dating."

Something about the word didn't sit quite right, but he was too busy enjoying the pressure of her ass on his thighs to quibble. "I guess we are."

"Don't guess. Believe." Her lips on his were a declaration and a promise. His mouth opened immediately and the kiss deepened, tongues tangling, tantalizing. He pulled her closer and she rose on her knees, curling over him. Her hands clamped his shoulders, her arms cradling her own breasts, plumping them so they brushed his jaw, his neck stretching to keep his mouth locked onto the deliciousness that was Lynn.

She wriggled off his lap and he groaned in disappointment—until she took his hand and tugged him up, leading him down the hall to her darkened bedroom. She set to work on his clothes, unbuttoning and unzipping and untucking. On his part, all he had to do was ruck her dress up and over her head. Unhooking her bra and thumbing her panties down was the work of an instant, and they fell onto the bed, a tangle of hot skin and quivering muscles and devouring mouths.

Their mating was fast and frantic, nearly silent in deference to the baby but possibly more intense because of that. He tried to slow down, to steep himself in her, but she was having none of it. She scored him with her nails, trapped him between her thighs, and he gave into her ferocity. A tug on her hair had her arching and pleading and a rush of liquid heat told him she was more than ready.

He scrabbled for a condom in the bedside table and plunged into her while she still shuddered from her orgasm. Her close-mouthed shriek flexed her throat as she tossed her head back and he rode her, engulfed in her depths, welcomed into her soul, until he, too, flew off the edge of eternity, his mind blank, his body shuddering, as he emptied himself.

CHAPTER TWENTY-FOUR

Lynn stood at Mrs. Whitestone's door, gripping a gift bag in one hand and Oscar's damp fist in the other. He'd insisted on walking from the car to the house. Luckily, she'd wrangled him into a snowsuit instead of his adorably tiny wool coat, so when he'd fallen and crawled several feet the suit had protected his clothes.

She had brought a change for him. Maybe two. Along with all the other paraphernalia an evening away from home entailed when you had a toddler, crammed into the large diaper bag that slipped from her shoulder at any move. She bounced to readjust it.

It was possible she'd over-packed. This would be their first evening with Benjamin's mother and she hadn't wanted to look unprepared or incapable. Not to the woman who had raised him.

Gift bag dangling from her pinkie, she reached to press the doorbell, hesitated, and dropped her hand. She needed another minute. Oscar was happily occupied, using his free hand to bat evergreen fronds sprouting from a decorative arrangement on the doorstep, so she closed her eyes and breathed deeply.

The last couple of weeks had swept by with unexpected ease. With the team in town, incorporating Benjamin into her life had been effortless. Their interactions at work, whether days in the office or evenings on game nights, hadn't changed, as by unspoken agreement neither had shared their new relationship with their colleagues. But he had spent several nights in her bed, and an afternoon with her and Oscar at a local Christmas tree farm, when he'd hauled her choice out of the field and strapped it to the roof of her vehicle, grinning the whole time.

He fit in so easy, in fact, that it occasionally made her *uneasy*. Tonight might be the night that ended that honeymoon period, however.

Without further useless reflection, she pressed the doorbell, rolled her neck, and pasted a smile on her face. Seconds later, the bright blue panel swung open, and a flood of sound and scent greeted her—chatter and music, roast turkey and boiled potatoes. Through an arch directly ahead, she caught a glimpse of Benjamin and his mother huddled over the stove. Other bodies, both big and small, hustled about. To her left, a large artificial Christmas tree blocked most of her view of a living room.

"Hi!"

She adjusted her gaze down.

The dark-haired girl was maybe ten years old and dressed for the season with a black, red, and white plaid skirt and a white, long-sleeved T-shirt adorned with a sparkling silver snowflake. "Are you Lynn?" she asked with inquisitive delight.

A tall blonde woman appeared from the bustling kitchen. "Don't be rude, Ella. She's Ms. Kolmyn to you."

"It's okay. You can call me Lynn. Both of you." She hovered in the open doorway, feeling distinctly overwhelmed. Big family meals hadn't been a part of her childhood or her life with Lance. Oscar apparently felt the same as he clutched her pant leg and let out a startled squawk.

"I'm Sadie Malhotra and this is my daughter, Ella. Let me take that." The woman plucked the gift bag from Lynn's fingers. "Come in. Ella will take your coat. I can't wait to get some baby cuddles, but we'll let him settle in first."

Sadie's cheerful acceptance of their presence eased her anxiety. As Ella disappeared down the hall, Lynn tucked the diaper bag behind a chair in the living room, hefted a clingy Oscar to her hip and followed Sadie into the kitchen. Kelly was setting the table with the help of a boy and girl that shared the same dark hair as Ella, and the air was so thick with delicious scents she could taste them.

Benjamin looked up, a smile lighting his face. With a quiet click, her remaining nervous tension vanished. She grinned at the frilly bib apron he wore to protect his clothes from whatever he was stirring at the stove. Before either of them could speak, Thea Whitestone approached. "Lynn. I'm so pleased you could make it. And Oscar, of course."

"Thanks for having us." They hadn't met since that awkward evening at the restaurant, and Lynn had rather expected her to be cold and formal. Instead, her eyes gleamed with wistful acquisitiveness as she stared at the baby. Her unabashed granny lust worried Lynn. When things ended between her and Benjamin, she didn't want to be responsible for breaking more hearts than her own.

She gestured hurriedly at the bag Sadie still carried. "I brought you a little gift. I hope you like it."

Sadie handed the bag to Thea. She dragged her gaze reluctantly from Oscar and opened it, removing a scented candle and a silver holder in the shape of a snowman. "Thank you. It's lovely. I know the perfect place for it." She vanished into the living room.

Lynn breathed a sigh of relief. One hurdle down. Fourteen hundred and fifty-two potential pitfalls left to go.

"Hey, there."

She latched onto Benjamin's familiar voice like a woman drowning at sea. Sadie left to mediate a dispute between her two youngest children and Lynn went to him, wishing she could lean into his strength and comfort, just for a moment.

"Sorry I didn't meet you at the door. Mom's got me working." He continued stirring the brown liquid bubbling in the roaster she assumed had held the turkey.

"Homemade gravy?" She leaned sideways, keeping Oscar far from the stove, and inhaled, closing her eyes in ecstasy. "You're forgiven. This is much more important than greeting me." She opened her eyes to find him only inches away. The heat that had yet to fade between them flared up and her gaze dropped to his lips.

"Don't I get a hello kiss?" His voice was husky.

She darted a glance at the chaos surrounding them. No one was paying them the least attention, so she gave him a chaste peck.

Amusement creased his cheeks. "I guess that will do for now." He looked past her. "Jujhar. Come meet Lynn."

She turned to see a tall man with coal-black hair and a generous beard approaching from the archway. He held a bottle of beer in one hand and a can of cola in the other. His dark eyes regarded her curiously.

"Hi. Nice to meet you." He placed the drinks on the counter and unerringly opened a drawer to extract a bottle opener.

"You, too." Benjamin had shared some of his history with Jujhar with Lynn. Enough that she knew meeting Jujhar and his family was an even bigger test than officially meeting Thea.

"I'm glad he got the guts to invite you. He's kept you pretty close to his chest." He popped the top off the beer and handed it to Benjamin.

"Ever think I was protecting her from you?" He took the bottle without losing the rhythm of his stirring and shot his friend a narrowed glare. "If you wanted to know more you could have asked."

"Uh-huh." Jujhar's grunt was disbelieving.

Maybe she should have been insulted Benjamin hadn't told his best friend much about her. Instead, she was relieved. Sure, she'd introduced him to the Silverberry Book Club, but no one other than Stephanie knew how much time they'd been spending together. Or that some of that time had been sleepovers—minus the sleep.

The fewer people who knew the depth of their relationship, the easier it would be when it ended.

Jujhar picked up the can of cola, pulled back the tab, and settled against the counter as if prepared for a long discussion. Oscar made a sudden motion toward his beard, and he smoothed it out of the baby's reach in an automatic gesture. "That's not for you, buddy."

"Sorry." Lynn stepped back, removing Oscar from temptation.

"No biggie. He wouldn't be the first to get a good tug in." He sipped his cola. "So, you work at the arena, too?"

Benjamin kept a close ear on the conversation between Jujhar and Lynn, ready to step in if things turned awkward. This was the first time he'd introduced a woman to his family—and Jujhar and Sadie were his family in every sense of the word—and would do anything necessary to ensure it went smoothly.

He also kept a wary eye on his mother. When he'd asked if it was okay to invite Lynn and Oscar to Christmas dinner—being held on December twenty-third as Jujhar, Sadie, and the kids were heading to Jujhar's parents in Surrey for the last week of the school break—he'd been pleased by his mother's quick agreement. His parents had effortlessly gathered people into their circle and holidays had always been filled with those who had nowhere else to go. He'd thought it would be perfect camouflage.

Since then, his spidey-senses had been sending

warning signals. A few things she'd said and done made him worry she thought wedding bells and an instant grandson might be in her near future.

A thought that made him alternately queasy and giddy.

When Thea announced all was ready for the feast, Jujhar led Lynn toward the highchair set out for Oscar, one that his mother still had on hand because of the Malhotra children. She cast Benjamin a wide-eyed look and he nodded encouragingly as he poured the gravy into a boat.

Everyone pitched in bringing dishes to the table, even four-year-old Elaine. Oscar watched open-mouthed, fascinated by the parade of people and food. It struck Benjamin that this might be the biggest gathering the toddler had ever seen. Lynn had no family in town, and while she was close with the Silverberry Book Club, he doubted they spent many noisy meals together.

He took a seat on the opposite side of Oscar from Lynn. She'd pulled a silicon bib and plate out of the enormous diaper bag she'd brought and placed a little of almost everything in front of him. He wielded his spoon with rather reckless abandon and Benjamin laughed.

"Sorry. You're sitting in the splash zone." Lynn's grin was wry and apologetic.

"Not a problem." And it wasn't. Having Lynn and Oscar with him tonight made him feel truly *home* for the first time.

Which was a thought to examine at a quieter time.

He stole a glance at Kelly, seated beside his mother. While he could never take the place of his father, the man made her laugh. It had been a long time since he'd seen her look so happy. Maybe that was on him, for not spending as much time with her as he should, but he decided that didn't matter. With her flushed cheeks and sparkling eyes, she looked ten years younger. He welcomed the man that made her that way.

Into one of those pauses that occur no matter what the size of a group, a phone trilled. Lynn cocked her head. "Sorry, that's mine. I left it in the diaper bag. I should have put it on silent." She pushed back her chair and passed behind Oscar and Benjamin to the living room. He twisted round in his seat, watching her just for the joy of it, as she dug out the phone and frowned at the screen. Swinging her hair out of the way in a gesture that made his stomach flutter with desire, she lifted it to her ear.

"Rupert? Is everything okay?"

Benjamin recognized Lynn's father's name from the online searches he'd done after learning her parents were musicians.

"What do you mean you're here?" Her tone rang with denial and disbelief. "No, of course I'm happy. It's just, I'm at a friend's for dinner. You caught me by surprise." Another pause. Her expression melted from shock to frustrated acceptance. "If I'd known you were coming, I would have arranged things differently. You'll have to give me some time. I'll be there as soon as I can." She swiped to disconnect and stared blindly at the Christmas tree's blinking lights.

Benjamin made sure Oscar was safely occupied with his meal and rose. Conscious of his mother and Jujhar's interested gazes, he drew Lynn out of the archway and deeper into the living room. "What's going on? Where do you need to be?"

She shook her head as if trying to realign her world. "My parents decided to surprise me by coming for Christmas. They're waiting at the airport to be picked up."

CHAPTER TWENTY-FIVE

Rupert Kolmyn was a compact, thick-set man with a bushy puff of curly, grizzled hair and a beard to match. His bulky Cowichan sweater made him appear even more barrel-shaped. "Crystal-Lynn! What took you so long?" He swept his daughter into an energetic hug that ignored her stiff-backed irritation.

Crystal-Lynn? Benjamin shrugged away his curiosity and set his expression to welcoming. *Crystal-Lynn* hadn't wanted him to come with her to the airport in the first place. He wouldn't make her regret his presence by teasing her yet couldn't help wondering what other secrets this impromptu visit might reveal.

He'd insisted on joining her, despite her assurance it was unnecessary. Behind that assurance had been irritation and disapproval and frustration, and he wanted to give her support, possibly even act as a buffer. Rupert hadn't even glanced at him, however, let alone noticed Lynn's aggravation. Maybe she'd been right, and he was superfluous.

She stepped out of her father's embrace. "If I'd known you were coming, I would have been waiting for you when you landed."

"We wanted it to be a surprise." Rupert's gravelly, whisky-fuelled voice was unexpected. He sounded nothing like the smooth tenor on the tracks Benjamin had downloaded.

"Well, it is." Lynn's sarcasm was heavy, but Rupert

didn't blink. She turned away from her father and with deeper affection greeted the thin, slightly stooped woman standing beside him. "It's good to see you, Mom."

Minerva had the same poker-straight blonde hair as Lynn, though hers was highlighted with silver. Her hug was more subdued than her husband's yet somehow more sincere. "I wanted to call. He wouldn't let me."

"It's okay." Lynn's tone was resigned and forgiving.

Minerva's eyebrows rose and her face gleamed with expectation. "So, where's my grandson?"

"He's with my mother." Benjamin stepped forward. "Hi. I'm Benjamin Whitestone. I'm Lynn's—"

"Friend. He's my friend." She shot him an undecipherable look. "I was having dinner with Benjamin and his family when you called. Since I was in a hurry to get here, it seemed simpler to leave Oscar there for now." She'd argued with both Benjamin and Thea about that but given up in her hurry to get to the airport.

"All right then. Let's get going." Rupert lifted the duffel bag at his feet and headed for the exit, clearly expecting everyone to follow.

"Here. Let me take that." Benjamin reached for the handle of Minerva's suitcase. "Is this all you have?"

"Yes." Her smile was faint. He wondered if years of standing in Rupert's shadow had faded her. "I'm used to packing light."

Lynn gave a snort that could have been agreement or dissent. The three of them moved through the automatic doors and down the exterior ramp leading to the short-term parking area. Rupert stood, vibrating with impatience, at the bottom, head swivelling from side to side.

Lynn led them through the dark, wintry night to her SUV. Benjamin stayed at Minerva's side. "If you're not too tired, you're more than welcome to come back with us. My mother insisted I extend the invitation."

"And it was a lovely offer." Lynn lifted the rear hatch and glared at Benjamin, her face hidden from her parents. "But I think I should just take you both to my house and go back and get Oscar while you settle in."

Rupert tossed in his bag. "I could go for some home cooking. The food on the cruise ship is nothing to sneeze at, but it's not like my momma used to make."

Lynn's retort was swift and sharp. "Maybe you would have more home cooking if, oh, I don't know, you had a home."

Rupert shrugged and made his way to the front passenger door, taking shotgun as if by right. "There's a price we pay for chasing our dreams. And that's one I'm willing to pay."

Lynn slammed the driver's door behind her with more force than necessary and stabbed the key into the ignition.

It relieved some of her frustration but not nearly enough.

She'd spoken with her parents only last week and they'd given no inkling that they were intending to come for the holidays. She had swallowed her disappointment and planned her days accordingly. Now her disappointment had morphed into a familiar anger at her father's disregard for other people's lives. Her schedule was screwed.

Yes, she had a schedule for Christmas holidays. Sue her.

In the back seat Benjamin was doing his best to draw her mother out. She'd been horrified by his offer to come with her to the airport. Introducing him to her parents would be fraught enough without adding in the current stressful situation. Not that he seemed stressed out by it, unlike herself. He had taken her unexpected announcement in stride, as had Thea and the rest of the adults.

Thea's smile, if anything, had grown wider at Lynn's announcement her parents had arrived without warning. "How wonderful that they've come to visit. Please, make sure they know they are welcome to come eat with us." She'd gestured at the heaping table. "There's more than enough."

Benjamin obviously got some of his laid-back, lack-of-conflict genes from his mother. Lynn was frantic at having to make up her spare room at the last minute. Thea couldn't have looked happier at having uninvited guests.

She hadn't missed the flicker of his eyelids when she'd jumped in earlier to prevent him from telling her parents he was her boyfriend or lover or whatever it was he was going to say. If she'd hurt him, it had been unintentional. But she needed to tell them in her own way, and in her own time.

Maybe she should have mentioned her new relationship when they were thousands of kilometres away. Too late now. She couldn't ban Benjamin from her life until they left, so they were bound to discover it sooner or later. Speaking of which...

"Do you know how long you're staying?" She struggled to keep her tone light. If only she'd had some advanced notice, she'd be thrilled they were here. She'd get there, but it would take a few hours. "Not that I'm rushing you, but I'll need to do a grocery run tomorrow so there's enough food in the house." The thought of battling the crowds on Christmas Eve made her scowl and clench the wheel tighter.

"We've got to be back in Miami by January second. The only reason we have this time off is the cruise line decided to go all Christmas all the time this week and brought in a different singer they thought fit the atmosphere better." Rupert put air quotes around the last four words, his disgust evident.

Lynn did the math in her head. Given the distance between Prince George and Florida, they'd probably have to leave the day before to get back in time.

Nine days. She could survive nine days. After all, wasn't this what she'd always wanted—a big family Christmas?

Her temples throbbed.

By the time Lynn fell into bed that night more than her head ached. Her neck was stiff from tension, her lower back twinged, and her shoulders were strained from pacing with Oscar in her arms as she'd tried to soothe him to sleep.

The first half hour or so at Thea's hadn't been horrible. Rupert charmed everyone as he plowed his way through two helpings of dinner. Minerva hadn't eaten much but glowed at the chance to hold Oscar.

The longer they stayed, however, the tetchier Oscar grew. Despite several hints it was well past his bedtime, it was only when she'd said she was leaving and Rupert could walk the few blocks home if he wanted to stay longer that she managed to drag him away. Oscar screamed the entire, thankfully short, trip, and had taken a long time to settle down. Minerva tried to help but he was having none of it. Lynn suggested she make up the hide-a-bed in her home office instead, and when Oscar finally wore himself out enough to sleep, her parents were in the spare room with the door closed. She had taken refuge in her own room with heartfelt relief.

She set her mind to relaxing every fibre in her body in the hopes that sleep would claim her. Despite the warm weight of her duvet, she was chilled, the sheets cool and slick. Tossing to her other side, she huddled deeper under the covers, searching for the elusive warmth, and then finally faced the truth.

She missed Benjamin in her bed. Missed the steady sighing of his breath, the dip of the mattress under his weight, the touch of his foot on hers as if he needed that tiny connection as he slept.

It would be the new year before he could stay again. Though she was committed to telling her parents they were dating, nothing on earth would make her comfortable enough to have him in her bed with her parents just across the hall.

Her sense of loss was stronger than she liked. It wasn't as if he'd spent every night with her since they'd decided to be...whatever it was they were. She counted back, growing drowsy as the sheets slowly warmed, and realized they had spent more than fifty percent of their nights together. It was rather lowering to admit that she slept better when he was there. She didn't think it was just the sexual exercise, either. She was certain her subconscious let her sleep deeper knowing someone else was there who might hear Oscar if he awoke.

She'd been in such a tizzy to get Oscar home, as well as still reeling from her parents' sudden appearance, that she hadn't even kissed Benjamin goodbye. Shifting on her elbow, she swapped her pillow for the one he used and buried her nose in it, searching for his scent. As faded as it was, it gave her some measure of comfort.

By tomorrow she'd be over her father's blithe disregard to her life and plans and be able to appreciate their time together. She had invited them, after all. She just wished she'd had some time to prepare.

What a way to end the year.

CHAPTER TWENTY-SIX

Benjamin's mother often spouted the old wives' tale that what happened on January 1 was a harbinger for the year to come.

If he believed in such things, he might as well crawl into bed for the next twelve months, because it was going to be a doozy. Not only had he broken his favourite coffee mug that morning, but his car wouldn't start. He'd had to call a taxi to get to the arena, where Levi had immediately ripped into him for being late. He'd bit his tongue as he usually did, but his temper was on high simmer by the time he stepped into the dressing room—to discover Valeri Nechayev regaling his teammates with tales of his drunken escapades at a New Year's Eve Party.

All of this, on top of not having a moment alone with Lynn for more than a week, set him to full boil.

Unnoticed by the players, he stood in the doorway, breathing fiercely through his nose, searching for calm. Nechayev was of legal drinking age but it defied team policy and violated Benjamin's expressed expectations. That he'd overindulged the night before a game flaunted the fact he didn't care what his teammates and coaches thought. Nechayev had been skating on thin ice for weeks, always pulling back his antics just before Benjamin snapped.

He'd taken one stride too far today.

They were now in the second half of the season and

Benjamin was running out of time. It was still mathematically possible for the Canyon Cats to qualify for the playoffs, but not if things continued as they had. If he wanted to atone for past failure by achieving future success, he had to make changes and make them fast.

"You're benched." His words were too quiet to be heard over the players' jokes and jeers, though they reverberated inside his chest like a gong.

The dressing room was a large space lined with benches in front of open lockers. Nechayev's assigned place was on the opposite side of the room. Benjamin stalked toward him, crossing the rubber mat flooring emblazoned with the Canyon Cats logo, bulling past half-dressed players. As the team became aware of his presence, the hubbub faded to a watchful silence.

"Take off your gear." Despite the rage coursing through him, he kept his tone mild. "You're not playing tonight."

Nechayev raised a disbelieving eyebrow. "Say what?" His accent gave the colloquialism an unfamiliar rhythm.

"You're benched. You broke my orders." Without waiting for a response, he traced a slow circle, turning his back on Nechayev and making eye contact with every player as he did so. "Anyone else out drinking last night?"

He waited.

Chisholm and Piiroinen raised their hands, shooting uncertain glances at Nechayev. They obviously didn't know whether he wanted them to bluff it out or join him in his rebellion.

One more hand lifted. Alternate Captain Gerald Dudas. Benjamin's heart sank. He would have bet good money that Dudas would never jeopardize his ice time by flouting team rules. While he wished he could only punish his problem players, he dared not show favouritism.

"The four of you will be watching from the stands

187

tonight. We'll discuss further penalties tomorrow. Get undressed. Avril will set your assignments before you go up." Players who were injured or healthy scratches were often asked to track statistics such as ice time, hits, and completed passes for the coaches' use. It was drudge work and most of them hated it, so was another level of punishment he could inflict.

He strode back to the door, aware every set of eyes tracked him. He turned to face the room. "The rest of you better be prepared to work your asses off. If you aren't, don't bother stepping on the ice."

The lights in the arena dimmed. On ice projections turned the glittering surface into a flowing fury of white water as the Canyon Cats' pre-game pump-up song boomed out of the enormous speakers hanging from the rafters. Lynn watched from a stairwell leading from the concourse into the arena proper. Fans trickled past, heading for their seats, as the players skated out onto the rink.

This was the third game the Canyon Cats would play since Christmas, but the first at home. They'd started the last half of the season with a two-game road trip, and Lynn had always planned to take those days off work. That meant she'd had plenty of time to spend with Rupert and her mother, and despite the bumpy start it had turned out to be a reasonably pleasant week.

That being said, she had waved them through airport security this morning with relief. As much as she loved her parents, a little bit of Rupert went a long way and her mother's well-meaning interference threw off Oscar's carefully orchestrated schedule. She couldn't wait to call her home her own once more.

And welcome Benjamin back into it without her parents' restrictive presence.

The house lights brightened as the rink announcer finished proclaiming the starting line-ups. Players fidgeted on the blue lines as the scattered crowd rose and a children's choir led everyone in the American and Canadian national anthems. Lynn let her thoughts drift to the days ahead.

The new Canyon Cats marketing coordinator would start on Monday, and while Cynthie had convinced Brewster to allow Lynn to work with his new hire for a short transition period, her days of being required to attend games were numbered. She couldn't help a pang of sadness at the thought.

The last week had been difficult for their fledgling relationship, what with her parents underfoot and Benjamin's road trip. They had barely had a chance to talk, and other than a few perfunctory kisses, no opportunity to be intimate. Even though they didn't always speak with each other on game nights, she enjoyed watching him behind the bench, and was subconsciously aware of him while she did her duties. Once the new marketing coordinator was on their own, she'd have one less excuse to spend time with him. The whole situation made her itchy.

Which in turn made her worried. Had she fallen too far, too fast? And if so, what was she going to do about it?

The choir finished and filed off the rink. Attendants rolled up the carpet as the rink announcer did his best to get the meager crowd chanting. It was time to get in position for the first fan event, which would take place about halfway through the period, but she lingered a little longer, watching Benjamin as he stood straight, tall, and stone-faced behind the players on the bench.

At the click of dress shoes approaching, she pressed up against the wall to allow the person to pass. Instead, the sounds paused, and Peterson Brewster came to stop beside her. The owner had a special suite next to those reserved for media and officials, which were in the top tier of stands above her head, opposite the luxury boxes rented out by local companies and corporations.

"Evening." He nodded an acknowledgment but remained where he was, not moving to ascend the next, longer flight of stairs that led to his exclusive aerie.

"Hello." She nodded back.

His eyes narrowed. Not at her, but at the five Canyon Cats preparing for the opening faceoff. "Where's Nechayev?"

He muttered the question under his breath, so she assumed it wasn't directed at her and didn't bother to answer. Now that he mentioned it, though, she didn't see the bane of Benjamin's existence in his usual place on the first line. And did the players' bench seem a little less crowded than usual?

Play began as Lynn did a quick head count. Only eighteen players were present, four less than usual.

Brewster had apparently reached the same total. He transferred his glare to her. "Have you got a copy of tonight's roster? Mine's up in my box."

Lynn flipped through the sheaf of papers clipped to the board she carried and found the printout updated before every game. "Here."

He scanned it, his expression thoughtful. "Nechayev, Chisholm, Piiroinen, and Dudas were last minute scratches."

Lynn had spent enough time around the team to realize these four players were a healthy chunk of the regular lineup. "Do you know why?"

"Not a clue."

A flash of emotion flickered behind his eyes. Lynn couldn't decide if it was irritation or satisfaction. Sometimes she forgot that Brewster *wanted* the team to fail. He did an excellent job of masking it in media interviews, and there were still no rumours of the team's possible defection floating about the community.

"It's going to be tough to win with such a depleted roster." She offered the comment and watched for any hint Brewster might have somehow orchestrated this himself.

"Yes, it will." Again, he remained impassive. No one seeing him would suspect a thing.

Suddenly the arena erupted in a roar. A horn blared and pulsing drumbeats rattled the rafters, making her sternum vibrate. On the ice, the Canyon Cats celebrated the early goal.

Brewster frowned. Catching Lynn's interested gaze, he smoothed out his expression and without further conversation swung around the corner and disappeared up and out of sight.

Lynn crossed her fingers as she, too, left her post. Maybe tonight wouldn't be as bad as she feared.

It was by no means a perfect game, but it was a win, and he'd take it.

Benjamin wasn't sure what to expect when he entered the dressing room after the final buzzer. During the game the team and staff had pushed aside personal issues, consumed by the pace of play and execution of strategy. The players deserved to celebrate the result, but would they be welcoming or wary at his presence?

He walked into an atmosphere redolent with the sweaty stink of physical exertion and the sweet tang of energy drinks. He'd asked them to work their asses off and they had. Now they drooped on the benches, heads hanging but eyes bright in a combination of elation and exhaustion.

Dudas was circling the room, congratulating his teammates while apologizing for letting them down. Nechayev, Chisholm, and Piiroinen stood off to the side, listening to the players giving blow-by-blow descriptions of each goal, each save. Nechayev glared, arms crossed, foot tapping, jealousy a green aura surrounding him. He was fiercely proud of his talent and skill—probably too proud—and watching others celebrate a win to which he hadn't contributed was subtle punishment.

It wouldn't do to let the team see him soften too much too soon, so Benjamin kept his post-game speech short and gruff. He gave credit where it was due, recognizing everyone's hard work and pointing out how the systems he'd beaten into them had produced results. But he also warned that one game did not a successful season make. Then he left them to their post-game cool downs and showers and headed for his office.

Lynn was waiting for him. She'd never done that before. She swivelled lazily in his chair, her hands clasped in her lap as if to prove she hadn't touched any of his belongings. His heart thudded once, strong and solid, as their eyes met across his desk. She sprang to her feet and hurried toward him.

"Great game." She gave him a quick, hard hug and his arms encircled her automatically. When she tried to step back, he pulled her in again so they connected from thighs to shoulders. She snuggled in with no protest.

"Thanks. They deserved the win." His hands, chilled from being at ice level for the last hour or so, gripped the slick nylon of the lightweight jacket that was her uniform on game nights.

"It must have been tough, without a full roster." Her inflection rose slightly at the end, but it wasn't a direct question. He briefly considered taking the out she'd left him, but instead found himself explaining the drama that had gone on before the puck dropped.

She stood quietly in his arms, studying his face. Her palms made soothing circles on his back, and he wondered if she was aware she was doing so. He kept his embrace light and easy, when what he wanted to do was crush her to his chest and claim the warmth and comfort of her kiss.

"You did what you had to do." Her lips curved up in a smile. "And, hey, you got the win. Maybe this will be a turning point."

"God, I hope so."

Her hands left his back and burrowed under his suit jacket, tugging his shirt loose from the waistband of his pants. He growled low in his throat as her fingers traced the sensitive skin of his abdomen. He adjusted his grip lower, cupping her ass and lifting her on her toes, to make sure she didn't miss the evidence of exactly how her touch affected him.

"We shouldn't be doing this. Not here." Her eyelids fluttered and her nails bit into his hips. "I've missed you."

The embers of lust that he'd kept banked for more than a week flared fiercely and his reply clogged in his throat. His kiss would have to do the talking for him.

Her mouth opened immediately and she hitched herself even higher, locking their lips together. The worries and frustrations of his day vanished in her heat.

He felt a quiet click deep inside, as of two puzzle pieces joining.

Nowhere near ready to study what that meant, he dragged his mouth away. She followed with a soft whimper that made his knees shake but he held himself out of reach. "I forgot to ask. Your parents got away okay?"

"Yes." Her husky voice was even rougher, more sensual than usual.

His skin rippled in response. "Invite me over, Lynn."

Her eyes were fever bright, her lips swollen. "Want to come over, Benjamin?"

"More than you could possibly know."

CHAPTER TWENTY-SEVEN

Lynn knew she was a control freak. It was a part of her personality she'd long accepted, might have been smugly proud of.

Wanting things to get done the right way—which was her way, of course—wasn't a bad thing, was it?

She gritted her teeth as she handed over her Canyon Cats files to the scrawny, barely-old-enough-to-shave young man Brewster had hired. She'd spent the week with Chue Kyong and while she accepted he was bright and intelligent and willing to work hard, she wasn't ready to let go.

Literally. He had to tug the folder out of her grip.

"Thank you so much." He clamped it to his narrow chest with both arms as if afraid she might snatch it back. "I appreciate your time. Is it okay if I call with any questions?"

"You're welcome, and certainly. Pop in whenever you like."

He waved goodbye to Sarah on his way to the interior exit and Lynn plopped into her desk chair, setting it rocking.

Sarah dug in her desk drawer, retrieved a nail file, and scraped it against her index finger. "I don't know why you're so glum. You've got your weekends and evenings back." It was after four on the first Friday in January and productivity had slowed to a crawl, if not a full stop. These were the darkest days of the year and even Lynn was having trouble finding her usual verve for work.

"I'm not glum. I'm just worried Kyong will mess things up." Other than the denial regarding her attitude, she wasn't lying. She was worried Kyong couldn't keep the momentum she'd built up during the last months. Despite the Canyon Cats' poor performance on the ice, several of her ideas, including the Adopt-a-Pet and an ugly Christmas sweater themed game, had created a lot of buzz. Attendance was hovering just below the danger line, though, and now she no longer had control of promotions and contests her gut churned.

The Canyon Cats were hosting the opponent nearest in the standings this weekend in a vital doubleheader. These would be the first home games she wouldn't be required to attend, and she was considering buying tickets for herself and Oscar. Maybe Stephanie and Peter, too, so she wouldn't look quite so pathetic. Not that she was going to gawk at Benjamin the whole game. She wanted to be there to show her support—for the team, not just him.

Yeah. For the team.

Cynthie poked her head out of her inner office. "Lynn? Have a minute?"

"Of course." Glad for the chance to think of something other than losing her influence over attendance, she strode past Sarah and into Cynthie's room. "What's up?"

Cynthie gestured her closer and spoke in a low voice. "I heard you with Chue Kyong. You've turned everything over, then?"

It appeared she wasn't getting away from her current least favourite topic quite yet. "Yes. I told him to stay in touch if he has any questions."

"You know as well as I do that we're not out of the woods on the attendance guarantee. I want you to stay involved."

"How? Brewster will wonder what's going on if I hover over Kyong's shoulder on game nights."

Cynthie shook her head. "Not with the on-ice stuff. We have to let go of that. But there are things we can do to promote the team in the community, things Kyong won't think of, and that Brewster can't kibosh."

"Like the senior citizen visits, you mean?" Lynn had set up a rotating schedule where players spent an hour or two each week in long-term care homes. The activity had garnered media attention, and she'd actually been able to track a bump in attendance on the game days following the visits.

"Along those lines, yes. A friend of mine is the executive director of White Spruce Mental Wellness Centre. He's always looking for ways to connect his clients with community role models. Do you think Benjamin Whitestone might be up to do a talk there? Something about teamwork and perseverance, maybe from the angle of his playing career as well as coaching?"

The idea caught Lynn's imagination and set it soaring. "Why stop at one talk? What about an entire mentoring program? Brewster might complain, but he doesn't control what Benjamin does in his free time. And I think he'd be excellent at it."

Cynthie nodded in satisfaction. "I'll leave it with you, then."

Benjamin stopped in his tracks. Lynn, bundled in a parka, winter boots, and fuzzy hat, continued on the snowy trail. Her hands met at her lower back, gripping the handle of the sled where Oscar sat enthroned, his arms sticking out stiff as a gingerbread cookie in his enveloping snowsuit.

"No." He shook his head. "I can't."

Lynn came to a halt and turned to face him, her brow wrinkled. "What? What do you mean?"

It was a gorgeous winter's day. The sky was a searing blue and fresh snow gleamed blindingly bright. The beauty of the scene mocked his inner darkness.

He was the *last* person who should be mentoring youth with mental health issues. He was stressed enough guiding his players, fostering their self-esteem while critiquing their game in a positive way. He knew the value of therapy and counselling, had participated in sessions during his listless career and even after his father's death. He hated to think how messed up he'd be if he hadn't taken those steps. But he hadn't exactly turned his life around, had he?

How to explain all that to Lynn without sounding like a fool? And a cowardly one at that.

The Canyon Cats had won both games of the home stand, the first such accomplishment all season. It was even sweeter since it was against the team they had to catch for any chance at making the playoffs. Nechayev, Chisholm, Piiroinen, and Dudas were serving five game suspensions for breaking the team's drug and alcohol prohibition. They would miss the next two games as well but would be available for the short weekend road trip after that. He was crossing his fingers that their return wouldn't throw off the groove the players seemed to have found.

The results had given him hope and he'd carried the warmth of that feeling to Lynn and Oscar's, where he intended to spend a pleasant, relaxing Sunday afternoon. Until she'd blindsided him with her mental wellness program idea.

"Benjamin?" Dropping the handle of the sled, she lifted one mittened hand to his shoulder. "Are you okay? You've gone pale."

The tip of her nose was pink with cold, her cheeks a matching rose. Her eyes, the same icy blue as the shadows on the snow, were filled with concern, searching his. He had to say something. "I'm not qualified to do that sort of thing. I'm not the right person." *Please don't ask me why*.

"What do you mean? You're perfect." Oscar fussed and she linked her arm through Benjamin's. Bending to retrieve the handle of the sled without releasing her firm grip, she began to walk, forcing him to follow. "You played in the NHL. Those kids will be excited to meet you. All you have to do is share your experiences about how you found success in life, despite disappointments."

It was easier to talk when she wasn't looking at him. "I haven't found success." He wouldn't claim that until he'd coached his team to the championships. Or at least the playoffs. Watching the chances grow slimmer had given him many sleepless nights, and the recent three game win streak hadn't solved his insomnia. "I was a washout as a professional hockey player, and I spent the last decade and more coasting from job to job. What kind of example is that for young people, especially those struggling with their own, much bigger problems?" Though his mother had absolved him of responsibility regarding his father, he hadn't forgiven himself yet. His palms sweat at the idea of recounting that story to Lynn. He tugged off his fur-lined leather gloves and the chill bit at his damp, exposed skin. He welcomed the discomfort.

"You don't consider yourself a success?" Her tone was curious, not condemning.

If he could have avoided answering he would have, but racing back to the parking lot and leaving Lynn and Oscar stranded wasn't an option. The wide, well-used trail wound up a slight incline between towering, leafless cottonwoods with gnarled bark. He drew in a deep breath so spicy with freshness it made him dizzy. Or maybe that was the conversation.

"Of course not." Why couldn't she see that? "As it stands now, my team is out of the playoffs. I have an owner actively hoping I'll fail, and the very real possibility that I'll be fired as soon as he achieves his goal to move the team. I live in a mostly empty, rented apartment and lease my car. What about that screams success?"

"I don't define it so narrowly. There are so many ways to gauge success." For several minutes there was only the sound of their boots crunching on snow, the shush of the sled's runners, the distant croaking of ravens, and Oscar's mostly unintelligible babbles. He began to hope she'd dropped the matter.

"You know what I see when I look at you?"

He was wrong. Apparently, she'd only been mustering her attack.

"I see a man who did his best, who never gave up, even when the odds seemed stacked against him." She kept her gaze forward, but he still felt pinned, like a forward crushed against the boards by the weight of a hulking defenceman.

"You don't know me then." The words tasted bitter. "I gave up. I gave up for years, running from job to job when things got tough. And I struggle everyday not to run again."

Lynn had known Benjamin's career as both player and assistant coach had involved several moves. She hadn't thought that deeply about it, other than to silently commiserate with him on the trauma of packing up and leaving and starting over again so many times. Given her own fractured childhood, that was what had stuck out the most.

But she had never pondered the *causes* of the moves.

"What do you mean, you ran away?" Her lips were dry, and not just from the cold. She'd gone into this relationship knowing he would leave someday to further his career. She hadn't considered that he might leave to avoid difficulties. If flight was his usual defence mechanism...

"Exactly what it sounds like."

"When you were a player and got traded, you didn't have any control over that." A thought that made her shudder. She would hate for anyone to have that kind of power over her.

"That's a handy excuse, but that's all it is. An excuse. If I'd been brave enough, I would have retired years before I did. I knew within a season that I'd never be the star everyone expected me to be, but I refused to admit it." He spoke with a clipped asperity she'd never heard in his voice before.

"There are what, a thousand players in the league?" She chose her words carefully, not sure what might ignite the explosion she felt simmering in the tense muscles under her hand. "Each team has maybe one or two true stars. Why put so much pressure on yourself?"

"It's what I'd worked for all my life. What my parents had sacrificed for. Do you have any idea how much it costs to give a child the opportunities they gave me?"

"No, I don't." She'd never been part of a team or a club, and even if she had, Rupert's constant uprooting would surely have disrupted any chance she might have had to excel.

"It's a lot. They never took a holiday. I don't count when they came with me to tournaments or training camps, because those trips weren't for them, they were for me. I cost them in time as well as money."

From what she'd seen of Thea, she couldn't believe his mother regretted a moment or a penny. Maybe his father had laid on the guilt. "The minute Oscar was born, I would have given him the world if I could and not counted it a sacrifice. Don't you think your parents thought the same?"

He was quick to defend them. "Don't get the idea they made me feel like I owed them. They didn't. That makes it worse."

She would need to unpack that later. For now, she

risked a quick glance. The brisk pace she'd set had brought faint colour back in his cheeks. He'd been rather alarmingly pale before. But his eyebrows were lowered in a scowl and his shoulders were hunched. "You may not want to hear this, but I think you're giving me reasons why you *should* do the mental health workshop, not why you shouldn't."

CHAPTER TWENTY-EIGHT

Lynn's words rang in Benjamin's head throughout the next week.

Could she be right? Could his feelings of failure and inadequacy actually make him a *better* coach and mentor?

She didn't badger him into making a decision. "All I ask is you think about it. Take a few days and get back to me when you're ready."

They finished their walk in quiet companionship and his turbulent emotions slowly calmed. The inner voice that had urged him to flee faded and by the time Oscar was in bed he was more than ready to accept Lynn's slow, confident seduction.

Their lovemaking was always intense, but that evening he sensed something more. In every languorous touch and deliberate kiss, Lynn was sending a message. A message he couldn't bear to interpret. Not yet.

To have her believe in him and then fail her, too, would be too much to take.

Home games on Tuesday and Wednesday and the road trip Friday and Saturday had prevented them from seeing each other since. That was the excuse he gave himself, anyway. He thought he caught a glimpse of her during one practice, yet when he looked again, she wasn't there. He couldn't decide whether she was allowing him space or had given up on him. His fingers itched to dial her number. He didn't.

He wished he had someone to talk to about his reluctance to do the mental health presentation, but the only person he wanted to talk to was Lynn. It was an ironically vicious circle that made his head ache.

The team arrived home early Sunday morning after the usual post-game, overnight bus ride. He passed out in his cold bed for a few hours, and then tossed a load of laundry into the wash and set aside what needed to go to the dry cleaners the next day. He opened the fridge, surveyed its meager contents—half a jar of jam, a stale loaf of bread, and a wilted head of lettuce—and shut it again. Pacing to the door that opened onto the tiny outdoor deck, he gripped the chilly railing and scowled out over the roof of the shopping complex below. The air took nippy bites out of his skin through the thin material of his T-shirt. He bore it as long as he could, but it soon forced him back into his soulless apartment.

Much like his office at the arena, he had spent no time making his home feel lived in. A copy of his parents' wedding photo hung on the wall but nothing else broke up the beige expanse. A dark grey sofa was placed under the photo, across from the television that he barely used, and a dinette table was tucked against the wall in front of the peninsula counter. He'd bought those three items, as well as his bedroom furniture, on a quick afternoon shopping trip the day he'd arrived in town.

He doubted it would take much more than four hours to erase all evidence he'd ever lived there. God, he was tired of living as if the axe was about to fall.

Before he could second guess himself, he pulled out his cell phone and tapped to connect to Lynn. She answered after one ring.

"Hi!" Just that single syllable released a coil of tension he hadn't realized was there. "Congrats on the road trip."

Her recognition of the Canyon Cats winning streak was gratifying, but not what he wanted to talk about now. "Thanks." His breathing was shallow, his pulse thready. Why was this so hard to do? "Uhm, I was wondering. Would you and Oscar like to come for dinner tonight?"

"To your apartment, you mean?" He deserved the shock in her tone. They'd been sleeping together for more than a month and he had never invited her over, let alone suggested a family meal.

"Yes," he said firmly. "To my apartment. I'm cooking. What would Oscar like?"

Lynn pulled off her glove with her teeth and tapped the apartment entry system screen. Oscar was perched on her hip, his diaper bag slung over her shoulder. A carload of supplies waited to be unpacked, but she'd never make it in one trip.

Benjamin's face appeared on the screen and her mouth curled to match his wide smile. "Hi. Come on up." The lock clicked and she pushed through. The apartment building was a newer one that had yet to become redolent of cleaning solutions and cooking smells, with a shiny tile lobby and a wall of glittering mailboxes. In the elevator she let Oscar press the button for the fifth floor, reminded herself to wash his hands the first chance she got, and watched the numbers click upward, butterflies dancing in her belly.

The doors slid open, and she stepped out. Benjamin appeared at the far end of the hall, striding toward her and Oscar, his smile undimmed.

"Hey." He lay a gentle kiss on her lips and then plucked Oscar from her arms. Her son went willingly. "I'm so glad you could make it."

She followed him into his apartment. His invitation had come as a complete surprise, and she had no idea what it might foreshadow. Though he'd welcomed her at his mother's for Christmas, that had still been one step removed from his own life. Tonight had to mean something, if nothing more than he'd forgiven her for putting him on the spot by suggesting the mental health workshop.

He tugged off Oscar's boots, set him down, and then removed his tiny jacket. Her son stood wide-eyed, absorbing the new space. "Let me take your coat."

She shook her head. "I have to get his highchair from the car."

"Give me your keys. I'll get it." He held out his hand. "It's probably better if you stay with Oscar, anyway. He might not be happy with just me."

Her son toddled into the living room. "Okay. Thanks." She didn't mention the portable playpen she'd brought. Benjamin wouldn't know what was in the black carrying case, and if things turned out differently than she hoped he didn't need to know she'd brought it along. She explained where she was parked, and he hurried away.

Toeing off her boots, she left them on the mat by the door, and then stepped deeper into the apartment. It was open concept, with a kitchen to her left, living room directly ahead, and a door and window looking out over a miniscule deck. The kitchen was well lit and airy, despite the dark January afternoon, with stainless steel appliances and faux stone surfaces. Savoury scents emanated from the oven and the counter was cluttered with clean but not yet put away prep dishes.

Despite the homey, lived-in appearance of the kitchen, the rest of the apartment was bare and cold. Not one knickknack or memento was displayed on the built-in shelving and the single framed photo on the wall only served to punctuate the overall barrenness.

Oscar had discovered a small crate placed on the floor between the wall-mounted television and the sofa. He was emptying it out with determination, and her heart clutched.

Toys. Benjamin had bought her son toys. To have at his apartment.

She was in so much trouble.

Benjamin stared at the door of his own apartment, folded highchair gripped in his tense fingers and held in front of him like a shield. The hall was silent, the soundproofing doing its job, and for a minute he felt the panicked certainty that Lynn and Oscar had left.

Since he had her car keys, he was being an idiot.

Rolling his shoulders, he opened the door. Oscar's giggles danced to greet him. Lynn sat next to him on the floor, driving a truck over his legs and up his belly, making a growling sound he assumed was her attempt at a motor. The toys he'd bought that afternoon while getting groceries were scattered about. From the oven, the roast with vegetables he'd put in an hour ago smelled just the way his mom used to make it.

Lynn looked up and grinned. His lungs squeezed at the warmth and welcome in her eyes, his heart suddenly taking up more space in his chest than usual. He smiled back, hoping he didn't look as strained as he felt. He really, really wanted this evening to go well. He wanted to prove to Lynn he was trying—trying to make her a part of his world, trying to work through his ingrained habit of running when the going got tough.

"Here, let me get that." She clambered to her feet and took the highchair from him. "There's a knack to opening it."

"Would you like some wine? Dinner won't be much longer." He moved into the kitchen, opened a cupboard, and took down the two wineglasses he'd also bought today. While he had the basic dishware essential to bachelor life, his stock hadn't run to crystal.

"Love some." She deftly clicked latches and pressed levers and flipped her wrist and the highchair unfolded. Before she'd arrived, he'd moved one of the dining chairs from the four-top table to make room for it, and she slid it into the waiting space.

"I have to ask." Keeping an eye on Oscar, still fascinated by the new toys, she reached across the counter and accepted the glass he gave her. "Why? Why did you invite us over?"

He'd planned for this question. While he wasn't ready to admit his deeper, personal reasons, he could give her an answer she'd accept. "I wanted to talk more about the White Spruce Mental Wellness presentation. I've decided I'll do it."

While he hadn't expected her to jump for joy, he had thought he'd get more of a response than a low, humming acknowledgment. She sipped her drink, pale blue eyes direct and candid, her expression mildly encouraging. "That's good news. But I don't want you to do it because you feel pressured. I didn't realize when I asked that it might be distasteful to you. The last thing I want to do is add more stress to your life. Not for something like this."

He joined her on the other side of the counter, leaning his hips against it. She shifted and he felt her gaze on his profile. "I think I have to. Raising the issue made me face things I haven't thought of in a long time. It has given me a different perspective on my career." Not that he'd accepted his failures. But he was beginning to believe they might not be as bad as he'd always thought.

"Good for you." She shifted again, this time mirroring his stance with her back to the counter and laid her head on his shoulder. The flowery scent of her shampoo curled into his nostrils, and he gave into the urge to rest his cheek on her head.

For a moment they stood in silence as Oscar crawled around the living room, babbling to his new toys and appearing completely at home. The ache in Benjamin's chest intensified until he wondered if he was having a heart attack like his father had. An emotion he couldn't identify bubbled and churned and threatened to overwhelm him.

He opened his mouth, preparing to jump off the deep end and tell Lynn a few of the thoughts racing through his brain. The beeping of the oven timer interrupted him before he could speak.

Not sure whether to be relieved or disappointed, he rubbed his chin on her skull and straightened off the counter. "Dinner's ready. Want to help me set the table?"

CHAPTER TWENTY-NINE

White Spruce Mental Wellness Centre was located in a repurposed school. The single storey, T-shaped building housed several complementary services under its flat roof, but Benjamin was concerned with only the one.

The wide glass door leading to the White Spruce offices was bland and discreet, with a simple logo etched on the top half. Nothing threatening about it. Yet he couldn't make himself unbuckle his seatbelt and go inside.

The day following his dinner with Lynn and Oscar, he'd spoken with Nishtha Sethi, the centre's executive director. Now here he was, a week later, parked outside the office, worms of dread crawling through his veins.

He'd made a commitment, and he was going to honour it, come hell or high water. To do it right, he would have to confront his past, not hide from it. He would have to be honest with the teenagers in the program, and that meant honest with himself.

He wasn't sure he was up for it.

As he stared at the door, a figure slowly approached from across the snow-covered playground. Head hanging, the face was hidden under the loose hood of an oversized sweatshirt inadequate for the late January freezing spell. Indecision and unwillingness were evident in the slouched shoulders, the hesitant steps. The person gripped the handle, paused, released it, and scurried back the way they had come.

Benjamin wasn't sure what made him open his door and call out. Maybe it was a sense of fellowship with someone who appeared as reluctant to seek help as he was. Maybe it was a test to see if he had the courage Lynn believed he had.

"Hey. Were you going in?"

The person stopped a step away from disappearing around the corner of the building. They glanced over their shoulder, and he glimpsed a spotty face and patchy reddish beard.

"I'm not too excited about it myself." Benjamin took a couple steps closer. "Maybe that's the reason I need to go in. I'm Benjamin."

For a moment he was certain the young man was going to flee, and so did he. Poised on the tips of his toes, his eyes skittered away from Benjamin and back again before he turned and answered. "Lee." A gust of wind blew off the baggy hood, revealing uncombed hair and a scrawny neck.

"Hi, Lee." He jerked a thumb toward the door. "I know one thing. It'll be warmer inside."

Hazel eyes stared out of a thin face and the knot of an Adam's apple bobbed. "I'm not scared to go in."

The denial, coming out of the blue, revealed the lie. Benjamin didn't call him on it. "You're not?" He shook his head. "You're braver than I am, then. I'm kind of terrified."

"I've been before. Once. They're not that bad." Another gust of wind had him hunching his shoulders. "They got coffee."

"I sure could use one." He went to the door and pulled it open. "How about you?"

Lee's shrug was an awkward mixture of insolence and despondence. He ambled past Benjamin, trailing the aroma of marijuana and body odour.

In the reception area, a woman with a thick brown braid and sloppy cardigan sat at a desk while another woman, about his age with a sleek fall of black hair and heavy eyebrows over intelligent brown eyes, stood behind her holding a blue file folder. Both smiled warmly as Benjamin and the youth entered.

"Lee! I'm so glad you came back." The woman with the folder rounded the desk and joined them in the tiny open space near the door. "The program's just starting. Same room. There's cookies and hot drinks."

Lee jerked a shoulder and strolled down the hall as if escape had never crossed his mind. Benjamin swallowed. If Lee could do it, so could he. "I'm Benjamin Whitestone. I have an appointment with Ms. Sethi."

The woman held out her hand. "I'm Nishtha. I'm so excited to discuss this program with you. Even more so now I've seen you with Lee."

Benjamin shook her hand, ducking his chin in confusion. "What do you mean?" All he'd done was walk in the building with the teenager.

"We saw him at the door. And we saw him leave." She tilted her head at the woman at the desk, who bobbed her head in confirmation. "Then we saw you get out of your car and the next thing we know you're both here. Lee came to group therapy a couple weeks ago, but we haven't seen him since. I don't know what you said, but we're so glad you convinced him to come back."

"I told him it would be warmer inside."

Nishtha grinned. "You know the first rule then."

"What's that?"

"Never lie." She waved the blue folder in the direction Lee had gone. "Why don't I take you on a tour first? Then we'll start hashing out the details."

With the uncomfortable sense that something life-changing had just taken place, but not sure exactly what, Benjamin followed her.

The Canyon Cats' unprecedented winning ways continued through the last half of January and into

February.

That was the good news.

The bad news was that attendance was *still* hovering just under the required minimum.

Lynn scowled at the spreadsheet displayed on her computer. It was all there in black and white. She had to come up with *something* to boost those numbers. Despite her belief in its value—to Benjamin, the kids in the program, and the Canyon Cats—the White Spruce Mental Wellness presentation was only a small piece of the solution.

It wasn't quite ten o'clock and she was already over her caffeine limit for the day, but frustration forced her to her feet and sent her to the coffeemaker.

Since the evening more than three weeks ago at Benjamin's apartment—which had ended earlier than she'd hoped when Oscar had refused to go to sleep in a strange room and she'd had to take her teary, overtired baby home—they'd spent more time talking on the phone than they had face to face. Six of the last eight games had been on the road, and when Benjamin was in town he'd focused on the team and the White Spruce presentation. She didn't begrudge that, not at all. As his confidence grew and flourished, her pride in his accomplishments, both on and off the ice, blossomed, too.

The White Spruce appearance was scheduled for the upcoming Tuesday. After so many games on the road, the Canyon Cats were home for all but one during the next four weeks, and it provided the perfect window of opportunity. Benjamin had met with the counsellors several times to prepare his talk, which she hadn't asked to see. This was between him and the teens. If he wanted to share with her, he would. If he didn't, that was his prerogative.

The coffeemaker finished its noisy procedure, and she took her mug back to her desk. As she sat, a text notification dinged from her phone. Benjamin.

Can you meet me under the stairs right now? We need to talk.

Her heart dropped into her belly. What now?

She rose. Sarah cast her an inquiring glance. "I need to clear my head. This project is making me crazy." She didn't say which project but had so many on the go Sarah could fill in the blank without making her tell an outright lie. "I'm going to walk the concourse for a bit."

Taking her coffee, she left the office and headed downstairs. The door to the catch-all space was ajar, and she stepped in. Benjamin was already there, pacing the cluttered room.

"What's going on?" She put down her cup and gripped his wrist to stop his restless movements. "You're worrying me."

"I have to cancel White Spruce." He twisted out of her touch and scrubbed his hands through his hair. "Brewster's booked a motivational speaker for the same day. I have to attend. I've been after him to bring this person in for months and he's always dissed the idea. I can't refuse to go after all that."

Lynn's mind raced. "Do you think he did it on purpose? Scheduled the speaker the same day to mess with White Spruce?"

"I don't know. He could have found out about it easily enough, as I have to put those sorts of things on a shared online calendar." He perched precariously on a rickety folding table and fisted his hands on his thighs. "I feel awful about this. As much as I hated the idea to begin with, I'd begun to look forward to it."

"We'll find another day." She visualized the schedule with its colour-coded blocks for events, games both home and away, meetings, and more. There had to be a white space big enough to fit it in.

"We can't."

"What do you mean, we *can't*?"

"Brewster made it clear he wants me to concentrate on the team and nothing else as we get into the final weeks. He congratulated me on the wins and says he doesn't want to jeopardize our chances of making the playoffs."

"But he doesn't *want* you to make the playoffs." It was her turn to pace. The room was so small she could only take three steps in each direction. "Does he?"

"I don't know what he wants anymore. Not that he was ever easy to read. But lately I've been getting the impression he's changed his mind about moving the team. Other than this thing with White Spruce, he's been very supportive of all the off-ice events. And even with this, he's making me miss it to do something I've been agitating for since I got here."

"I don't trust him." Of that, Lynn was certain. "He *has* to have an ulterior motive."

Benjamin took out his phone. "I have to go. Practice is starting soon."

She stopped in front of him and laid her palms on his chest. "It's all going to work out."

His smile was half-hopeful, half-pessimistic. "If you say so."

"I do." She pressed a kiss to the corner of his mouth. "We'll talk more later."

Back in her office, she stared fiercely at her computer screen without really seeing it. If only she could figure out what Brewster was up to. She didn't believe he'd given up his secret plan to break his contract and move the team.

An email notification popped up on her screen and she clicked through, eager to escape the hamster wheel of her thoughts.

She read the message and stared.

Benjamin had just taken a bite of sandwich, intending to eat a late lunch at his desk now the morning practice was over, when his office door burst open. Lynn stood in the opening, flushed and triumphant.

"You'll never guess what I just did." She strode forward, planted her palms on his desk, and grinned. "You're going to love it."

The last time she'd said something similar she'd been proposing the White Spruce presentation. He hurriedly chewed and swallowed, the hairs on the back of his neck standing up. "Am I?"

"I need one last big hurrah, something to really push the Canyon Cats attendance over the edge. And what should show up in my email this morning?" She paused expectantly, eyes flashing like blue stars.

"I have no idea. But I'm sure you'll tell me." He willed his pulse to slow. He had to stop expecting the worst all the time.

"Sylvester Armstrong is coming." She wiggled her hips and bopped her shoulders. "Sylvester Armstrong!"

His hovering dread congealed into an icy ball in his lungs, forcing him to breathe shallowly. *Say something. She doesn't know what this means.* "Well done. That's quite the coup." It was. Armstrong would draw huge crowds to any appearance. He'd been voted to attend the all-star game multiple times, held numerous team scoring records, and hadn't been afraid to throw a few punches. Off the ice, he was a respected spokesperson for various charities and endorsed a top-of-the-line sports brand. He was the epitome of Canadian hockey excellence.

He was everything Benjamin wasn't—and had wanted to be.

"I can't believe I got him." Lynn beamed. "He had a cancellation, and I scooped him up under everyone's noses. He's going to do an autograph signing, a public skate, and an appearance of the last home game of the season."

He couldn't throw cold water on her excitement. Not again, not after his reaction to the mental wellness event. He *couldn't*. She chattered on, her words unintelligible through the avalanche of his memories.

Armstrong was his nemesis, the symbol of everything that had gone wrong in his own career. The fact he was oblivious to Benjamin's continued existence only made it worse.

As juniors, they'd been considered near equals, lauded by the media, sought after by scouting staff. They'd been drafted the same year—Armstrong in the first round, Benjamin in the second. Other players would have been thrilled to go that high, but to him, it was the first of many disappointing performances. Two minor injuries didn't help his ice time, and when coupled with an inability to gel with his linemates, the result had been predictable. He'd been traded away at the end of the season. While Armstrong's star rocketed to the stratosphere, his had fizzled and died, sucked into the black hole of mediocrity. He'd been passed from team to team. Unwanted. Unneeded.

"Benjamin?"

He dragged himself back into the present. Lynn stared at him, head cocked to one side, and he scrambled to catch up with the conversation. "That all sounds great. I'm sure it will be a huge success."

"When I looked up his bio, I saw you'd been teammates. I thought this might be a nice surprise." Her voice lilted up at the end.

Bang went the slim hope she hadn't noticed their connection.

The last time he'd been traded he'd ended up on Armstrong's team. By then their roles were firmly entrenched, him on the fourth line—if he played at all— and Armstrong on the first. Toward the end of that season, a hit resulting in the third concussion of his career had placed him on the injured reserve, and he'd finally taken the hint. He'd retired from the major league, vanishing into the wilderness of European hockey.

He'd received no fanfare, no goodbye party, no

special television coverage. His departure hadn't made a ripple. Not like when Armstrong had retired almost fifteen years later after a legendary career.

He clutched his pen, the thin cylinder bending in his grip, and groped for a reply that would deflect her implied question. "I'm amazed you realized. I played for a lot of teams. Do you have them all memorized?"

He'd hoped she'd laugh, but instead her eyes narrowed. "Yes. Was I naive, thinking you might be friends? I imagine it's a job like any other—you like some colleagues and not others."

She was skating dangerously close to the truth, and he couldn't bear to have his pettiness exposed. "We got along fine, but we were teammates for less than a season. It was an honour to share the bench with such a talented player." It took all his concentration to sound professional, not resentful.

Lynn pulled one of his visitor chairs closer, sat, and propped her elbows on his desk. "You don't have a problem with him coming, do you?"

"Of course not. It will be good to catch up." The lie tasted like ash.

Her wrinkled brow smoothed out and the gleam returned to her eye. "Good. I think this will be great, will really punch up the attendance." She bit her lip, and he braced for more unpleasant news. He shuddered to imagine what it could be. "Also, I have a favour to ask."

His jaw ached and he had to loosen muscles he hadn't realized he was clenching in order to speak. "What's up?" *Please don't ask me to host Armstrong.* That would add insult to injury.

"He's going to be in town for three days and two nights, including game night. The first evening he's agreed to have dinner with fans—it will be a contest of some sort, not sure what—and I'll need to chaperone that. I thought maybe you could look after Oscar for me. Stephanie will be out of town for work, and I try to avoid asking Mikayla on school nights. And he really likes you..." She trailed off, her brows raised in a silent appeal.

Cool relief flooded his veins. "I'd love to take care of him." It would serve the double purpose of helping out Lynn and giving him an excuse to avoid Armstrong.

Working with Nishtha at White Spruce during the last few weeks had helped him view his career in a new light. Most great coaches hadn't been superstar players. He needed to take his failures, mistakes, and disappointments and learn from them. Use them to be the coach his team needed.

Having to stand in Sylvester Armstrong's shadow one more time would be just another lesson.

CHAPTER THIRTY

In the weeks leading up to Sylvester Armstrong's appearance, Lynn tried to forget about the frisson of worry that had tickled her spine at Benjamin's reaction. The bleakness she thought she'd seen flash across his face never returned, even when the other man's name was mentioned. As far as she could tell, his attention was fixed on the team and little else.

Yet something didn't feel right. He did nothing she could point to and say *there, that's what I mean.* His nervous excitement when White Spruce agreed to postpone his presentation until the season was over was genuine, and he continued to treat her and Oscar with his usual warmth and kindness. But when he held her in his arms and made love to her, there was a distance between them, a loss of connection and intimacy. No matter how many times she told herself she was imagining things, she couldn't shake it.

Her misgivings returned in full force the evening before Armstrong was due to arrive. As had become habit on non-game nights, she and Benjamin were curled up on her couch watching reruns of a nineties sitcom while Oscar slept down the hall.

Dozing in the cradle of his arm, she said, "Will you come with me to the airport tomorrow, for moral support? I'm feeling a little overawed at finally meeting Armstrong. I've only talked to his manager, never to him. I get the impression he's a bit...difficult."

"No." Under her head, Benjamin's shoulder stiffened. "I don't have time."

"He arrives at eight in the morning. We'll drop him off at the hotel and be at the rink by nine, easy." There were only four games left in the season, and while the Canyon Cats had clawed their way into contention, every game, every point mattered desperately. Benjamin had few free hours, but if he had time to cuddle on the couch, he had time to come with her to the airport.

"Trust me. You don't want me there."

She unwound from her tucked position so she could see his face. "What do you mean? If I didn't want you there, I wouldn't have asked." She was beginning to believe she wanted Benjamin in every aspect of her life, for as long as he'd have her. The idea of going back to the days when he wasn't there to help with Oscar, to make love to her, to watch silly television shows, was— well, it wasn't to be borne.

"I'm sorry, but I can't." He pushed up from the sofa and strode to the large window overlooking the street, his back to her. "You'll be fine. You won't let him intimidate you."

Had he emphasized *you* at each repetition or was she hearing things? "I asked this once before, Benjamin. This time, tell me the truth. Do you have a problem with Armstrong?" She shifted to her knees, sitting on her heels, her weight pressing into the soft cushion.

"It's not him." The floor-length curtains were drawn against the darkness outside and he fidgeted with the edges where the fabric met. "It's me."

She choked back a laugh and earned a glare over his shoulder. "Sorry. You don't mean to be funny. But can you please explain what's going on?"

He was silent so long she thought he wasn't going to answer. Then he sighed and turned to face her, feet shoulder-width distance apart, hands clasped behind his back, like a soldier at ease. But there was no ease in his stance. None at all.

"He had the career I wanted." He spoke through tight lips. "The career I'd dreamed of since I was old enough to lace up skates. I don't blame him. That's just the way it went. But the least amount of time spent having it rubbed in my face, the better."

"Who's going to rub it in your face?" She clambered off the couch, took two long strides, and jabbed him in the chest. "Who? You think I would do that? Armstrong?"

A muscle flexed in his jaw. "No one will *do* anything. It's just the way I'll feel."

"Fine. Get over it."

His expression iced over. "Get over it?"

Apprehension wriggled in her belly. She didn't want to hurt him, but it was time for some tough love. "Stop feeling sorry for yourself. So you didn't have the career you wanted. Sometimes life sucks. But you can either let it keep on sucking or make plans to change its direction."

"You think I feel sorry for *myself*?" His short, brittle laugh held no hint of amusement. Her disquiet grew. "This has nothing to do with me. It has to do with my parents, who I disappointed. With my teammates, who I let down. With my coaches, who I frustrated."

She waggled her fingers in a dismissive gesture, even as her stomach sank at the pain creasing the skin around his eyes. Had she made a mistake with this approach? It was too late to back down now. "Excuses. All of them. You need to take a hard look at yourself. If you're still telling yourself you don't deserve good things because you didn't achieve your teenage goals, you're crazy."

"It's not just that." His eyes darkened, haunted by ghosts she couldn't see. "You don't know the worst of it."

"Then tell me." She softened her tone and laid a

palm on his chest. "Help me understand why you're so hard on yourself. It has nothing to do with Armstrong, not really. Does it?"

He moved away from her touch and scrubbed his hands in his hair. "No. Not really." His gaze flickered to her but settled on a distant point over her shoulder. "I told you my father died of a heart attack. What I didn't tell you is that I was talking on the phone with him when it happened."

"Oh, Benjamin." She stretched out a hand toward him, but he jerked back. "That must have been awful."

"We were talking about my career. I was accusing him of not supporting me, when all he'd done every moment of my life was do exactly that. It was a stupid argument, and if he hadn't died we would have sorted it out and all would have been good. But he did die, and I'll never have that chance. When Brewster offered me the coaching job, I vowed to win the championship. It wouldn't bring my father back, but it would prove to everyone I'd disappointed in the past that I wasn't a washout. And right now, it looks like I'm going to fail at that, too. I guess Armstrong's visit underscored all that."

Her heart cracked at the despair blazing from his expression. "You're not a washout, Benjamin. Failing doesn't mean *you* are a failure. It just means you're human."

"Well, then I'm more human than most."

Her initial irritation returned, only slightly tempered by his confession. How could he not appreciate how much he had to give? "If you can't see what you've accomplished, all the good you've done, no amount of *telling* will fix that. You have to realize it for yourself."

His eyes were dark in his pale face, his lips pressed together in a thin line. "I've got to go."

She wanted to wrap herself around him and not let go until he'd absorbed her belief in him. Instead, she perched on the edge of the couch and twined her fingers together. "Think about what I said, Benjamin. You deserve good things. All you have to do is believe."

Benjamin pushed the treadmill speed up another notch. As coach, he had full access to the team gym whenever he wanted. At this time of night, he had it all to himself. He was alone. Solitary.

"Just the way I like it." His mutter was barely audible over the pounding of his feet.

Sweat slid down the bridge of his nose and he swiped it away with the back of his wrist. He'd come here directly from Lynn's house, needing to release the tension twanging in his muscles. His heart thundered, pulse thrumming in his ears, yet it still wasn't loud enough to drown out her parting words.

She was wrong. *So* wrong. Belief wasn't enough. If that were true, he would have fulfilled his father's dreams years ago. Would have found redemption and forgiveness by now.

Her admonishment to get over it punched like an enforcer's fist deep into his soul. He'd tried. He really had. How could she not have noticed? He felt like he'd turned himself inside out over the last weeks, focusing on the future, on the team, on Lynn and Oscar.

And still it wasn't enough. He was still consumed by his failures.

He punched the velocity higher. His thighs burned, his calves cramped, his lungs heaved. He welcomed the pain.

It was nothing compared to the agony twisting his heart.

He loved Lynn. He wasn't exactly sure when the revelation had come to him, but her challenge tonight had solidified it. She was strong and intelligent, caring and passionate, and the world shone brighter when he was with her. The dark places inside him were vanquished by her light.

He wanted to be the man she deserved. The man she believed him to be. But every time he thought he took a step toward that future, he let his doubts pull him right back.

He set the treadmill to max and ran faster than he ever had before.

Because that's what he was good at. Running away.

The next morning, he slouched on a bench in the dressing room, surrounded by well-dressed Canyon Cats awaiting the arrival of Sylvester Armstrong. Lynn had arranged a private meet and greet for the players before the public events began. The babble of chatter flowing around him held an edge of excitement, and even Nechayev and his cronies appeared less cynical than usual. Since their suspension after New Year's, he'd had little to complain about regarding their performance on the ice, but he suspected they'd simply become more adept at hiding their attitude.

He stretched his neck and winced. Every muscle in his body throbbed. Even his fingertips pulsed with pain. Resting his elbows on his knees took some of the strain off his back, but it wasn't only the punishment he'd inflicted with the treadmill that caused the aches. Wondering whether his actions last night had been the last straw for Lynn clawed at him, sawed at his breath as if the air was laden with razor blades.

He wanted another chance. *Needed* another chance. And that meant talking to her. But he couldn't do it today. She'd be too busy with Armstrong. Then Friday and Saturday were game days, and it would be his turn to be too busy. It would have to wait until Sunday.

The door swung open. All conversation stopped.

Lynn walked in and his vision dimmed. Except for her. It was as if she stood in a spotlight, her wheat-coloured hair gleaming golden, the blue scarf draped over the shoulders of her close-fitting tan coat the same pale tint as her eyes.

Eyes that searched the room before locking with his, spearing him with their directness.

He realized he was standing, had even taken a step toward her, and forced himself to remain where he was. A frown creased the delicate skin between her brows.

Cheers and clapping shocked him from his trance. The players' shrill whistles, hoots, and hollers heralded the arrival of the guest of honour. He was ushered in by Brewster and stood beside Lynn, nodding and smiling and waving, accepting the accolades as his due.

He hadn't seen Armstrong in person since the last day Benjamin had played in the national league. He wasn't as tall as he remembered and the buttons of his suit, revealed by his unfastened overcoat, strained slightly over his belly. When he retired, he'd apparently abandoned the strict regimen necessary to stay at the top of his game. Much like his hair had abandoned the top of his head.

Petty satisfaction flushed Benjamin, and he let himself enjoy it. He'd take what he could get.

CHAPTER THIRTY-ONE

Lynn's worries about Sylvester Armstrong's sense of entitlement were unfounded. He was blunt and forthright and knew what he wanted and needed. But he was also polite and professional.

The lack of drama with her celebrity guest only gave her time to stew over the ongoing drama with her recalcitrant lover.

She hated being wrong, but she had to admit she'd handled Benjamin badly, underestimating his deeply ingrained belief in his own failures. While she tended to gloss over her mistakes, move on as quickly as possible, he obviously felt his own errors more profoundly, even obsessed over them.

Well, this was one mistake she wouldn't ignore. She needed to talk to him as soon as she found the time.

She stood beside Brewster and watched Armstrong charm the young players. He regaled them with stories of his triumphs while modestly including anecdotes of when things didn't go as planned. His patter was practiced and polished and she had to respect his skill.

After the first searing glance they'd shared, Benjamin had kept his attention on their guest, his expression noncommittal and detached. On the other hand, her own gaze constantly made its way toward him. Never once did she catch him looking at her.

Frustrating, irritating, bullheaded man.

After Armstrong finished his casual but prepared speech, he circled the room, speaking to each player individually. This wasn't the appropriate place to have a discussion with Benjamin, and he appeared to want her to keep her distance, but she should at least say hello. Maybe she could show him without words that things weren't over, that she wanted to fix what was broken.

And maybe he'd ignore her. She'd hurt him badly, and he didn't look ready to talk.

As she dithered, Brewster called across the room. "Benny. Can I see you for a minute?" He jerked a thumb over his shoulder, indicating the hall outside.

He wound his way through the loose scrum of players. "Of course." Without a glance at Lynn, he preceded Brewster out the door. It closed behind them with a note of finality.

"Can we go to your office?" Brewster didn't wait for a reply but headed to the room two doors down the corridor.

Benjamin followed. It was a relief to be away from Lynn's penetrating gaze, but it was rarely a good thing when Brewster wanted to chat. "What's going on?"

Brewster waved him in and shut the door behind them. "We won't be going public with this until the regular season ends, so keep mum. But you need to know now."

The room shrank. Benjamin heaved air into his lungs, let it out slowly. "Know what?"

"I've sold the Canyon Cats. The league still needs to approve the deal, but it's done. Next season the team will be in Woodbury, Minnesota."

Benjamin reached behind him, found the edge of his desk, and lowered himself onto it. "You sold the team?"

Brewster nodded. "I had a different plan at the start of the season, but then this offer came along."

By *different plan* Benjamin assumed he meant *sabotage the team to lower attendance so I could move it*. His molars ground together, and he pressed his lips tight. Confronting Brewster about that now was pointless. This news went a long way to explaining his change of heart a few weeks ago. He would have wanted them to succeed in order to get the best price he could.

Benjamin couldn't regret the wins. Every point had kept his dream of reaching the championships alive. His mouth was so dry he had to work saliva into it before he could speak. "What about the staff? What happens to us?" Levi may have been a thorn in his side all season, but that didn't mean he wanted to see the man lose his job. And unlike Avril and Ryan, who were only in Prince George because of their careers, he'd been born and raised in the town. It was his home, the Canyon Cats his passion.

"That's what I want to talk to you about, Benny." Brewster crossed his arms over his wide chest. "The new owners are open to keeping you on. Say they've been impressed with what they've seen so far."

Not even Brewster's use of the hated *Benny* could distract him from the import of his words. *You*. Not Avril or Levi or Ryan. Just Benjamin. Instead of relief, all he felt was the heavy weight of guilt sinking lower on his shoulders, followed immediately by an even more breathtaking conclusion.

This was exactly what Lynn had worried about—that his career would tear them apart. That he would have to make the choice between her and Oscar and proving himself as a coach.

Was this a sign? Did this opportunity, coming so close on the heels of her challenge, signal he wasn't meant to be with Lynn? With Oscar?

He wanted to vomit.

"Don't think it's in the bag, though." Brewster's gruff voice pulled him back from the whirling pool of doubt and confusion. "They want results before they start any discussions."

Results could only mean one thing. He clutched the

knot of his tie and wiggled it, trying to ease the tightness in his throat. "If we don't make the playoffs, I don't get the job."

"It's not quite that simple, but in general, yes. Also, they want to meet you. Tonight."

The shocks were coming hard and fast. Benjamin blinked away dizziness. "Tonight? They're in town?"

"Two of them. It's a consortium, but the major shareholders are here. Dinner tonight, and of course they'll be in the owner's suite tomorrow and Saturday."

"I have plans." He couldn't let Lynn down. She'd hate him enough once she learned of the sale.

"Change them. But remember, this is all confidential until we make the announcement." Brewster pulled open the door. "You have a chance to keep your job, Benny. Don't screw it up."

Lynn glanced at the clock on her phone. Brewster and Benjamin had been gone for several minutes but she couldn't wait for them any longer. It was time to get Armstrong to his next event.

"Excuse me." She tapped the elbow of the player in front of her. Her head barely reached his shoulder, but when he looked at her his chin was covered in pale fuzz, his cheeks rounded with youth. God, they were just babies. "It's time for Mr. Armstrong to go."

Obligingly, he nudged the player next to him and a way opened to the centre of the circle. Armstrong nodded at her approach and wrapped up whatever he'd been saying.

"It's been great to meet you all." He clapped shoulders and shook hands as he wound through the throng, moving with purpose but no obvious haste. "I'll be watching from the stands tomorrow night, wishing I was out there with you."

Moments later they were in the corridor under the bleachers. He plucked his phone from the inside pocket of his suit and flicked his thumb over the screen. "The Rotary luncheon is next, right?"

"Yes. Then the public skate followed by an autograph session." Everything was laid out in a precise schedule that allowed for the bare minimum of delays. "At seven the winning bidder will meet you for dinner." Armstrong had allowed himself to be auctioned off as a fundraiser for the local hospital.

"You're coming along, right?" His dimples popped, the silver in his faint scruff of a beard glinting. "Not that I'm afraid to be alone with fans, but conversation can be a little stilted until they realize I put my pants on one leg at a time just like they do."

"Of course. That was the deal." She wasn't immune to his charm, but preferred Benjamin's true modesty to Armstrong's practiced humbleness. Mind you, Benjamin's modesty also irritated the hell out of her, and not only because he couldn't see the good in himself, the good that was so obvious to her.

She needed to apologize for last night. She'd been wrong to challenge him as she had. He needed support, not criticism. It would take time and privacy, though, and that would be in short supply over the next few days.

"Great." Armstrong's eyes flickered to her feet and back up again. It was by no means a leer, but it certainly conveyed masculine appreciation. "I'm looking forward to it."

Behind him, the door to the head coach's office opened. Brewster appeared, followed by Benjamin. Lynn rocked forward but halted with one foot in the air when his gaze met hers only for an instant before skittering away. His tie was slightly askew and if anything, he looked more tense and brittle than he had in the dressing room.

What had Brewster done now? She *knew* he was still up to no good, evidence of the last weeks to the contrary.

"It was an honour to meet you, Sylvester." Brewster's voice boomed off the concrete walls and floor. He held out his hand and Armstrong shook it. "I'll see you tomorrow night at the game. As my guest, of course."

Benjamin halted at Lynn's side. He kept his back to the other men and spoke quietly, still not looking at her directly. "I have bad news."

"I got that impression." She checked to make sure Armstrong and Brewster were engaged with each other and not paying attention. "What's going on?"

"I can't look after Oscar tonight."

That was so far from what she'd been expecting that she blinked in confusion. "What?"

"I have to meet some people. It has to do with the team, but I can't say anything more. Not yet. I have to go to this meeting. I'm sorry."

"You promised." She scrambled to think of an alternate caregiver. "You *promised*."

"I know." He hunched his shoulders and dipped his head. "I wouldn't break it if it wasn't important."

More important than Oscar. More important than her. It might be a mild example of what she'd feared all along, but it was still crushing. "Who are these people?" He made a dampening motion with his hand and her temper flared. "Don't you shush me."

He shot a worried glance at Brewster. "I can't tell you. I'm truly sorry."

"Lynn?"

Biting back the retort burning her tongue, she drew a calming breath and turned to Armstrong in time to see Brewster disappearing at the end of the hall. She hadn't heard him leave. "Yes?"

"We're going to be late." He frowned, tapping his phone against his palm.

"I'll be right there." She faced Benjamin. His expression was pinched and tight, but his dismay was worthless to her. "Fine. I'll deal with it. I've got to go."

CHAPTER THIRTY-TWO

Lynn sat in a sea of suits—pants, pinstripe, and skirts—and fumed. Armstrong stood at a podium on a low dais at the front of the hotel banquet room and did his spiel for the second time that day. It wasn't the same speech he'd given the boys in the locker room, but it was familiar enough that it didn't hold her attention.

To be fair, she wasn't sure anything could at the moment. Hurt and disappointment warred inside her.

And not just because Benjamin had let her down. Because she had let herself forget what they had was only temporary. He hadn't hidden how important his career was to him, but she'd ignored all the signs that, when push came to shove, he would choose it over her and Oscar.

Rolling laughter rippled through the audience. Armstrong was a pro, telling the same stories she'd heard this morning from a new angle, one that would resonate with the business managers and owners who had paid to attend this Rotary luncheon.

She took a bite of roast beef and stabbed a steamed asparagus spear but left the Yorkshire pudding alone. Why couldn't they serve salads at these events? It was only midday. If she ate the whole heavy meal, she'd be asleep by two.

Her phone vibrated, the screen lighting up. Smiling apologetically at the heavy-jowled businessman sitting on her right, she lowered it to her lap and read the text from Makayla.

Sorry, Lynn. I've got basketball tonight. Do you want me to ask my friends?

She'd had little hope the teen would be available on a school night at such short notice, but with Stephanie out of town she had few options. And while she appreciated Mikayla's offer, she'd rather not leave Oscar with a complete stranger if she could help it.

She tapped back. *Let me try someone else first. I'll get back to you.*

Applause broke out and she rose along with everyone else to join the standing ovation for Armstrong. She was pleased the crowd was so appreciative, but did he really deserve such an accolade? It wasn't like he'd won the Nobel Peace Prize or cured cancer.

Damn Benjamin for making her so cranky.

Armstrong took the seat on her left and nodded complacently as the others at the table added their personal thanks. She lifted a hand to touch his arm and then drew it back. While she didn't mind his casual flirting, she didn't want to give the wrong impression, either. The motion did its job by catching his attention. He lifted an eyebrow.

"I have to make a quick call." She waggled her phone. "I'll be right back."

"And I'll be right here. Waiting for you." The innuendo was light yet unmistakable. She would have to tread a fine line between encouraging him and pissing him off.

Ah, the perils of the modern career woman.

Winding her way through the tables she nodded and waved at several acquaintances without stopping to chat. In the wide hall outside the banquet room, she found a quiet corner and searched her contact list for Helen Mansfield.

The matriarch of the Silverberry Book Club answered after two rings. "Lynn! How are you? We missed you at the last meeting."

"I'm sorry. I've been a bad Silverberry this year." What with working so many evenings, not wanting to leave Oscar when she did have a free night, and spending time with Benjamin, she had only attended one club meeting since December. Which was partly why her as-yet-unvoiced request made her feel like she was taking advantage of Helen.

"There's no such thing. You know what I say, once a Silverberry, always a Silverberry. Are you coming Tuesday? We're painting Ukrainian Easter eggs."

"That sounds great." Not the painting part—Lynn was all thumbs when it came to detailed art—but the getting together with her friends part. As much as she cared for Benjamin—even her current disenchantment wouldn't allow her to deny that—he owed her nothing. Today had been a rude wake-up call, a painful reminder of the temporary nature of their relationship. She needed to spend more time with those who truly had her back.

The door behind her opened and a pair of suited men strode out. The luncheon was breaking up. "I have a favour to ask. I need a sitter for Oscar. Tonight. I know it's last minute, but I have a business dinner I can't miss, and my arrangement fell through."

"You know I'd love to take him. But what about Benjamin?" Helen had met him once more since the Christmas party, when he'd picked Lynn up at the January book club meeting—learning how to throw pottery with a local guild—after she'd had one too many of Helen's Red Shoe Martinis.

"He was my arrangement. He bailed on me."

"I'm sure he had a good reason."

"All he said was he had to meet some people and it was important." A wriggle of worry wormed its way past the sting of his rejection. He'd never been secretive before. What was going on?

This time when the doors swung wide, they stayed

open as a stream of well-dressed men and women filed out. She had to get back to Armstrong. "Can you come to my house, or should I bring him to you? I need to be free by six forty-five."

"Nathan and I will come there. It is okay if he comes, too, right?"

"Of course. You're not some randy teenagers I have to worry about making out on my couch."

Helen's raunchy laugh rang out. "We may not be teenagers, but we haven't forgotten what making out is. But don't worry. We'll behave. See you later."

The potential purchasers of the Canyon Cats were pleasant, personable men. One owned the largest car dealership in Woodbury, the other an agricultural equipment franchise that had locations across Minnesota. The others in the consortium were not quite as rich but well off enough to risk investing in a junior hockey team.

Benjamin learned all this during the dinner Brewster had insisted he attend. He nodded and smiled and made appropriately agreeable noises while wondering what the hell had been so important he'd had to break his commitment to Lynn. Nothing that had been discussed couldn't have waited a few hours. While he understood the power of networking, it hadn't been worth letting her down.

By the time Brewster drove the four of them back to the hotel, he was exhausted from making nice and wanted nothing more than the quiet sanctuary of his own apartment. But when one of the men suggested a nightcap in the hotel bar, Brewster—who had picked Benjamin up and was his planned ride home—thought it was a fabulous idea. Benjamin had no choice but to follow them into the lobby.

As the automatic doors wheezed wide, Lynn and Armstrong stepped out of the romantically lit restaurant tucked behind the reception desk. Benjamin's step faltered and he hurried to rejoin the other men, who paused in the middle of the large space. Brewster was talking, though his words were unintelligible through the buzz of awareness humming in his ears.

Lynn wore a silvery blue dress that hugged her hips and dipped between her breasts. High heeled shoes emphasized the curve of her calves, her tan coat was draped over her arm, and her rich blonde hair, piled on top of her head, revealed the soft skin of her nape. His fingers itched to touch her there, to trail his tongue behind her ear where dangling earrings sparkled and flashed.

His hands curled into fists when Armstrong leaned in, his lips almost brushing her cheek. Whatever he said made her laugh, her chin lifting. The warm, sensual sound rolled across the lobby and set fire to something raw and primitive inside him.

Lynn was *his*. The sight of her with another man crystallized his scattered thoughts. His career was in flux and his life a mess, but in that instant it didn't matter. It was time to fight for what he wanted.

And he wanted Lynn.

"Excuse me." He ignored Brewster's raised eyebrow at his interruption. "There's someone I need to talk to. It was great meeting you." He offered his hand to the two out-of-towners then to Brewster. "Thanks for the meal. I'll find my own way home."

He'd never been one for confrontation but, as he stalked across the shiny tile floor, he realized he was looking forward to this one. If he and Lynn broke up, now or sometime in the future, it would be because of something he had done. Not something he had avoided.

"Hello, Lynn. Armstrong."

She swung around, earrings swaying, eyes widening. "Benjamin. What are you doing here?"

He dropped his arm over her shoulders and stared

at Armstrong. "Enjoying your time in Prince George?" *You might have had dinner with her, but she's not available for anything else.*

"I am, yes." His gaze slipped from Benjamin to Lynn and back again, his lips pressed tight at the corners, understanding dawning.

That's right. Get the message. He snugged Lynn closer. "It's a great hockey city."

A wry grin lightened Armstrong expression and he shrugged as if to say *can't blame me for trying.* "Well, I should hit the sack. We have another busy day tomorrow." In a gesture that made the hackles on Benjamin's neck rise, a move that had to be for that reason only, he drew Lynn's hand to his lips and kissed her knuckles. "I'll see you tomorrow. Goodnight, Lynn."

Armstrong strode away and Lynn stared after him, the back of her hand damp from his kiss.

"What did I miss?" She narrowed her eyes at Benjamin. "And whatever it was, what right did you have to do it?"

He stepped away from her, lifted her hand, and rubbed the sleeve of his coat on her knuckles as if eradicating Armstrong's caress. She'd felt nothing at that charming yet ironic gesture, but her belly fluttered at the hot look in Benjamin's eyes, the firm clasp of his hand.

"Can we talk?" He tugged her into a sheltered alcove, shielded from the main lobby area by two huge ferns in tall urns.

She jerked her hand free and planted her fists on her hips. "Oh, *now* you want to talk."

"I'm going to tell you something I'm not supposed to." He glanced over his shoulder, and she leaned sideways to follow his line of sight. "See those two men with Brewster?"

She caught a glimpse just before they vanished into

the bar on the opposite side of the lobby from the restaurant. "Barely."

"They're the new owners of the Canyon Cats. Or will be soon."

She gaped, and then shut her teeth with a click that rattled her brain. "They're what?"

"It's going to be announced at a media conference at the end of the regular season. But you have to keep it under wraps until then."

"Of course." Questions and comments fought for attention, her mind whirling. "So that's why Brewster was so agreeable all of a sudden. He was selling the team."

"Yes."

"This is great news." Excitement bubbled. "Brewster obviously wanted out. New owners will bring new blood to the team, breathe life into it. I can't wait for Cynthie to find out."

"You don't understand." Benjamin's tone was grim. "The new owners are from Minnesota. The team is moving, Lynn. And they want me to go with them."

CHAPTER THIRTY-THREE

Behind the lightly applied blush on her cheeks, Lynn paled. Her mouth opened and closed and the muscles in her neck flexed as she swallowed. Benjamin waited, poised on the balls of his toes, ready to take a punch.

"Move? To Minnesota?"

He nodded, his neck stiff with tension. "Yes."

"And they want you to go with the team." Her tone was flat. It wasn't a question.

"Maybe. That's not a done deal yet. They want to see how the last few games go." He'd done it. He was all in. The decision to stick it out, to see how things went between them was with Lynn now. No more hiding, no more avoidance.

"And you want to go with them." Again, it wasn't a question.

"If the Canyon Cats leave town, there's nothing for me here." He was talking about his career, but even as he said the words he realized he wanted her to say that *she* would be here for him. She and Oscar.

She recoiled, her chin lifting, her arms crossing in self-defence, and a glassy sheen flooded her eyes.

A different interpretation of his words blazed across his mind. "I didn't mean it like that!" His breath scraped in his chest. "Lynn. I wasn't dismissing you and Oscar—"

"It's okay." She unfolded the coat from her arm, plunged a hand toward the sleeve, and missed. He

239

reached for the collar to help hold it and she swung away from him. "Really, it's okay. We knew this day would come, right? It was only a matter of time."

"No." He had no idea what he was denying, but it was the only syllable his brain could conjure up. *I love you* made it as far as the tip of his tongue but disintegrated at her look of distress.

She managed to get one sleeve in place and twisted her other arm to get to the other. "When did you say they were announcing?"

He answered by rote, his lips numb. "When the regular season is over." After the two games this weekend, there was a home-and-home series against their nearest rival the next. "Probably a week from Monday."

"You'd think they'd wait until after the playoffs. Why disrupt the team while they're in the post-season?"

Her tone was calm, professional, but she spoke through gritted teeth and a tendon flexed in her jaw. She buttoned her coat with short, fierce twists of the shiny brown disks.

"I guess they don't think we'll make the playoffs." At the moment, he didn't care about the very real chance he would fail in his goal to make the championships and rewrite history while honouring his father. All he could think of was how he'd hurt Lynn with his careless words.

"I've got to get home." She shoved her hands in the pockets of her coat and pulled out her keys and phone.

"Wait." He side-stepped to prevent her from leaving, his hands hovering midair. She folded her arms and huddled into herself. It as good as shouted *don't touch me.* "I'm sorry. I really screwed this up. Can I go with you so we can talk? We need to figure out what this means to us."

"Us? How can there be an *us* if you're leaving town?" Her voice wavered, the evidence of her pain a thousand cuts to his soul. "My life is here. Oscar's life is here. If you go to Minnesota..." Her shoulders rose and fell helplessly.

"I told you, that's not a done deal." His desperation had him repeating himself.

She met his gaze. Like the slow fading of lights in a theatre, her expression dimmed. The lines at the corners of her eyes and mouth, the lines he rarely noticed, deepened. Her hand cupped his jaw gently, her thumb rubbing the short bristles on his chin. "Goodbye, Benjamin."

She swept past and he could do nothing but watch her leave, her touch burning like a brand on his skin.

Lynn pulled to a stop in her driveway but left the ignition running. She needed a minute before facing Helen and Nathan.

Her hands gripped the steering wheel at its apex, and she lowered her forehead onto them, suddenly too tired to stay upright.

Benjamin was leaving.

What a time to realize she loved the jerk.

Tears prickled and she sniffed. She'd been such an idiot. She thought she'd been safe, because that's how Benjamin felt. Safe and comfortable and easy to be with. Oh, there was heat in the bedroom, heat that hadn't waned in their weeks together. But she'd thought that, because she wasn't obsessing over him all the time, she wasn't in love. Because wasn't that what falling in love was? A burning, awkward feeling that nothing was right in your world unless you were with that person? While she'd missed him during his frequent road trips, she hadn't pined for him, spent sleepless nights yearning for his return.

What a time to realize the difference between infatuation and love.

Her experience with Lance had also taught her confusing lessons. She'd thought she'd loved him—why else would she have planned to marry him, have children with him? When he'd left, she'd been angry that he'd ruined her plans, her life's agenda. But it hadn't taken her long to adjust her expectations, to achieve her dream of being a mother in a different way.

What a time to realize she'd never been heartbroken.

Because she hadn't experienced this soul-tearing black hole of emotion before. It was as if all her vitality, her joy, her *self* had been sucked into nothingness. All that angst she thought she'd managed to avoid had come home to roost with a vengeance.

The curtains twitched. Helen or Nathan must have heard her arrival and wondered what was keeping her. She turned the key and climbed out, her bones aching as if she'd been body-slammed by a professional wrestler.

She didn't have the luxury of wallowing in her misery. She had a full day with Armstrong tomorrow, though she didn't have to attend the game tomorrow night since Brewster was playing host from dinner on. Once she'd brought her celebrity guest to the airport Saturday morning, she'd quarantine herself and Oscar in the house and focus on their new future.

Her and her son. Just the two of them against the world.

Friday's game was a disaster on so many levels.

Not only did the Canyon Cats lose—and badly—but that loss was a direct result of two coaching errors that could be laid at Benjamin's feet. His mind hadn't been with the team, but at home with Lynn.

He should have been more depressed about the results, given his future as a coach depended on these next few games and that every loss kept him a step further from his redemption. But misery over the colossal mistake he had made off the ice left no room to worry about those he made on it.

Aware of Levi standing just behind his shoulder, ready to pounce, he addressed the morose players in the dressing room.

"I owe you an apology." A couple of heads lifted but most avoided looking his direction, focusing on unlacing skates and unbuckling equipment. "My head wasn't in this game, and I screwed up."

A few sideways glances. Levi's aura grew even more disapproving. He'd think this was yet another show of weakness, but it had to be done. Avril and Ryan, waiting in his office for the post-game conference, would hear a repeat of this apology as soon as he saw them. If he expected his players and staff to own their mistakes, he had to do the same.

"We can still make the playoffs. The Wolverines lost tonight, too, but we can't depend on them to clear our route. We can't afford any more losses." He wasn't telling them anything they didn't know, and he could feel their attention drift. "So, we won't lose. I won't allow it."

That drew a few more glances. He waited, silently urging them to be open, to be receptive. Maybe Lynn was right. Maybe the first step to achieving a goal was believing to the marrow of your bones you could do it.

"How are you going to do that?" For once, Nechayev sounded curious, not condemning.

"I believe in you. In all of you. I need you to believe in me." He had all eyes now. "I'll learn from tonight's mistakes and not repeat them. Losing isn't an option. So, we won't do it."

A tap in the adjoining shower room dripped, clearly audible in the silent room. Expressions ranged from doubt to speculation, hope to confusion. But he had them thinking, and that's what he wanted.

He nodded. "See you tomorrow."

Levi followed him into the hall. "You think telling them to believe is all you need to do to make them win?"

He stopped and faced the older man. "We've had our differences during the season, but I've never once thought you weren't a good coach. You understand the players, know the systems, work hard. But belief is something you can't teach. You have to feel it. And if any of us"—he narrowed his eyes to make sure Levi understood he was included in that—"don't believe right down to our toes that we can win, we won't."

"You know the odds—"

He held up a hand. "Believe, Levi. I meant it. Losing isn't an option. So, we won't."

He'd already lost Lynn. He wouldn't lose this, too. It was all he had left.

CHAPTER THIRTY-FOUR

Lynn spent a miserable weekend pretending everything was just fine. Stephanie was back from her work trip, and she joined her and Oscar for dinner on Saturday and a trip to the pool on Sunday afternoon. And if she cried herself to sleep each night, curled into a ball to muffle the sound, no one knew but her.

She'd felt a spurt of vicious glee when the Canyon Cats lost on Friday. Benjamin didn't deserve to win, not after he'd been such a jerk. But she couldn't hold onto her righteous anger, and when the team won on Saturday, she'd been reluctantly pleased.

As much as she wanted to hate him, choosing to focus on his career didn't make him a bad man. He wasn't like her father—tossing aside everyone else's wants and needs for his own selfish reasons. And he was nothing like Lance—who had promised to marry her and then vanished with scarcely a look back. Benjamin didn't owe her anything—not stability, not a future, not love. They'd had great sex and enjoyed each other's company and that was it. If she'd been foolish and fallen in love with a man whose life was destined to take him away from her and Oscar, that was her own fault.

Their short-lived romance was over. It was time to revise and rework her plans. Again. As soon as she had the energy.

She took refuge at her desk on Monday and Tuesday, entering and exiting the office by the exterior door to lessen the chances of running into Benjamin. She didn't think she could keep up her facade of everything's fine if she came face to face with him. Neither Sarah nor Cynthie commented on her wan complexion or occasionally red-rimmed eyes. Cynthie was thrilled at the success of Sylvester Armstrong's visit, which had pushed their attendance levels to a record high for the season. She crowed over the fact Brewster wouldn't be able to break his contract, and Lynn had to pretend to share in her excitement. The sale wouldn't be announced for several days yet, and no matter how wounded she felt, she wouldn't betray Benjamin by telling the secret he'd shared.

Between the stress at work and not sleeping at night, she was exhausted by Tuesday evening. The Silverberries were meeting at a local art studio to try their hand at painting Ukrainian Easter eggs, and as much as she wanted to crawl under the covers and hide in the dark, she forced herself to stick with the plan. Leaving Oscar in Makayla's capable hands, she allowed Stephanie to chauffeur her downtown. She was so weary in both body and mind she dozed off for a moment or two on the way, but if Stephanie noticed she made no comment.

The studio was in a converted warehouse with breeze block walls painted white and blindingly bright lights hanging over stained and scarred tables. The other Silverberries had gathered in a far corner and Helen waved them over with a wide grin. Nathan was by her side as usual, with Penta, Natalie, and Terrance seated at the barstools ranged around the tall table.

She did her best to keep up her side of the conversation, asking Penta how her children were and discussing the local political scene with Natalie and Terrance. It was a relief when the instructor called for everyone's attention.

Focusing on directions required too much effort and she hoped the others were paying attention. When everyone reached into a bowl set in the middle of the table, she did so too. After choosing a hollowed-out egg and picking up a sharpened pencil, she stared at the smooth white surface, her mind as blank as the shell.

Stephanie spoke, her words camouflaged by the chatter and laughter of the other Silverberries. "Any time you want to go home, just let me know. We'll make up an excuse."

Apparently, Lynn hadn't been hiding her distress quite as well as she'd thought. "No. It's okay. This will be fun."

Benjamin had become a fixture around the house, especially on Sunday afternoons, and Lynn had had to tell Stephanie something when he hadn't shown up last weekend. But she'd kept it to the bare bones—that Benjamin had a job opportunity in another city and that Lynn had decided it was best if they didn't see each other anymore. Given the fact that he hadn't tried to contact her once since Thursday night, it was obvious he had decided the same thing.

She drew a faint line around the egg's equator, and then another from the pointier tip, under the base, and back up again. There. She'd made a start. That was all she needed in life, too. A new start.

"Peter asked me to marry him."

Stephanie's voice was so quiet Lynn didn't think she'd heard correctly. "He what?"

She shot her a glance but didn't repeat herself. With a quick look around the table to make sure everyone else was engrossed in their work, Lynn leaned in and spoke just as quietly. "What did you say?"

Stephanie's expression was bleak. "I said no." She dipped the tiny stylus they'd each been given in the beeswax and held it over the flame, and then traced one of the pencil lines she'd drawn on her own egg. "I like him. A lot. But I'm not ready for that kind of commitment. He's the first man I've dated since my surgery, and we've only known each other a few months."

"Well, aren't we a pair." Lynn blew out a long breath and drew a star inside one of the quarters she'd marked off on her egg.

"It's different for you." Stephanie concentrated on her work. "As much as I enjoy Peter's company, I always felt something was missing. But with you and Benjamin…I thought you were pretty special together."

"Not special enough to stop him from putting his career first." Lynn was shocked at the bitterness in her voice and strove to speak reasonably. "It's not like we had an understanding, had ever talked about the future. I don't blame him for looking out for himself."

"Are you sure about that?" Stephanie lowered her egg into a jar of bright yellow dye and sat back on her stool, wiping her fingers. "You don't sound like it. And if you didn't talk about the future, how could he know what your expectations were?"

Lynn frowned as she finished the last star on the simple pattern she'd drawn. "We'd only been together a few months. Why would we have talked about the future?"

Stephanie's chuckle was tinged with sadness. "You're a planner, Lynn. We all know that. You would have been outlining your next steps from the day you met Benjamin."

"I certainly did not." Was that how her friends saw her—staid and strict and structured? "For once in my life I was going with the flow, seeing how things went. And look where that got me." She held her stylus over the flame, dipped it in the beeswax, held it over the flame again and began tracing the pencil lines on her egg.

"I watched you with Benjamin. You were so good together, so good for each other. You love him, don't you?"

Her lip trembled, the truth ready to spill out. "I don't want to. He's the wrong man for me. If it's not this job, it will be another one in another city. And then another. That's the nature of the business. I don't want that for myself, or for Oscar."

"You're scared. I get that." Stephanie knew all too well the terrors that transitions wrought. "But are you scared of change—or scared of love?"

Jujhar shuffled sideways on the scarred wooden bench, making room for Benjamin as he stepped off the ice and through the gate at the end of his shift. "Nice shot, man. My dog could have stopped that one."

Normally the good-natured teasing would have slipped off his back like oil on water. But everything stung a little harder these days. "Oh, shut up."

He'd been looking forward to the drop-in recreational game, eager to release some of the restlessness coursing through him. Though body contact wasn't encouraged, the flow of the game allowed for scrums in the corner and shoving in front of the net. Between that and the exertion of skating he was hoping he'd get his first good night's sleep in a week.

An offside pass drew a whistle and he and Jujhar headed back onto the ice. The scrape of his blades on the slick surface, the heft of his stick in his gloved hands, even the bulk of his equipment under his logo-less jersey were ingrained so deeply into his soul he couldn't imagine a life without them.

But if he wanted to have Lynn, the odd beer-league game might be all he'd have left.

The idea wasn't as terrifying today as it had been a month ago.

Back on the bench a minute later, Jujhar squirted water into his mouth, his shoulders heaving. Despite his regular workouts with the Canyon Cats, Benjamin's heart thundered along with the rise and fall of his lungs.

What Jujhar said next did nothing to calm him. "You know I wouldn't ask you this, man, but Sadie is pestering me. She wants to know how things are going with Lynn."

The play swept past the benches, shouts for a pass and cheery profanities ringing to the heavy metal rafters above. The last thing he wanted to do was answer, but Jujhar's elbow in the ribs told him he wouldn't get away with simply ignoring his friend.

"It's not." He pulled off his glove, shook his hand to ease his cramped fingers, and put it back on. "She broke up with me."

"When?"

"A week ago tomorrow." He knew it down to the days, hours, and minutes but didn't want to sound any more pathetic than he did already.

"What did you do?" A whistle and boisterous cheers signalled a goal. "Hold that thought. Time to redeem our team."

Two shifts later, after Jujhar had scored a sweet one-timer off Benjamin's cross-ice pass, he picked up the conversation. "So, how'd you screw up?"

He resisted the urge to squirm. Sweat dripped into his eyes and he used his forearm to wipe it away. "I said something stupid."

"That's a given, bud. What exactly did you say?" Beads of moisture clung to Jujhar's beard. He squeezed it out like a dishrag.

"I may have given her the impression I was leaving town for a new job because she and Oscar weren't important to me."

Jujhar stared. "Yeah, that would do it."

"I didn't mean it. The words came out wrong and she wouldn't let me explain. Not that I blame her. I would have been too pissed to listen, too." They shifted down the bench to make room for other players coming off the rink. The stench of well-used gear battled for supremacy over the crisp freshness of the ice. Less than a minute remained in the game, and he doubted he and Jujhar would have time for another shift. "You know the stupidest thing? I don't even know if I want to coach anymore."

"Really?" Jujhar's dark eyes met his through the double screen of their visors. "I thought you loved coaching."

"I love the game, love working with the kids. But I just kind of fell into it. It was what ex-players did, you know." He'd had no idea of the politics involved. Thinking about the stress of Brewster's sabotage and then the sale of the team made his gut clench. "Am I too old to go back to school?"

The third period buzzer sounded. The teams lined up for handshakes and then headed to the dressing rooms. No fancy lockers for recreational players—just wooden benches and rusty hooks. He and Jujhar took the spaces reserved by their equipment bags and bent to unlace their skates.

Jujhar resumed the conversation. "School, huh? And take what?"

"Psychology?" Hearing how his voice lilted up at the end, he cleared his throat and tried again. "Psychology. I'm thinking of becoming a counsellor. Like coaching, but not." He had Lynn to thank for this new vision of his future. As terrified as he'd been when she'd first suggested the mental wellness presentation, working with the staff at White Spruce, even his brief interaction with Lee, had reminded him how important a therapist's role could be, and the thought of becoming one had stuck like a burr in his mind.

Jujhar whistled. "That's quite the commitment. How long would it take?"

"A while. I'd need a B.A. first, then decide what track to follow." Setting his skates to the side he pulled off his damp socks and rubbed his feet dry with a towel, and then yanked his jersey over his head and unbuckled his elbow pads.

"You could go to the university here."

"I know." It would take him several years to become

qualified. The cost wasn't an issue—he had a nice little nest egg from his time in the national league. His salary had been tiny compared to most players, but generous nonetheless, and he'd had an excellent financial advisor. But was he ready to invest so much time into such a dramatic change at his age? He'd be in his forties before he could start practicing.

All his adult life he'd been waiting for things to fall into his lap, taking the good with the bad, coasting with the tide. If he decided to do this, it would be on him. He wouldn't be able to blame it on anyone or anything else.

He'd wasted enough opportunities. He couldn't let any more go by.

With or without Lynn, he was going to build a new life, right here in Prince George. He'd keep connecting with his mother, with Jujhar and his family, make new friends. And maybe someday, when he'd shown Lynn he was serious about growing roots, she might talk to him again.

He had two things left to do before he could put any of those plans in motion, however. Drag the Canyon Cats into the playoffs and then make a run at the championship. Not for his dad, not for his past, but for the players who had put their heart and soul into the team, for the fans.

For himself.

CHAPTER THIRTY-FIVE

Stephanie's words echoed in Lynn's bones.

Are you scared of change? Or are you scared of love?

What if she was scared of both?

Stephanie hadn't let her off the hook even after they'd returned home with their brightly coloured eggs safely nestled in small cardboard boxes. They watched through the front window until Makayla's front door had opened and closed, and then she confronted Lynn again.

"It comes down to a simple question. What would be worse—leaving Prince George with Benjamin, or Benjamin leaving Prince George without you?"

Lynn's throat swelled and she headed into the kitchen, avoiding Stephanie's inquiring gaze. She had a rarely used eggcup in a cupboard somewhere, and she opened random doors as she sought frantically to remember why she'd vowed to never move again. "This is my home. I chose this city. It's the first place I've lived for longer than a few months. No one can make me leave it." Like her father had made her leave everywhere she'd lived before.

"Home isn't a place," Stephanie said gently. "Home is the people you love."

"I loved Lance." At least at the beginning she had. It wouldn't serve her purpose to admit her feelings had weakened long before he'd left her. "What good did that do me? At almost forty years old I had to start over, adjust all my plans. I don't think I'm strong enough to do that again." There it was. A wooden hourglass-shaped object hiding behind a gravy boat.

"You're assuming you'll have to. What if you don't? What if you and Benjamin are meant to be?"

She turned and stared, tiny box in one hand, wooden cup in the other. "You're serious. *Meant to be?* Benjamin's not my soul mate." A shiver snaked down her back as she said the words. She didn't believe in fated love. She *didn't*.

But was she willing to throw away a future with Benjamin, the man she loved more than she'd ever thought she could, without a fight? Without giving him a chance to explain himself?

"You're going to drop those." Stephanie took the box and eggcup from her nerveless fingers and set them on the table. "I know you had an unsettled childhood, moving from place to place at the whim of your father. But do you honestly see Benjamin dragging you and Oscar along with the same sort of selfishness?"

"He wouldn't mean to be selfish. He'd do it thinking it was best for us all. But it would still be uprooting Oscar over and over again."

Stephanie paused at the top of the stairs, her hand on the latch of the baby gate. "Staying rooted in one place doesn't guarantee happiness. But growing roots *with* someone, that's something to cherish."

As the days passed, Lynn examined her own feelings in a way she never had before. She didn't consider herself a coward. But was it possible all her careful planning had disguised a fear of new experiences? Had she chosen to stay in one place not to build stability, but to hide her timidity?

Did Oscar deserve a mother who was that fainthearted? Or did he deserve parents with lives that fulfilled and nourished them?

Benjamin had obviously taken her goodbye to heart.

He hadn't reached out to her at all since that night in the lobby of the hotel. If she wanted another chance with him, she would have to take the first step.

Which was why she took the baby monitor into Stephanie's room at three o'clock on Sunday morning, shook her friend awake, explained what she was planning, and drove to the arena parking lot to await the team's arrival home after the final game of the season.

The atmosphere in the Canyon Cats bus was still jubilant hours after they'd boarded. Everyone should have been sleeping during the overnight drive, but no one was, too pumped up at making the playoffs with a road win against the Wolverines.

"We did it." Nechayev clutched the back of Benjamin's seat and swayed with the motion of the bus. For the first time he could remember, the young player's eyes were bright with joy and satisfaction. "You said we would, and we did."

"You deserve it. All of you. Everyone worked their asses off to make it happen." They'd also received a little help from the hockey gods. An untimely bout of food poisoning had kept the Wolverines' top scorer out of the line-up and eased their way. That fact didn't negate the results. "You should try and get some rest. Everyone should. This is only the beginning."

Nechayev returned to his seat and after a while the chatter faded into rumbling snores and breathy sighs. Benjamin remained wide awake, head resting against the glass of the window at his shoulder, watching the yellow line flash past, the occasional oncoming headlights blinding him for an instant before disappearing.

He wished he could be as excited about making the playoffs as the team was. Damn it, he *should* be excited. It was, after all, a necessary first step in reaching the championships, which had been his objective all year long.

Somewhere along the way, though, his goal had changed. Well, maybe not his goal, but his desperation to reach it. He'd wanted to win for his father, to prove his belief in Benjamin hadn't been misguided, simply postponed. His mother's acceptance and Jujhar's forgiveness, both of which he'd been granted without having to justify himself, had eased the guilt and anxiety he'd felt for so many years, had made achieving his ambition less penance and more an homage.

And then there was Lynn. Lynn, who had welcomed him into her home, into her life. Who he had fallen in love with, even though he hadn't realized it until it was too late.

No. He shook his head, blinking the exhaustion from his eyes. It wasn't too late. It couldn't be. He just had to figure out how to get her back.

He must have drifted off because the next thing he knew the bus was hissing to a stop outside the arena. It wasn't yet four in the morning and the world outside the wide windshield was black and bleak. Vehicles waited, some with exhaust curling from their tailpipes, others covered in a dusting of light snow.

Levi rose from his seat across the aisle, stretching and yawning, and then made his way to the back of the bus, waking players as he went. Benjamin gathered his belongings and waited, as was his habit, for everyone to exit before making his own way down the stairs.

Movement in a sheltered alcove at the side of the arena caught his eye and he froze one step from the ground.

What the hell is Lynn doing here?

An icy wind bit Lynn's ears and wriggled its way down her neck. Taking a deep breath, she stepped out from the doorway. Benjamin stared at her a second longer, and then lowered his foot the last step to the ground and paced toward her.

"What's going on? Is everything okay?" His dark, intense gaze warmed her to her fingertips.

"Everything's fine. Everyone's good." God, she loved this man. His first thought was never for himself.

"Then why are you here?" A shout drew his attention over his shoulder. "I've got to grab my bag so the bus can leave. Don't move."

She huddled next to the building until he returned, his compact suitcase gripped in one hand. "It's freezing out here." He hitched his messenger bag on his shoulder and wrapped his free fingers around her wrist. "Let's sit in my car."

He led her to the vehicle and released her to fish the fob out of his pocket and beep the locks. "Get in."

She sank onto the stiff, chilled upholstery and shut the door behind her, relieved to be out of the brisk breeze and faintly terrified to be enclosed in such an intimate space with Benjamin. He opened the rear door behind the driver's seat, tossed his bags into the back, and then climbed in behind the wheel. Starting the engine, he turned the heater to max.

"It'll take a minute to warm up, but it's better than outside." He flicked the wipers on. They swept arcs through the thin film of snow on the windshield.

Cold air rushed out of the vents, and she directed them away from her face. She should say something. Now she was with him, though, all her carefully prepared speeches had vaporized. She could feel his gaze on her profile and swallowed, her mouth arid.

"Why are you here, Lynn?" His words were barely audible over the whirr of the heater.

She lifted her chin and turned to face him. "Congratulations on making the playoffs."

"Thanks." The hint of defeat in the taut syllable confused her. He should be celebrating. He'd done what he'd set out to do. Knowing the Canyon Cats' season wasn't over yet was one of the reasons she'd raced willy-nilly into the winter night to meet him when he got off the bus.

Her heart beat so high and fast she wondered if she was having a panic attack. Putting this off any longer wouldn't ease her symptoms. She sucked in just-starting-to-warm-up air and blew it out through pursed lips. "I know how busy you'll be over the next few days. I wasn't sure when we'd have a chance to talk. That's why I came."

"What do we have to talk about?" His expression was wary. She couldn't blame him. She hadn't been quite rational when they'd last spoken.

She set about easing his guardedness as best she could. "I owe you an apology for the other night. When you told me about your chance to coach for the new owners." The announcement of the sale would be made tomorrow morning. Now Benjamin had dragged the team into the post-season, they could announce he'd continue as head coach at the same time. That was the other reason she'd had to talk to him today. She had to tell him how she felt before anything formal had been announced. It was the best way she could think of to show him she was serious. About him, about their relationship.

Also, if what she told him changed his mind, it would be better if nothing was public yet.

God, she hoped he changed his mind.

"You owe me nothing." His tone was firm. "You've never hidden that you don't want to leave Prince George. I didn't expect anything else."

"Not that. I'm apologizing for accusing you of not caring for me and Oscar. I know you do, and that when you asked what was left for you here if the team moved you weren't talking about us. I'm sorry I took it that way."

His stiff shoulders softened. "I didn't mean to hurt you."

"I know." This was the tricky bit. "I think I know why I took it so poorly."

"Why?" The lights from the dash lit his face from below, sharpening his cheekbones, glinting off the whites of his eyes.

Here goes nothing. "Because I've fallen in love with you, and I don't want you to go."

His face went blank. "Say what?"

She gritted her teeth. "I love you. Don't worry, you don't have to say it back. But I thought you shou—"

Benjamin's mouth clamped over hers. With a moan she shifted onto her knees to lean over the console separating them. One hand gripped the back of her skull and the other her hip, dragging her closer. Desperation and desire flared in her belly, coiling and uncoiling like a spring ready to snap.

Well before she was ready, he pulled away. "What if I want to say it back?" His lips whispered against hers as if he couldn't bear to stop tasting her even as he spoke.

She nibbled at the corner of his mouth, the rasp of his whiskers burning her lips. "Go right ahead." Eager to feel him under her palms, she tugged off her gloves and laid her hands flat on his chest, stroking and caressing.

Giving a muffled groan, he lowered his forehead to her shoulder. His hair rustled against the nylon of her collar. "I can't. Not until after the playoffs."

Her soaring relief sputtered and stalled. His intense reaction to her confession had seemed a wordless confirmation that his feelings matched hers. That he'd choose her over hockey.

Had she been wrong? And if she was—what now?

She sank back, taking away his support, and he raised his head. "I understand. This was a bad time to throw this at you." She kept her tone light despite the dark chasm cracking under her ribs.

He tapped her thigh with a fingertip. "It certainly

wasn't the greeting I thought I'd be getting this morning." The smile curving his lips didn't quite reach his eyes. "It's just...I have to focus on the team right now."

"Of course. I said I understand." Dawn was hours away, but the sky had lightened from midnight black to charcoal grey. Her car was the only other vehicle in the parking lot. "You've got a full plate."

She reached for the door handle, suddenly frantic to escape. His grip on her elbow stopped her. She turned her head but couldn't meet his eyes.

"Yes. More than you know. Nothing is settled yet, and I don't want to jinx it. Will you look at me?" Reluctantly she lifted her gaze. His eyes searched hers and she struggled to hide the gaping wound carving a hollow in her chest. "I promised you once that I would never ghost you again. Be patient with me a little longer? Until the playoffs are over?"

She rubbed her aching temple. "Of course. You know where to find me when you're ready."

CHAPTER THIRTY-SIX

There was no Cinderella run for the Canyon Cats. The euphoria of squeaking into the playoffs evaporated the first time they played the top-ranked team in the division, and though they put up a fight, they went out in the first round, four games to none.

Benjamin had the satisfaction of knowing the players and coaching staff had done their best. They hadn't rolled over and died but had been beaten by a better team. His chance to redeem himself by winning the championship was over. Not just for this season. For good.

And he was at peace with that.

The morning after their final loss, he knocked on Peterson Brewster's door and entered when bid. The bluff businessman seated behind the desk waved him to a chair. "You wanted to see me?"

"Yes." He sat, keeping his feet flat on the floor and resting his palms on the arm of the chair. "I wanted to let you know I'm turning down the head coaching job in Minnesota. I won't be moving with the team."

Brewster's eyes narrowed. "I recommended you for that job. The new owners wanted to clean house, but I told them you deserved a chance."

"And I thank you for that, for your faith in me. But I'm not the right man, not for this. I think you should throw your support behind Levi."

Brewster's eyebrows rose. "Levi? You don't even like

the guy."

"Maybe not, but I respect him. He's a good coach, is extremely knowledgeable, and the players respond to him. Most of all, he wants the chance to prove himself."

"And you don't? I can't believe you're throwing this away, Benny."

Certainty filled him with euphoria. "It's Benjamin."

Brewster's forehead wrinkled. "What?"

He repeated himself with quiet confidence. "It's Benjamin. Not Benny." Standing up, he extended a hand across the desk. Brewster took it with a confused air. "And I'm not throwing away anything. I finally know what I want, and it is something other than hockey."

He wanted Lynn. It had been more than two weeks since she'd shocked him with her declaration of love. More than two weeks since they'd last spoken. He hoped he hadn't left it too late, but he'd had to put all the pieces in place first. He needed to *show* her how he felt, not just tell her.

She'd said she'd be patient. He prayed she'd meant it.

It had been the longest two weeks of Lynn's life. Even longer than the final two weeks of her pregnancy, which she swore had lasted seven years.

Alone in the administration office, Cynthie and Sarah having left for lunch, she opened her cooler bag and took out the sandwich, apple, and granola bar she'd packed that morning. She'd taken to eating at her desk and working through her break so she could head home earlier. The less time she spent in the same building as Benjamin the less chance she might snap, race to his office, fall onto her knees, and beg him to make a decision.

She had experienced a glimmer of hope when the announcement the Canyon Cats were moving to

Minnesota hadn't included a mention that the head coach was moving with them. But there were many possible reasons for that omission, and the continued suspense consumed her. She couldn't sleep, could barely eat, and was running out of the patience she'd promised.

It went against every instinct she possessed, but she'd given Benjamin the space he'd asked for, swinging from hope to despair, anticipation to terror with every beat of her heart. She'd placed her future in his hands, relinquished all control.

She was going to kill him if he broke up with her now.

Her resolve had cracked last night. Knowing it was her final chance to see Benjamin behind the Canyon Cats' bench, she'd left Oscar with Makayla and used a staff pass to get through the gate. The arena was sold out—a fact that should have thrilled her but barely registered through her Benjamin-induced haze.

Though they put up a valiant fight, the Canyon Cats had lost a heart breaker in overtime. The entire game, she'd stared hungrily at Benjamin as he'd paced behind the players, exhorting and encouraging. He'd looked in his element, and a revelation had slapped her like an open palm.

She couldn't ask him to give that up. It would make her as selfish as her father, expecting Benjamin to abandon his passion in order to soothe her fears. When the time came and he told her he was moving to Minnesota with the team, she would be nothing but supportive and loving. It was the right thing to do.

Too restless to remain at her desk, she shoved her lunch kit in a drawer and jumped to her feet. Her three-inch heels weren't made for long walks but would suffice for a couple of circuits around the concourse to clear her head. She pulled opened the interior office door, took two steps into the concourse—

—and barrelled into Benjamin.

Every cell in Benjamin's body reacted to the weight of Lynn leaning against him. His arms encircled her, steadied her, and then refused to let go. She stared at him with wide blue eyes, an O of surprise parting her lips, a flush rising in her cheeks.

"Sorry. I wasn't looking where I was going." Her voice was breathy and low. Though she was stable on her feet, she clutched the lapels of his sport coat.

"I was coming to talk to you." A tremor shivered through her, and he drew her closer. "The playoffs are over."

She nodded. Her tongue flicked across her bottom lip and his mouth dried. His hands slipped to her hips, warm and curvy and she gave a little wriggle that sent all the blood in his brain south.

The crash of a push-bar on a nearby door echoed off the concrete walls and gruff voices reverberated, growing louder. "I'm going to text you an address. Will you meet me there this afternoon? Bring Oscar."

"Where is it?"

The voices were nearer, heavy steps a drumming counterpoint to the as-yet indistinguishable conversation. "I'll include directions. It's not far."

Two men rounded the far corner of the concourse. Damn it, he didn't care who saw them. He kissed Lynn with passion and determination and promise. She tugged at his jacket and returned his caress with equal zeal. The footsteps passed them, accompanied by low chuckles.

Breathing heavily, he dragged his mouth away. "I'll text you."

He felt her stare on the back of his neck as he hurried out the main doors of the arena and into the parking lot.

With grim precision, Lynn followed the GPS directions to the address Benjamin had provided. She had no idea what this was all about as he'd refused to answer any of the questions she'd peppered at him via text.

She ended up on a rural road just a few minutes out of town. At first, older homes on large lots lined both sides, but then the populated area was replaced by a densely wooded patch. Benjamin's car was parked on the side of the road not far past the last driveway. She pulled in behind.

He strode toward her and opened the rear door as she climbed out of the driver's seat. Oscar babbled a cheerful greeting as Benjamin unbuckled him from his car seat. Apparently unfazed by the fact he hadn't seen him in weeks, he settled onto his arm and patted his cheeks.

"Benamin."

Lynn stared. Benjamin stared back.

"Did he just say...?" Benjamin swallowed and reared his head back to look at Oscar. "Did you just say my name?"

Oscar patted his cheek again. "Benamin."

Tears prickled on the roof of Lynn's mouth. "I guess he did. He must have missed you."

Looking shell-shocked, Benjamin stood stock still. Lynn's heart beat once, twice, three times before he broke out of his trance. "I missed you, too, little man."

The swell of love staggered her. She couldn't let fear keep her from sharing in something so wonderful as the sensations coursing through her. Stephanie was right. In a tug-of-war between leaving her home with Benjamin, or Benjamin leaving her and Oscar, there was no contest.

They belonged together. All three of them.

She took Benjamin's free hand and snuggled up next to him. "So. Why are we here?"

He shook his head and blinked. "Right. I have

something to show you."

"Go on then. Show me."

He used his chin to point across the road. "There. What do you think?"

She lifted an eyebrow. "Trees? What do I think of trees?"

"I've put an offer on the lot. I thought it might be a great place to build a house. Raise a family."

She gripped his bicep as the earth shifted under her feet. "You bought land? Here? But you're moving to Minnesota."

"No to both."

It was her turn to shake her head. She had to do something about the buzzing in her ears. Obviously, she wasn't hearing clearly. "I'm confused."

"I put an offer on the lot. But it's conditional. If you don't like the area, don't like the idea, I can get out of it. As for Minnesota"—he rolled his shoulder, the muscles under her hands flexing and bunching—"I turned down the job."

"I need to sit down." Lynn opened the driver's door and lowered herself onto the seat. Benjamin shifted Oscar to his other arm—the boy had grown like a weed since he'd last seen him—and watched her carefully.

Waiting.

It wouldn't be April for a few more days, but spring was in the air. The breeze was soft and scented with the smell of melting snow and water-filled ditches and budding leaves. The seasons were changing, and so was his life. No matter what Lynn decided, he had designed a new game plan.

He hoped she'd help him play it.

"You're not going to Minnesota." She looked up at him, her brow creased, eyes dazed. "But I thought..."

"So did I. We were both wrong." A muted barking reminded him he had other news. "Just a second."

He strode to his car and opened the rear door. A lolling tongue and laughing eyes greeted him. With one hand he unclipped the safety harness and took up the leash. "Come on, Scout."

The black and white dog leaped off the seat. Benjamin nudged the door shut with his hip while Oscar crowed and squirmed and Scout dragged him toward Lynn.

"Lynn, meet Scout." The dog planted his front paws on her knees, leaving muddy prints before Benjamin could tug him off. "We need to work on his manners."

"You have a dog?"

He was rather enjoying her poleaxed expression. "I do. Since last week. I tried to get Rascal, but he'd been adopted months ago." Scout zigzagged back and forth on the road, nosing an invisible trail until he reached the end of his leash. Whining, he looked over his shoulder at Benjamin.

"Come on. Let's take a look at the lot."

She followed him across the gravel road. A roughed-in driveway crossed the ditch, the culvert underneath shiny and new, and led through a band of trees to an open area that was showing signs of being reclaimed by nature.

"Will you let Scout off the lead for me? He won't go far." Despite being a rescue, the dog had bonded quickly and didn't stray far from Benjamin's side. The fact he had a pocket full of pepperoni probably didn't hurt.

She unlatched the leash and Scout set off to explore. It was actually his second visit to the lot, since he'd come along when the real estate agent had shown it to Benjamin a couple of days ago.

Between attempting a playoff run, the search for property, and becoming a dog owner, it had been a busy couple of weeks. And as much as he was determined to start anew for his own well-being, it would be joyless without Lynn.

She stood at his shoulder, surveying the scraggly

space. In his mind's eye he saw a modern home, a well-kept yard in summer, a backyard rink in winter. Could she see their future here? Or only his delusions?

He cleared his throat, nerves sparking with anxiety. "The current owners got as far as putting in access and clearing this space. Then the wife died, and the husband decided to sell."

"You're going to build a house."

He couldn't blame her for sounding dubious. "Well, not with my own hands, but yes. I told you I wanted to show you something. Well, I wanted to show you I'm in this for the long-haul. Anyone can buy a ready-made house. But committing to building one—that takes months. Months of planning and dreaming and compromising." He touched her chin and turned her face toward home. "All the things I want to do with you."

"You're staying." Her eyes shone with wonder. "You're not leaving. You got a *dog*."

Oscar struggled in his arms, and he lowered him to the ground. He wore bright yellow rubber boots and a rain suit that covered him from neck to ankles. A little mud wouldn't hurt him. He toddled off a couple steps then plopped down next to a pile of rocks.

"I love you, Lynn." He kissed her to the accompaniment of Oscar banging stones together and Scout barking at an irate squirrel. "I'm never going to leave you."

She burst out laughing.

She couldn't help it. Her joy had to go somewhere, and since the ground was too muddy to tackle Benjamin, she let it loose in laughter.

"Are you going to let me in on the joke?" His eyes were amused but she could see his uncertainty. He probably hadn't been expecting guffaws when he'd confessed to loving her.

"I have also been speaking with a real estate agent." She giggled and snorted. "I wanted to know how much I could get for my house. I figured we would buy one in Minnesota when we moved there."

Benjamin's mouth dropped open. "You were planning to move? Because of me?"

"Of course because of you. It was pretty simple in the end. Life with you or without you. I choose with you, no matter how uncertain your career. Because you are the one thing I am certain of."

He hugged her fiercely. His whiskers caught in her hair when he spoke. "Speaking of careers. You understand I won't be coaching anymore, right?"

She blinked and pushed just far enough away to see his face. How had it escaped her until now that, if he was staying in Prince George, he'd have to find a new job? She blamed it on too many shocks to her system. "What are you going to do?"

"I made some decent investments when I was playing, so I can afford to buy this land, build a house, and still have a buffer." His gaze darted away, landed on Oscar, tracked Scout as he snuffled the edge of the clearing, and came back to her. She watched in fascination as his cheekbones reddened. "I thought I'd go back to school. Take psychology or social work. Maybe become a counsellor."

His ambition floored her. There had to be a story behind it, given his initial reaction to the White Spruce presentation, but she could ask about that later. "Wow. That's perfect."

"You think so?" His expression was bashful and hopeful.

Tenderness blossomed in her chest, and she wrapped her arms around his waist, rested her head on his shoulder. "You'll be an amazing counsellor. I just know it."

Later that night, Lynn watched Benjamin sleep. Across the hall, Oscar snored softly in his crib, and Scout had made himself at home on the couch in the living room.

She'd once thought of being with Benjamin as colouring outside the lines. Instead, she'd found a fierce, abiding love between them.

He had called his real estate agent and finalized the offer on his lot. Scratch that—on *their* lot. The legalities still had to be figured out, but he had been firm on that point. They were buying the lot together. Would build the house together.

For once in her life, Lynn didn't need to have the future mapped out in detail. She trusted Benjamin, and she trusted herself. Together, they could handle whatever surprises the future held.

He stirred and opened his eyes, his lids drowsy. "You're awake."

"I'm too excited to sleep."

"I thought we took care of that. You know, before." He waggled his eyebrows.

They'd made love with an intensity that would have frightened her only a couple of weeks ago. But in the shiny new glow of their commitment, it had only seemed natural.

It hadn't been enough though. She didn't know if she'd ever get enough of this man.

"I guess you were wrong." She lifted the covers and slid onto him, skin to skin, heart to heart. "We'll have to try again."

"I'm up for that." His hands slid from her ass, up her spine and under her arms to cup her breasts. "All you have to do is ask."

"Consider this me asking." She fused her mouth to his.

Thanks for reading
Loving Between the Lines.

Reviews and ratings are a great way to help other readers discover new authors. Just a line or two is all that's needed—or simply click the number of stars you think it deserves. I encourage you to post your honest opinion at the retailer where you purchased your copy, on GoodReads and BookBub. Thank you so much!

Visit my website to discover more titles in the Silverberry Seduction Seasoned Romance Series.

I'd love to stay in touch. Subscribe to my newsletter and you'll immediately receive a free read, be able to tag along with my dog-walking adventures, find out what I'm reading when I should be working, and other randomness...along with all my writing news, of course! Find the sign-up form on my website, www.brendamargriet.com.

Lynn's Slow Cooker Sausage and Peppers

8 – 10 uncooked Italian sausages (can be any flavour)

1 onion, sliced
3 peppers (any colour), sliced
5 – 6 cloves garlic, chopped
1 bag baby potatoes (or equivalent amount of regular potatoes cut in large cubes)
1 tbsp salt
1 tsp Italian seasoning
¼ tsp dried oregano
½ tsp crushed red pepper flakes
1 28-ounce can diced tomatoes
¼ cup water

1 bay leaf

Brown sausage in frying pan. Set aside.

In large bowl mix next ten ingredients. Spoon enough of this mixture into greased slow cooker to cover bottom. Add layer of sausage, more sauce, another layer of sausage, and the rest of the sauce, covering the sausages.

Add bay leaf. Cover and cook on low for 6 hours or high for 3 hours. Remove bay leaf before serving.

ABOUT THE AUTHOR

Brenda Margriet writes savvy, slow burn, contemporary romances with ordinarily amazing characters. In her own ordinarily amazing life, she had a successful career in radio and television production before deciding to pilfer from her retirement plan to support her writing compulsion.

Readers have called her stories "poignant," "explicit and steamy," "interesting, intriguing and entertaining," and "unlike any romance you've read before" (she assumes the latter was meant in a good way).

Join Brenda on social media—she is most active on Facebook and Instagram. And you can always discover more about her and her books on her website, brendamargriet.com.

ALSO BY BRENDA MARGRIET

SILVERBERRY SEDUCTION SEASONED ROMANCE
Secrets Under the Covers
Loving Between the Lines
Turn the Next Page
Strictly by the Book
Too Good for Words
The Complete Silverberry Seduction Series
(e-book only)

TIMELESS SEASONED ROMANCE
After Words
Richly Deserved

THE BENDIXON SISTERS SERIES
Allegro Court
Gateway Crescent
Crossroads Corner
Taking His Measure: The Complete Bendixon Sisters
Series (e-book only)

STANDALONE READS
Mountain Fire
Reserved for You
No Life But This
When Time Falls Still
The Promise of Frost

Read excerpts and find buy links at
www.brendamargriet.com